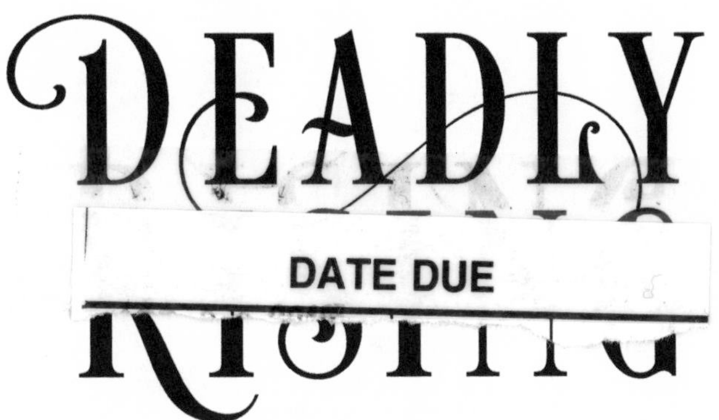

BOOKE TWO IN THE BOOKE OF THE HIDDEN SERIES

JERI WESTERSON

everafter ROMANCE

EverAfter Romance
A division of Diversion Publishing Corp.
443 Park Avenue South, Suite 1004
New York, New York 10016
www.EverAfterRomance.com

For more information, email info@everafterromance.com

First EverAfter Romance edition October 2018.
Paperback ISBN: 978-1-63576-460-4
eBook ISBN: 978-1-63576-459-8

LSIDB/1810

To Craig, with all of his magic and delights

CHAPTER ONE

I stood back, hands on hips, and watched as Barry Johnson, handyman and owner of Moody Bog Hardware, hung my new door. There had been nothing wrong with the last one...until some bikers and a demon creature destroyed it two nights ago.

You'd think saying that would be odd, but it wasn't anymore, not to me.

He dropped the last pin in the hinge and there it was. He swung it and closed it. Opened it again and stood back. "Ay-yuh. There you go, Miss Strange."

"You can call me Kylie, Barry. I feel we've bonded these last few days."

He chuckled. "We have a hard time getting used to flatlanders in our little town, Miss—Kylie—that's folks not from Maine."

"California is as far from Maine as I can imagine," I said. And truly it was. But for better or worse, I had chosen Maine as my new home, and I looked on at my door proudly. A "Shaker-Style Three Light," the accompanying literature had said. It was solid and sturdy, something I was likely to need, since demons and bikers were now a common occurrence.

"You did a great job, Barry. And with the window repairs too."

"No problem, M—Kylie. That must have been some fight Doug and his biker friends had in there. Funny them being in a tea shop at all."

"He was drunk," I was quick to add. That was the story I'd decided to go with. It made as much sense as anything.

"Looks like you've fixed up your shop mighty quick. Open for business again?"

"Two days closed right after my grand opening? That's two days too long. So yes, we are open. Again!"

"Good. I'll send the missus in. She's a tea drinker and has been wanting to try something other than teabags."

"I'll be happy to set her up."

He saluted as if touching the brim of a cap he wasn't wearing. "I'll be collecting my things and getting out of your hair, then."

"Thanks, Barry. I mean it. You really worked fast."

He saluted again, gathered his tools, dropped them into his toolbox, and walked up the blustery street toward his store.

I ruffled my hair and observed my shop anew. *Strange Herbs & Teas* was carved in gold letters above the door. That didn't begin to describe what went down here these days.

I opened the door again, hung the store bell, and closed it, satisfied with the tinkling sound. Walking over the threshold, I sighed. It was back to normal. Or whatever served as normal in Moody Bog. The town itself was quaint and old world, and I had fallen in love with its tree-lined streets, its surrounding hills and farmsteads. The pioneer in me loved this shop—*my* shop. Old built-in shelves that reached the ceiling. Apothecary jars full of teas on the buffet. I filled my shelves with teapots and tea paraphernalia of my stock and trade: colorful china cups and saucers, distinguished infusers of brass and stainless steel, dessert plates, brown betties, tiered plate stands, cozies, towels, books...anything you could want. I kept the herbs inside carefully marked wooden drawers. Unusual herbs. Hard-to-get herbs, with exotic names and origins.

The fireplace against one wall with two cozy wingback chairs facing one squashy sofa made the perfect little nook for both customer and proprietor, since I also lived here. With small side tables placed about the space with samovars for tea tasting, I deemed it perfect.

"Now all I need are customers."

A tingle across my shoulders made me turn. I knew that feeling. The Booke. It wanted my attention.

I passed through the swinging door to my kitchen. There, on the kitchen counter, where I distinctly had *not* left it, was the Booke. Yes, it liked to follow me around the house—around the town sometimes. It was large, like an old family Bible. Of ancient and unknown origin, I had found it bricked up in my shop wall and oh how I wished I had left it there to rot. But the best I could figure, it somehow called to me, making me break through three-hundred-year-old brickwork to free it. And once I'd opened the cover...

Even though I didn't want to touch it, my hand came up and involuntarily smoothed over the ancient leather of its binding. I ran my fingers over the gold embossed words "Booke of the Hidden."

"What do you want, you stupid Booke?" I whispered. Because it did want. It wanted to be open and cause havoc. It served as some sort of Pandora's box, once opened releasing supernatural creatures into the world. And I, the now not-so-proud owner of the damned thing, was tasked with closing it again. Not so easy a feat when I had to recapture all the beasties now running free. The most recent one was a succubus and hadn't that been fun. And as far as I could figure, the last owner of the Booke, one Constance Howland from 1720, the same person who built this house I now called my home, was chased off a cliff by a "dark man," a demon who was attached to the Booke. Or so the legend went.

With immense willpower, I stepped back, my hand jumping to the amulet hanging from my neck. The face of a demon, tongue extended, eyes made of rubies. Not something I would have picked for myself. Wearing it secured my safety against the demon of the Booke. But just where that demon was…well. Erasmus Dark drove me nuts! He was arrogant, a pain in the ass, pushy…and…sexy as hell.

"Don't think about him, Kylie," I admonished myself, but it was of little use. I couldn't *stop* thinking of him. Tall, dark, brooding, with an English accent. We'd had a…well. An "intimate moment," which had been a mistake. I couldn't tell if he was using me or not…"Don't be an idiot. Of course he was using you." But two nights ago, he had disappeared when Baphomet was summoned and I had just as quickly sent the god back to the Netherworld with my chthonic crossbow…

No matter how many times I said that sentence it never got less weird.

Still, it meant that Erasmus was sent away too. I didn't want to think about it. I would much rather think about Sheriff Ed. Wouldn't it be better to think about a human man than a supernatural one?

"Just one more stupid problem in the great life of Kylie Strange," I murmured, leaving the kitchen to once again survey my shop.

And then the sheriff's black and white Ford Interceptor SUV pulled up in front on the gravel parking area. I could see him through my newly repaired front window.

I automatically smoothed my hair, tugging the loose strands up over my ears, and brushed at my sweater.

Sheriff Ed Bradbury himself got out. He was a tall man, dark haired, square jawed, broad chested. Every adjective you could think of. A fine specimen all around, especially in his uniform, though most of it was covered with a thick jacket with a fake fur collar. His deputy got out the passenger door and stood, looking up distastefully at my shop sign.

Deputy George Miller had a small dark mustache and carefully groomed hair. He never seemed quite fond of me. Not like Sheriff

Ed. In fact, he waited outside, stomping around, cold air clouding his face, as the sheriff walked up to the front door and pushed it open. The bell above the door jangled merrily.

He doffed his Smokey Bear hat and smiled. That grin was heart melting. "Hey."

"Hey, yourself," I said, trying not to fidget.

He gestured with his hat toward the shop. "Looks good as new."

"Yup. Barry Johnson just got done installing the door."

"I like it," he said, swiveling here and there to get a good look at the place, before he squared on me again with those intense eyes. "And how are *you* doing?" He took a step closer. "Are you okay?"

My hand went to my throat, covering the amulet that always felt hot under my touch. "I'm fine. Open for business. I mean… my *business* is open for business. The *shop*, I mean…jeez. Just forget I said anything."

He ducked his head, hiding a grin. "Yeah. I, uh, just came to tell you…that Doug and his gang have been released."

"Oh?" Doug and his biker gang, known as the Ordo or, more particularly, *Ordo Dexterae Diaboli*—Order of the Right Hand of the Devil—had trashed my place with the help of the late succubus.

"Yeah." He ran his hand up over the back of his neck. "We really couldn't hold them. Not if you weren't going to press any charges. Kylie, I'm sorry about my brother. I told him to keep his gang of idiots away from you. But as you might have guessed, he isn't too fond of listening to anything I have to say."

Well, I *had* pleaded for leniency. I was of the mind that Doug could be reasoned with, maybe even eventually help us. Of course, Ed didn't know anything about what was really going on, and I wanted to keep it that way.

"I told you it was okay."

He moved closer still. I was staring right at his seven-pointed-star badge, shiny and bright. And close enough to get a whiff of his spicy cologne. "If anyone harasses you in any way, or if you ever feel unsafe..."

"I know I can call on Moody Bog's finest." I smiled up at him to try to wipe that concerned look off his face. When I pressed a hand gently to his chest, the frown fell away. "I know I'm in good hands."

He was leaning in. He was going to kiss me, and as much as I had enjoyed it on our date, I couldn't help but slip away from him.

"Kylie," he said, his voice a little gravelly. "I know there's a lot on your mind but...I'd like to take you out again."

I said nothing as I felt him approach.

"I mean, I thought we were having a good time...till that owl took me out of the game."

It hadn't been an owl. And wasn't that part of the problem? Should I get involved with Ed when so much else was going on? So many unbelievable elses? So many secrets?

"Sure," I said. I wanted to kick myself. Not even a pause for reflection. *Way to go, Kylie!*

Ed's demeanor changed again. Straightening his shoulders, he smiled, clutching his hat to his side. "Well that's...that's great. Would tonight be too presumptuous?"

The bell above the door sounded and we both turned. Deputy George stuck his head in. "Sheriff, got another goat theft on our hands. The Mason farm just called it in."

"Jeezum, another one? That makes three this week."

"Kids, you reckon?"

"I don't know. Let's keep an eye out for homeless camps, campfires in the woods and such."

"Think someone's eatin' 'em?"

"Well, I'd hate to think what else they'd do with them."

The deputy's mustache twitched.

"I'll be out in a minute, George, okay?"

Deputy George looked me over, managed not to sneer, and closed the door as he left. He thrust his hands in his parka pockets and paced on my gravel, surveying Lyndon Road.

Ed gazed at me with a gentle smile. I guessed he wanted an answer to his question. I hesitated. "How about tomorrow night?" I offered. "Gotta get things squared away here."

He looked around again, sizing up the shop, which looked pretty squared to the both of us, and nodded. "All right then." He leaned over and this time it would have been too awkward trying to duck away from him. His lips touched mine. It wasn't a quick peck either, but the promise of more to come. Ed laid it on me, and feeling bereft, lonely, and not a little aroused, I leaned into him, accepting the gentle offering.

When he pulled away, his eyes had a glazed-over look about them. I was feeling a bit fuzzy myself.

He nodded, said nothing, and affixed his hat on his head. Looking over his shoulder at me, he left, closing the door behind him. I leaned against one of the wingbacks.

The coven liked Ed. They'd be ecstatic.

And speak of the devil, Jolene Ayrs, junior coven member and my teenage assistant, walked in just as Sheriff Ed's Interceptor pulled away. She dumped her backpack with the Hello Kitty skull patch behind the counter.

"Was that the sheriff just here?" she gushed, adjusting her clear plastic-framed glasses.

"Never you mind, young lady."

She chuckled and looked around the renewed shop. "How about customers?"

"None yet. I'm a little worried."

"But didn't you say everyone at the Chamber of Commerce meeting was pretty excited by this place?"

"That was before I broke into Ruth Russell's library."

She sank. “Oh yeah.”

“I’m sure she let everyone know that I’m a sneaky thief and to steer clear of my shop. Though Barry from the hardware store was friendly enough.”

“We’ll know more when the coven meets tonight,” she said. “I think Doc wants to meet here, if that’s all right.”

“More than all right.” I snuck a glance toward the kitchen, resisting the silent call of the Booke. “It’s probably for the best.”

Nightfall. I had loved those first early fall nights in New England when I knew nothing of the Netherworld or demons or haunted Bookes. The nights full of the smell of nearby woods, of smoky chimneys. The bright reflected eyes of foxes and deer gazing at me from my wooded backyard. But now the night was full of portents and danger. And now I could never be sure about those eyes in the woods. What was next? What had the Booke released that now lurked out there? Erasmus had warned me that the nightmare was far from over, that more creatures were roaming and waiting to strike.

So I was glad to have met what I like to call “my coven,” that is, the local Wiccans. Not that they were much of a coven before all this happened.

Doc Boone arrived first, white haired and with a little glint in his blue eyes.

He was followed soon by semi-goth Nick Riley, local barista. He liked his black-dyed hair, black nail polish, black clothes…but that seemed to be as far as it went. I hadn’t asked if he was going to college, but it didn’t seem likely if he was always hanging around Moody Bog.

Seraphina Williams pulled up in her hybrid car and entered my establishment, casting a whiff of strong perfume. She wore clanking layers of necklaces and bracelets, and swishing Boho shawls and chiffon. Somewhere in her late forties, she was clearly fighting the march of time. Or was she older and doing a better job hiding it than I realized?

No one in the little village knew what was truly going on. The Wiccans had gone from a small, barely tolerated bunch on the fringe, chalking pentagrams and waving smoky bundles of sage to little effect, to now, somehow, some of the strongest mages around. Not that I was all that versed on mages. I had met a few folks like them back in California when I ran my old boyfriend's herb and tea shop, but this was different. Very different.

Only our little coven knew about the supernatural happenings. Well, and Doug Bradbury's biker coven. Did I mention that Moody Bog was slightly unusual?

Doc Boone got right down to it. He was straight out of Central Casting as the kindly old retired country doctor, complete with white hair, round middle, and crinkly eyed smile. But he was all business when it came to spells and charms.

"We need to use a very strong protection spell for Kylie's shop," he said in a strong Maine accent.

"Won't the Booke negate that?" I asked.

"We were successful last time. I should say, *Jolene* was very successful with her potion." He bowed to her and she grinned, blushing.

"But that kept…" I bit my tongue. I had been about to say that that had kept out Erasmus. Yet that was exactly what they wanted to do. And it was probably for the best. But it was hard to see it that way when my heart wasn't in it.

Seraphina's half-lidded expression of serenity never wavered. "What did you have in mind, Doc?" she asked in her breathy tone.

"I've been doing some reading," he said, taking the cup and saucer I handed him with a nod. "And we need to do something stronger. More than just salt on the perimeter or a potion."

Nick grabbed the delicate teacup with his hand, lifting it by the rim instead of the handle. "What's left?" He sipped loudly and glanced at Jolene as she perched, legs folded beneath her on the rocking chair, snorting at the way Nick drank his tea.

"A spell," she said. "A very powerful spell."

Nick slurped again. "Do you think we can?"

Doc took the teacup by its handle and sipped properly. "If you'd asked me a week ago, I would have said no. But ever since Kylie opened that book…"

"It gave you powers," I said quietly, thinking of Doug's Ordo gang. Because it gave them powers too. And that was *not* a good thing.

I toyed with my cup, spinning the spoon around and around, even though the sugar had long since dissolved. "But what about… Erasmus? Will it keep him out too?"

They all looked up. They knew about our tryst, and Doc spoke for all with his frown. "Yes, Kylie. It should keep him out as well."

"But what if I need him? He helped me last time. Isn't that why he's attached to the Booke? To help the Chosen Host?"

Seraphina laid a hand gently on my arm. Even as heavily made-up as she liked to be, there was a natural beauty to her strong features. "Kylie, we don't know anything about his true motivations. Everything we know about him and his connection to the book comes from him. And we know that demons lie."

Everyone was silent except for the sipping of tea and the crunch of a cookie.

I couldn't stand it anymore. I stood and gathered the empty plates and leftover teacups on the tray and took the whole thing to the kitchen. Running the hot water in the sink with a few squirts of soap, I began vigorously washing the dishes.

To tell you the truth, I didn't know how long I was at it. Only when Nick came in and looked me over did I seem to snap out of it.

"Hey, Kylie," he said, frowning a bit. His black-dyed hair drooped over his forehead. "You, uh, done there? 'Cause I think they're super clean now."

I'd been leaning over the edge of the sink with my arms resting in the now cold water. The plates and cups were neatly stacked on the dish strainer. I hadn't remembered finishing. "Yeah, sure. I just..." I flicked my hands toward the sink and grabbed a towel. "I just spaced out a little, is all."

"I just wanted to let you know," said Nick as I followed him back to the shop, "we've got a hell of a spell!"

I cringed a little. I wished he wouldn't throw around the "H" word. You never knew who was listening.

CHAPTER TWO

Doc hovered over a thick book not unlike my Booke of the Hidden. Perhaps not as old but certainly nothing new. He'd had to make a special request from the Bangor branch. The cover said *Daemonolatreia*.

"Now ordinarily," said Doc, "this would be used to trap witches, but it does have an obscure paragraph that discusses just what to do to protect yourself, including a bit about the Craft. And then I found more in some microfiche. I copied it down." He was plainly using it as a bookmark. "I used some modified language from the *Liber Loagaeth*. From my research, I was definitely on the right track."

Seraphina and Jolene both nodded sagely.

I tried to follow his explanation, but clearly it was beyond me. They asked to use some of my herb stash, which I gladly handed over. Anything to keep whatever was out there staying out there.

Doc produced a piece of chalk and held it up. "I presume you won't mind if I mark your floor again? And this time, Kylie, could you not cover it?"

I nodded. My customers would just have to put up with the odd pentagram here or there. If I ever got any customers again.

Doc began chalking the pentagram in front of the fireplace and Nick followed him, waving a burning herb bundle over each corner Doc marked. But he wasn't done with one pentagram, creating a seven-pointed star around it. Funny. It reminded me of Sheriff Ed's badge.

Once Doc was finished at last, Jolene set a burning white pillar candle in the center and Seraphina placed smooth, flat stones at each triangle of the seven-pointed star. They were black river rocks, the kind you'd see in a Japanese garden.

They all stood around the chalked marks, joining hands. Doc gestured toward me. "You too, Kylie. This is for *your* protection, after all."

I joined the circle, standing between Nick and Jolene. Everyone bowed their heads and closed their eyes. I tried to follow suit but couldn't stop peeking.

Doc lifted his head, eyes still closed, and spoke in an authoritative voice, "Arise! Arise! We call upon the Archangel Sandalphon amid the Souls of Fire and the Angel Nalvage, who keeps the ancient words; we call upon the god Enki and the god Marduk for your ancient wisdom, and upon the mighty Shammash, who lights the way. Command the evil to leave this house, to protect it from that which would cause its inhabitants harm! Guard window and door. Command them, O mighty gods and angels! Bar their way. Hold this place fast in the palms of your hands. Place your seals upon the stones we offer."

If I had not seen their powers before or beheld what could come from gateways to the Netherworld, I would have laughed it all off as nonsense words. But now I knew better. I said nothing, not wishing to stop whatever magic they were weaving. And there was magic. My skin tingled with it, the hairs on the back of my neck stood straight up, and then I saw a glow. The pentagram and the star around it were glowing with an eerie greenish light. Threads of light—magic—followed the chalked pentagram and the other star, reaching toward the stones. The whole floor beneath our feet was aglow with lit threads and symbols, the stones rimmed with halos. The black surface of each stone had been perfectly smooth, but now as I watched, a tendril of fire etched a different symbol onto all the stones until each stone was glowing too.

Something banged against the kitchen door. My head snapped up. I looked at the others, but they seemed in a trance, swaying together, eyes closed while Doc chanted his indecipherable names and commands again.

The kitchen door banged once more and I jumped. All at once it burst open and the Booke was there. I tried to pull away, but Jolene and Nick had death grips on my hands. They didn't even seem to know I was there, struggling to get away.

The Booke hovered. It was not pleased by what was going on. After all, I supposed it was evil, too, and didn't like the command for it to leave. It fought. It glowed under a purplish halo that grew darker and angrier, like a bruise. I didn't want to interrupt Doc if what he was doing was working, but I also didn't want to piss off the Booke.

"Doc," I rasped when he seemed to have paused. "Doc!"

He slowly opened his eyes, but they were unfocused, as if he wasn't really there.

"Doc!" I cried again. The Booke was hovering closer, menacing. I tried to tell it to back off, screaming in my head, but it wouldn't listen.

He shook his head and looked at me, eyes slowly returning back to normal. His gaze darted toward the Booke. With the cessation of the chanting, the Booke fell to the floor with a loud report, startling everyone else awake in the circle.

"Whoa," said Nick, edging away from the damned thing.

I knelt and gingerly picked it up. I felt nothing from it—no vibrations, no ill will. Setting it on the nearest table, I stared down at the Booke.

"Did it work?" asked Seraphina, swiping her hair out of her eyes.

Doc picked up one of the stones. Must have been hot because he tossed it like a hot potato from one hand to the other. I could clearly see the symbol etched on it.

"Looks that way," he said. Once it had cooled enough to hold in his hand, he examined it closely.

I studied the stone over his shoulder. It was engraved with what looked like a stylized bull. "What does that symbol mean?"

"Mithra," said Doc softly. "Renewal, creation, immortality."

Nick cradled one in each hand. "And those?" I asked. One looked like a horse's head, the other a goat. The goat reminded me too much of our old pal Baphomet.

Nick shook his head and deferred to Doc.

Doc looked them over, then the others in Seraphina and Jolene's hands.

"The horse...see these Gaelic symbols? I'm almost certain that this refers to the ritual bath in horses' blood that the ancient Irish kings took to imbue them with strength and agility in battle. And the goat—see the Hebrew glyphs—is the scapegoat. These others..." He touched the two in Seraphina's hands. "Hmm. Greek. *Ἰφιγένεια*. Iphigenia. Her father sacrificed her so that his ships could sail to Troy. And this one is Aztec..."

I was sensing a pattern here that was making me nervous.

"Never mind," I muttered. "They all have to do with sacrifice, right? From every culture and time."

He nodded.

"I guess we know who that's directed at, then."

"Now Kylie, I wouldn't read anything into it."

"Are you kidding me? These are the symbols your angels and gods chose to protect me. But it's also a little message, right? It's all about sacrifice. And *I'm* the one being tied to the stake!"

"Now Kylie..."

I grabbed the Booke without meaning to before stomping out of the room. When I noticed it was in my hands, I slammed it down to the nearest flat surface. "You know what? I don't intend to be anyone's sacrifice. Opening that Booke was a mistake. I never meant to. And I think it's rude of the Powers That Be to make it *my* fault and then punish *me* for it. I'm just not going to be sacrificed and that's final."

I was breathing hard and hadn't noticed that my face was wet with tears until I wiped angrily at them.

Doc's hands suddenly closed over mine. He held them fast while looking me in the eye. "Kylie, we will not allow anything to happen to you. We're here to help."

"Yeah," said Jolene in a small voice. "But how?"

She was always the one with answers. A whiz at research and tech, Jolene could always be relied on to find solutions. But if *she* wasn't sure, what chance did *I* have?

He gestured with his rock. "We've already done it. Our spell. Now you and Seraphina take your four rocks and put them at the cardinal points of the house. These last three." He put them on my open palms. "Put one in the bedroom, one in the kitchen, and the last in this room. Doesn't matter where. It's your protection."

"The Booke didn't like it."

"As well it shouldn't. It knows we're fighting back. That should reassure you."

It should but it didn't.

I slowly climbed the stairs and opened the door to my bedroom. When I saw the four-poster, I immediately thought of Erasmus, who had taken me right there on that quilt. Where was he? "Erasmus, I could really use your advice about now." But of course, he wouldn't be answering. Either he was long gone or...or this spell would keep him away.

I stuffed one rock under the mattress.

Back downstairs, I tucked one rock on a kitchen shelf so it would be unobtrusive, and then came out to the main room, where my Wiccans watched me with anxious faces. I steered clear of the pentagram, put the last rock by the coal scuttle I used to hold kindling, and wiped my palms down my sweater as if rubbing away something distasteful.

⁂

Rain angled down, streaking the window glass. The bedroom was cold in the morning so I quickly grabbed my bathrobe and wrapped myself up. Downstairs, the coffeemaker was brewing. The promise of coffee sent me into the shower.

There were going to be customers today, I vowed, scrubbing my hair with citrus-scented shampoo. Lots of customers, and then I had a date tonight with Ed. Everything was going my way, right?

I let the water rush over me. Apparently, I had been standing there for a long time. Longer than I realized because the water had turned cold. I had never been one for particularly long showers, especially coming from droughty California, but the feeling of the water and steam was intoxicating. With a shiver, I quickly turned off the shower, listening to the music of the old pipes as they creaked and banged, before toweling off.

Dressed, hair combed out, earrings in place, amulet hidden under my oatmeal heather sweater, I trotted downstairs, got my cup, and began brewing teas for my samovars.

I walked around to each window to open the curtains and let in what sunshine there was to offer. The room sprang to life with the scents of spicy herbs and aromatic teas. Shiny tea things, colorful towels, and gadgets caught the light. I walked toward the fireplace but paused at the brink of the chalked pentagrams. *Screw it.* I strode right over it and knelt on the stone hearth to light the kindling under a stack of birch logs. Once that was going merrily, I placed the screen in front of it and readied the samovars and the bite-sized pieces of pecan loaf.

It was still early. When I glanced out the window, the rain had stuck the autumn leaves fast to the street. The trees across the way were still in full fall bloom, with bright yellows, oranges, and burgundies. Their vibrancy was only slightly dampened by the drizzle. I could even forget for a moment that those were the woods where I had hunted a succubus. I wondered what was out there now, for surely the Booke hadn't been idle.

I also took a cursory glance around for a familiar figure in a long duster…but saw no one.

The next time I looked at my watch, it was time to turn over the closed sign to "open." As luck would have it, there had been enough intrepid tourists coming off the highway to pop in and make purchases. One woman even bought the expensive English tea set that I had been beginning to think was a marketing mistake.

The customers were all so cheerful, but some wondered why I didn't have pumpkins on my porch or Halloween decorations in the windows.

"It's so Sleepy Hollow here in this little village," remarked one woman from Texas.

She didn't know how right she was. I just didn't feel Halloweeny when every day was Fright Night. But when I grabbed my broom to sweep the leaves off the front stoop and gazed down the street to other houses and businesses decked out for the fall and Halloween, I began to feel as if I was letting the village down in this second week of October.

I was feeling better about Halloween in general, though, especially after my good morning of sales. I grabbed a quick bite for lunch and rinsed my dishes, luxuriating in the dish soap, the warm water, and got back to the shop later than I realized.

I happened to glance out the window and there was Jolene, standing on the porch. I expected her to come through the door, but she was just standing there. Looked like she was staring at the rain.

I knocked on the window glass until she suddenly looked up at me. She seemed puzzled for a moment before she shook off her raincoat on the porch and hung it on the hall tree by the door.

"It's wet out there, I'm tellin' you," she said, wiping her glasses on her sweater.

"What were you looking at?" I asked.

"Huh?" She replaced her glasses on her nose and blinked.

"Never mind." I walked past her to the hall tree and grabbed my own coat.

"Was it something I said?" she asked, watching me button up.

"I'm going over to the market to get some pumpkins. We need to Halloween up this place."

"Oh. I never mentioned it because...well. Because I thought you had enough real Halloween on your hands."

"Me too." I grabbed a few bucks from the register. "But I'm getting over it. See you shortly."

Like a real "Maine-ah," I decided to eschew the car and walk. But as I got several yards from the shop, I began to regret my decision. I hurried my pace, hunkered into my mackinaw, and ducked my head.

Soaked and chilled, my feet splatted through the market. I chose the roundest pumpkins I could find in the bin, ones with good stems, and loaded them in my cart, along with some mini pumpkins. I even picked some witchy things, like twig brooms, pointed hats, and four cornstalk bundles that I planned to tie to the front porch posts. I sniffed some pumpkin spice candles and it gave me an idea to make my own pumpkin spice potpourri to sell.

I rang it all up with the cashier, dumped the miniature pumpkins in my coat pockets, and carried the two round pumpkins under my arms. The rest would be sent on in an hour or so.

Trotting with my awkward bundles, I finally ran the last few yards. I plopped both pumpkins on the porch. They were going to look very picturesque with the cornstalks. I went inside, sighing at the warmth.

"You didn't come back with anything," said Jolene, staring at me, arms akimbo.

"Yes I did." I pulled the little pumpkins out of my pockets like a magician performing a trick and she laughed. "I thought we could put these around. More is being delivered from the market. And I thought we could make our own pumpkin spice potpourris. Put them in those gold voile bags and tie them with a ribbon. Would be a nice impulse buy."

She seemed delighted to be doing something. "I'm learning a lot from you."

"Planning on going into retail?"

"My parents are in it. But I was never excited about the nursery. Maybe because I *had* to work there. And it was always cold, being outside and watering plants. It's nice and cozy in here."

"Choose your retail wisely, I always say."

"So you did this before, right? In California?"

"Yup. I was business partners with my boyfriend, Jeff. *Ex*-boyfriend. Never go into business with a boyfriend. Unless you have lots of written contracts."

"Was he a jerk?"

"He was the dictionary definition of a jerk." She and I assembled our herbs and spices as we talked, pulling out the cubbies and laying them on the counter. I got out a wide wooden bowl for us to mix all the ingredients together, and soon our conversation mellowed with the aromas of cinnamon, cloves, dried shredded ginger, nutmeg, and allspice. I added star anise for looks.

"He cheated on me," I went on, "he stole from my checking account, pretty much all the things you don't want in a boyfriend."

"Do you think Mr. Dark is better than Jeff?"

I pulled up short, the small bag hanging limp in my hand. "Um…Mr. Dark is…different. Anyway, I'm dating Sheriff Ed." I slowly began filling the bag again.

"I approve."

"I'm so glad." But her mention of Erasmus put a damper on my enthusiasm. I had been looking forward to tonight. I mean, I still was but…well.

I let her talk about high school, the various boys that were in her classes—all stupid, apparently—until we tied up the last bag. We'd done ten. I figured that was enough to start.

I checked my watch. We had a few hours till closing. I worried that the rain would keep customers away, but these Mainers were made of heartier stuff. Several ladies—even some from Ruth Russell's knitting circle—came in. They didn't seem to care about my hijinks at her house, or maybe they secretly applauded it. I got the impression that Ruth Russell wasn't as universally adored as she liked to think. They each bought a potpourri and some flavored herbal teas that I had blended myself. I also managed to talk them into a tin of herbs for roast rubs.

All in all, it hadn't been a bad day. Just as Jolene was leaving for the night, my Halloween stuff arrived from the market. I tipped the high school kid, who said his shy hellos to Jolene (who didn't seem to think *he* was all that stupid, judging by the blush to her cheeks), and set them inside. There would be time to arrange them tomorrow. I turned the sign to "closed," waved to Jolene, locked the door, and began closing curtains.

I yanked the curtains sharply at first, and then…just stopped. I was transfixed by the sunset's dying light playing on the rain rivulets running down the window panes. They trickled down in straight lines and sometimes, without rhyme or reason, took sharp turns to make new downward rivers. It was hypnotizing. When

I finally shook myself loose and looked at my watch again, a full twenty minutes had passed.

Embarrassed for daydreaming, I quickly closed the rest of the curtains and hurried upstairs to change. Ed had texted me earlier and said he was taking me to a more rustic, homespun sort of dinner. So I thought jeans would be in order, a lacy bra, and a slightly tighter sweater.

I turned to and fro in front of the mirror. Not bad. I couldn't decide whether to let my hair grow longer or keep it trimmed. It hung just to my shoulders and had a nice swing to it. Longer might get in the way of working, though. In the summer, I often wore it in a ponytail.

My watch said seven fifteen when I trotted downstairs. Ed was there at the door on the dot.

He was in his civvies: a leather bomber jacket, dark sweater over a button-down shirt, and dark jeans. I'd forgotten how handsome he was. He leaned in to give me a quick kiss, maybe to remind me what I had to look forward to.

Grabbing my coat, I accompanied him to his car, the sheriff's black and white Interceptor as it turned out. I looked around at the dash, at the CB radio, the laptop attached to the center console, the holsters for guns. As he started the engine, he checked the radio. "Sorry," he said when he saw me noticing. "We've had a missing persons case and I want to monitor the situation."

"Missing person?" My heart grew cold. Had it begun again?

"Yeah," he said, backing up and aiming down the street into the heart of Moody Bog. "A jogger. Went missing yesterday morning. We searched the trail but didn't see anything. We never really had much crime here, but sometimes there are outside elements, like Hansen Mills."

Hansen Mills was where his brother Doug had his biker gang. They had warned me about staying away from Hansen Mills, but

I figured, sooner or later, I'd be invited back, and by "invited," I meant "abducted." Again. I wondered if that's what happened to the jogger.

"I hope it's not anyone I know. I mean, I've only met a few people..."

"Nichole Meunier. Ever hear of her?" When I shook my head, he turned into the rain and switched on the windshield wipers. "She usually kept on her place down in the hollow. Organic farmer. A friend called when the animals started making lots of noise."

"How awful. Is anyone taking care of the animals?"

"Her neighbors. We're a pretty tight bunch here in Moody Bog. We take care of our own."

And know each other's business, was the other unspoken thought. Ed already knew about my transgressions with Ruth Russell, but never went into detail. I was dying to ask how much he'd heard but kept silent.

We didn't drive far. There wasn't any driving too far within the precincts of Moody Bog, though there were other homesteads up in the hills surrounding the town center, and, apparently, some farms "down in the holler."

We moved down the curve of the road. On the right was a white clapboard church, just like in postcards. Idyllic. Steeple and all. But there was a secret there too, one I had yet to explore. Why had the custodian put a pentagram in his closet? I had run into him at the Chamber of Commerce get-together, and he seemed like a crusty old bird. But he wasn't part of my Wiccans. I had to find out more about him. I didn't want any of Doug's Ordo offshoots anywhere near me.

"Kylie, did you hear me?"

Oh shit. I hadn't. "I'm sorry, Ed. What did you say?"

"I said that I hoped you'd like some of our local fare. Are you a fish fan?"

"Very much. Ate a lot back in Huntington Beach." And speaking of where I came from…"Hey, Ed, have you ever heard the name 'Strange' mentioned when the locals talked about the founders?"

Before answering, he pulled into what looked like a shack on the crest of a hill overlooking the dark Atlantic below. There was light coming through the gingham curtains and plenty of cars filling the surrounding parking lot.

He got out and came around to my side just as I grabbed for the handle. I couldn't recall ever having a man open the door for me before, and here was Ed doing it a second time. I blushed as I got out. The rain had let up, so we walked like normal people instead of running inside like something was after us. The restaurant smelled of butter and crab cakes and toasty loaves of bread.

We grabbed a gingham-covered table in the busy and tiny restaurant, with a small votive candle flickering between us, and paper napkins at our places. Peeling off our jackets, he took both and hung them up by the door. I guess there was no chance of someone walking off with mine with the sheriff present.

"It's cute," I said of the restaurant.

"And it's real good home-cooked food."

"You must go out a lot. Or do you cook?"

"I cook a little, but not like this. I do a good clambake, though."

I smiled. It was all so cliché, but I guessed clichés came from some grain of truth at one time or another.

The waitress came up with her notepad. "Hi, Sheriff. Hi, Ms. Strange."

"Oh…hi…" I checked her nametag. "…Megan. You can call me Kylie."

"Will do! What can I get for you folks tonight?"

"I'm going to let the local order for me."

Ed smiled. "We'll both have the chowder and lobster rolls. And a couple of Bog Brews." He smiled again. "That's our local microbrew."

We settled in and he leaned toward me, resting his arms on the table. "So…to answer your question about the 'Strange' surname…I can't say that I have heard it associated with the founders. I would have told you to ask Karl Waters, but…" We both seemed to give him a moment of silent memorial. But if "Strange" was not a founder name, then chances are Ruth *wasn't* my cousin. Except that I had seen the name on her papers, hadn't I? "Ruth Russell would know more about that," Ed went on. "But speaking of Ruth…I heard a rumor about that Knitting Social. You never did get done telling me what exactly happened."

I dropped my head on my hand. "Jeez. I am really embarrassed about that. I don't know what you heard, but that's all I was doing in her library, just looking for relatives…and I found them."

"Really?"

"By the way, what exactly did you hear?"

"A few things. That you were stealing something from her, that you crashed her party—"

"I was invited!"

"That you made a scene and had to be thrown out." He was looking at me steadily.

I rested my hands demurely one over the other. "I didn't make a fuss," I said primly. "I took *myself* out of there…*before* she could throw me out. She caught me. But I wasn't stealing anything. I was just looking."

"Why didn't you just ask her?"

"Because I believe in asking forgiveness rather than permission. She might have said no."

"She'll certainly say it now."

"I know. But I plan to go to the library and see if anyone else has any archives. Someone must."

"And you really did find your name?"

"I thought I did. I was pretty rushed. But if it *is* true, then it looks like Ruth and I are cousins...distant, but still. I...recently remembered that my grandfather lived somewhere hereabouts. I used to come here for the summer when I was very small."

"To Moody Bog?" He seemed surprised that anyone *would* come here.

"I'm not sure of that. I don't remember where we were exactly. And my mom...passed away a few months ago. There's no one left to ask."

"I'm so sorry, Kylie. Were you close?"

"Yeah. We were. And it's funny that I didn't remember anything about Maine before. But I think the last time I was here I was six. So that was over twenty years ago."

"I'll ask around, if you'd like. I know some old-timers who might know."

"That would be great. Thanks."

We chatted some more. He told me about his home life, giving me a few insights about Doug, the black sheep, who couldn't seem to fit in. I talked about California. Our beers arrived and not too long after that the clam chowder in small bowls, with a heap of warm rolls in a basket. I gorged myself on the savory soup and soft bread. And then the lobster rolls arrived. Hoagies stuffed with chunks of mouth-watering lobster. I was happy to devour it all.

We each had another beer and hung out some more to let our food settle. I would have liked to take a walk, but once we got outside, it was bone-chillingly cold. Instead, we got into the car and Ed gave me a driving tour of the area, pointing out the highlights, the different neighborhoods. I saw the high school, the combination elementary and junior high, some of the farms, though we couldn't see much in the darkness. The clouds had cleared, though, and the moon and stars gave their own light to the freshly rain-swept countryside. I could make out the occasional barns and farmsteads in the distance, their chimneys puffing with blue-gray smoke lit by starlight.

Between the rustic fences lining the road, the warm vintage street lights, the cozy houses with their pumpkin-clad porches, I liked Moody Bog. I felt good about most of its inhabitants, especially the handsome sheriff. But the effect was slightly dimmed by what else was here, what *I* had unwittingly brought to it. And I began to wonder if I had ruined the idyllic nature of Ed's village, if I was responsible for changing it in ways that could never be repaired. People had died, after all. And that was on me.

Something had to be done about the Booke. It couldn't be allowed to harass some other little town in another three hundred years. Bricking it up in a wall had obviously not protected the town as Constance Howland had thought.

Ed's phone chimed. He clicked it and put it to his ear. "Bradbury here." He listened, offering an occasional, "Yeah…yeah. Okay. I'll talk to you in the morning."

"Police business?"

"Yeah." He tightened his hands on the steering wheel. "Someone else has gone missing between here and Hansen Mills. The daughter of one of the dairymen up there. My deputy is on it with the help of the staties."

"Oh. Do you have to go?"

"No. They've got it covered, but I'll be briefed early tomorrow."

"How old was she?"

"She was about twenty, I think."

"Do you think this has to do with the other one? The jogger?"

"Not enough evidence yet to link them. But it's suspicious. You know, one of the things I like about being sheriff here is the lack of big-city crime. Like I said, we have the occasional theft and kids getting out of hand, even the occasional bit of drunk driving. And it's not as if we weren't trained." He shook his head. "Dammit, I know every one of these people here. They're *my* people, and I take it personal when someone murders or kidnaps them."

What could I say? I wanted to comfort him, offer him platitudes like "You'll get 'em, Ed." But I knew that was a lie. Because you couldn't arrest a succubus. And I'd already killed it. How would he ever resolve this for himself? I could see how mired we would soon get with the layers of lies I would be obliged to tell him, and I didn't like the look of it.

"Then these goats went missing," he went on with a grumble.

"What about them? Someone planning a barbeque?"

"If it were only that simple. Last time this happened it was my *brother* doing his stupid witchcraft. He was *sacrificing* them. Can you believe that?"

I sure didn't like the sound of *that.* I wondered if Doc knew the kind of spell you did with a goat sacrifice. Probably too many to nail down.

Ed huffed an exasperated sound. "And the worst part of it is I kept it off the record. Do you know how much trouble I could be in if that ever got out? I can't let it go a second time. You see what I mean about Doug getting third and fourth chances? I don't know what to do with that idiot. If only he'd dump this stupid witchcraft crap." He glanced at me sheepishly. "I don't mean any offense. I know you and Doc's Wiccans are close."

"But they don't do animal sacrifices. Frankly, I can't see any of them having the stomach for it."

"That's good to hear." He looked relieved. "I mean…I was pretty sure about them, but to have you vouch for them, that means a lot to me."

The smile he offered meant a lot to *me.*

He pulled up in front of my place, put the car in park, and turned off the engine. I could see him wiping the police business out of his mind. "But we aren't supposed to be talking about that. This is a date."

"Would you like to come in?"

"Love to."

We unbuckled, but he was damned fast getting out and coming around to open my door, almost before my seat belt could reel itself in.

I unlocked the front door, switched on a lamp, and hung my coat on the hall tree. "Would you like some coffee? Or how about some relaxing herbal tea?"

"I'm not much of a tea drinker."

I faked an arrow to my heart. "Right where I live!"

"Sorry. I guess I'm not your demographic."

"That's okay. Coffee…or something else? I have brandy."

He followed me into the kitchen and didn't speak as I pulled down a bottle from the cupboard. Since I didn't own snifters, I grabbed two wine glasses. "I hope this is okay. I'm not a connoisseur, I'm afraid, but someone gave this to me and they seemed to know what they were talking about, brandy-wise."

I prepared a tray with brandy and glasses and brought it to the living room area, where I ran the shop. Ed got the fire going as I poured. He looked down with a frown at the pentagram on the floor, but he didn't ask and I didn't offer.

As we sat together on the sofa and sipped, I realized that this was exactly what I had been looking for when I left California: a man like this by my side, the future sprawled before me.

I turned to Ed with a pensive expression. He put down his glass, suddenly slid forward, and cupped my cheeks. There was no hesitation on my part. I met him halfway. His mouth was soft and warm and he opened to me. The sweetness of it soon turned to heat. I wrapped my arms around his neck, bringing him closer. The brandy-flavored kiss deepened. I felt his heart thudding against my chest…or was it mine? I just wanted more of him. He drew back only enough to nip at my lips, my chin, and then to drag sucking kisses down my throat to the base. He murmured a soft, "Kylie…" before his lips moved up my neck to my ear and left soft kisses behind it.

His hands were at my waist and slowly crept lower until fingers slipped underneath my sweater's hem, teasing my tingling skin. I was this close to lifting that sweater up myself, but I liked the feel of his large hands, the nipping and hard breaths at my neck. My hands were doing a bit of exploring on their own. He had a hard, muscled chest. I could feel that even through two layers of sweater and shirt. And just so he knew exactly where I was in the process, I dropped my hand to his lap…and squeezed.

He jolted for a second, breath hitching, before his hand seemed to get the go-ahead and slid fully up under my sweater, and with a groan I felt in my bones, he found a handful of breast.

I threw back my head and let him push the sweater up over my lacy bra. He dropped his head there and I clutched his hair in my fingers, gasping at his warm lips and breath. My eyes were half-lidded when I tilted my head just that much.

The curtains to the front window were slightly parted and I happened to glance toward them. I wasn't worried that someone would see. My shop was yards and yards away from the nearest house and surrounded by woods.

First, a shadow. Then, a figure appeared in that small opening and glared through the window. Erasmus!

CHAPTER THREE

I screamed. Ed sprang back and fell to the floor. I stood and yanked my sweater back down.

Ed looked up at me with glazed-eyed shock. "What…what…?"

"I'm sorry! I'm so sorry. I thought I saw a…a rat. Um, right over there!" I pointed vaguely away from the window.

Ed made a half-hearted laugh and leaned his arm on his upraised knee. "A rat? Seriously?"

"Yes. I…I have to put out a trap."

"Right now?"

"Yes. I'm sorry. I just hate those kinds of things. I can't stand the thought of them."

"Well…I'll put it out for you then…"

"No, that's okay. I think the mood has effectively fled."

He dropped his head and ran his hand up over his sweaty neck. "Okay. All right."

"I'm so sorry."

"That's okay." Clearly it wasn't. Especially after he rose. Those were some *tight* jeans. "I'll…leave you to it then. If… you're sure."

"Yes." I hugged myself.

He nodded, resigned. He strode to the door and grabbed his coat but didn't put it on. I sympathized. I really did.

Erasmus's timing was superb as always.

Ed turned at the doorway and took my hand, pulling me in. His kiss was rough at first but then softened. "I had a good time tonight. Despite..." He gave an exasperated sigh. "At least this time I wasn't knocked unconscious."

"There is that. I'm really sorry. Maybe...*your* place next time. If you still *want* a next time."

"I do. I'll cook. And I promise, there will be no rats...or owls... or badgers or anything else."

"It's a date."

"I'll call you." He kissed me again, turned, and got into his car.

I hugged myself in the cold and watched him drive away. Once he was down the road, I leaned into the doorway and retrieved my coat, slipping it on.

"Erasmus!" I rasped, peering into the shadows. Had I imagined it? "Erasmus, where are you?"

"Here."

I whirled. And there he was, in the flesh. Dark hair flopping over his brooding eyes, mouth twisted in a sneer, black leather duster hanging from his shoulders. Ed was suddenly forgotten. I almost stepped forward close enough to be in his personal space, but then held back. "Where have you been?"

"Away. But I see you wasted no time."

"You *told* me to move on."

"I didn't know you could so easily take it to heart."

"That's not fair."

He turned away, duster whirling around him. "What have you and your little Wiccans done? I cannot gain entrance."

"They...did a spell. To keep evil away."

"Ah." He frowned.

"You were gone. I didn't know where you were. I didn't know if you were coming back."

"I am tied to the book. You know this. There is nowhere for me to go."

I breathed, giddy with relief. He was all right! I wanted to punch his face.

"I'm going to need your help," I said.

"I know."

He said nothing more and I sighed, leaning against the rough clapboards. "Do you know what's out there? Ed said that two women are missing."

Still he didn't speak. But I watched his profile, watched him lift his head. His patrician nose sniffed the wind. "Something…" he said quietly.

I moved closer to him then. Without thinking, I laid a hand on his arm. His head snapped down, looking at my fingers on his sleeve. Drawing them back, I mumbled a quiet apology. He huffed a noise, dismissing it.

"Do you still have the crossbow?" he said.

"Of course."

"And my amulet?"

I tugged it out from under my sweater and showed him. He glanced at it and turned away again. "You never tried to summon me."

"I didn't see the use. You just vanished."

"Sometimes I must. But you bear my amulet. I told you. All you need do is call."

"So…literally? I just go outside and call your name?"

He sighed dramatically. "Yes! What about all this seems so hard for you to grasp?"

And there was our old irascible Erasmus.

"I get the concept, idiot."

"What did you just call me?"

"We don't have time for this. And it's *cold*. Could you just find out what's out there and let me know?"

"I'm not your servant."

"And yet I have this." I held up the amulet. "And you come when I call. Isn't that the definition of—"

"Off you go then." He made ushering movements with his hands.

I laughed. I couldn't help it. I was relieved. I wanted to hug him. He'd hate that. It made me want to hug him all the more.

Turning toward the front door, I stopped. "Are you sure you can't get in?"

"The house is warded."

"Are you sure there are no loopholes?"

His gaze slid toward mine. "Are you wondering if you'll be safe… or about a way to get me…*inside*." He said the last so salaciously my throat went dry. I swallowed.

"You're a…naughty demon, aren't you?"

He turned his face but not in time to hide his smile. "Get inside before you freeze."

"Do you need anything? I have brandy."

He frowned. "Brandy? I wouldn't mind."

I hurried inside, snatched up my glass, and filled it again before running back outside. "Here you go."

He took the glass by the stem and held it up to the moonlight. Then he dunked his nose inside the bowl and sniffed.

"It's supposed to be decent stuff."

He gave me an "I'll be the judge of that" look. He sipped, rolled it in his mouth, and swallowed. Tilting his head, he shrugged.

I rolled my eyes. "I think you're full of it."

"I beg your pardon. I have lived for thousands of years. I've certainly had my share of spirits."

"Sure. But this doesn't compare to Netherworld booze, blah, blah, blah."

He postured with the glass still aloft. "There's something not quite right about you."

I grinned.

He drank while I stood there, hands thrust in my coat pockets, trying to keep warm. I didn't want to go in just yet.

"So..." he said. He stared down into his glass. "You, er, went on another *date* with that man."

There was a part of me that reveled in his obvious jealousy. Then the realization struck me that he had probably been hanging around even though I couldn't see him. "Were you following me?"

He considered, as if he didn't quite understand the question. In the end, he merely ignored it and took another drink.

I crossed my arms. "And so you were reduced to a peeping tom."

"I am nothing of the sort."

"I *saw* you through the window."

"Because I couldn't get in."

"So how long were you planning on standing there?" I was tapping my foot now.

He shrugged one shoulder and drank.

"Perv."

"I'm not the one throwing myself at the nearest male under forty."

He knew he'd gone too far. Before I could explode, he downed the brandy and offered me back the empty glass. "Thank you."

I grabbed it out of his hand with the idea of throwing it against the wall. He raised a hand. "Don't you think it would be wise to do a little hunting?"

I stopped in mid-throw. "What? Now?"

"Of course now."

"But we don't know what we're looking for."

"That shouldn't stop the Chosen Host, now should it?"

I hated when he called me that. "Let me get a hat…and my crossbow."

I took my knit hat from the hall tree. The chthonic crossbow whistled in the air, coming toward me from its hiding place upstairs. I put out my hand automatically and caught it. Chosen Host stuff.

I grabbed a scarf, wrapped it around my neck, and locked up the place. "A-hunting we will go," I hummed. "Where to?" I asked.

He raised his face and sniffed the air, then pointed toward the forest behind the house. "Let's try that way."

I hated the idea of hunting blind…but I couldn't help but feel a little thrill to be with Erasmus again. Which was completely stupid and wrong. I could have been in the strong embrace of Sheriff Ed… and a fine embrace it was. If only I hadn't looked out the window. Had I left those curtains open slightly on purpose? Freud 1, Kylie 0.

I stuffed the crossbow under my arm and dug my gloves out of my mackinaw's pockets. The crossbow hadn't loaded itself. I checked. It had the habit of picking just the right quarrel from its many hiding places on the hilt. Each one—ten, to be exact—was made of a different wood, point, and fletching. The crossbow knew just what was needed to defeat whatever beastie was about. And a good thing, too, because the Booke didn't come with an instruction manual. It enjoyed its mayhem. I felt *that* much coming off it.

I gripped the crossbow again, ready when it was. But the woods were dark, and the moon was setting. And I had forgotten my phone again.

I followed Erasmus. He moved noiselessly, like he always did, while I, the stumbling, bumbling human, made the biggest racket crunching through leaves, breaking twigs and branches in my path, and swearing as I tripped again and again.

"Is there no sound you can't make?" he sneered at me.

"It's not easy to do this in the dark, you know."

He didn't bother turning back or replying. A subtle shaking of his head sufficed.

We traveled downward. There was a bit of a path, which made the going easier. The forest ahead seemed to rise, hills emerging around us. I tried to note where we were in case we got separated. I knew he'd try to protect me. It was his job, though I was a little sketchy on the whole demon/Booke dynamic. The Booke was, apparently, far older than the Powers That Be, and they assigned a demon to close up the Booke whenever it was opened. They didn't like the idea of things existing over which they had no control.

"Erasmus?"

He slowed to a stop, sniffed the air, and then finally turned. His eyes were deep holes in the dark, but they glittered from starlight, making them seem more human.

"The Booke is still such an enigma," I said. "The Powers That Be don't like it, but their big plan was to put a demon on it? If they are so powerful, couldn't they have come up with a better solution?"

"I don't like talking about them."

"Why? Are they eavesdropping?"

"Beelze's tail, I hope not." When he looked back at me he must have seen the concern in my eyes. He stopped to face me. "They cannot see or hear what transpires on this plane except through the eyes of their own demon servants."

"Like you."

"Not quite. In order to communicate with them, I must travel to the Netherworld."

"What's it like? Is it very Dante's Inferno?"

He sneered. I guess no one likes their world reduced to a cliché. "No. I do not know why you creatures give such credence to the unremarkable ramblings of a bad poet. He's never been there, I can assure you."

"Okay. But...what *is* it like? Do you...like it there?"

He turned abruptly and headed into the forest again. I double-timed it to catch up. "I wouldn't say I necessarily 'liked' it. It is familiar."

"Are you saying you like it better here?"

"I said nothing of the kind."

"But…do you?"

He kept walking. "There are certain aspects of this place to recommend it."

I couldn't help but smile. And wonder. Was one of those things…me? *That's stupid, Kylie. Don't think that. Not for one second.*

Then I thought about the day he left. It was so messed up in so many different ways.

"Why *did* you go away?" I blurted. "Was it because of Baphomet?" *Good save, Kylie.*

"Do not utter his name. He might think you are summoning him."

"Oh shoot. Okay. How about…'Goat Guy'?"

He stopped again and turned, mouth hanging slightly open.

"Was that why you had to disappear? Do you and…Goat Guy…have a conflict of some kind?"

I saw him incredulously mouth the words "Goat Guy" before he answered. "We…well. It is a long-standing animosity. Demons and gods typically don't get along."

"I didn't know that."

"As I have mentioned before, your ignorance on the subject is astoundingly unparalleled."

"You're such a sweet talker," I murmured. But remembering that day sent chills down my spine. "You were transparent, like you were fading away."

"It happens."

I almost asked but his unwavering gaze told me that the subject was closed. Yet something else was still troubling me. I really didn't know his full purpose. Guarding the Booke, yeah, I got that. But chasing the last Chosen Host to her doom? That was something I really wanted to—*needed* to—nail down. "Your tattoo." I pointed vaguely toward his chest. "We discovered that it means 'follower.' Or…'assassin.' So…which is it?"

"You're very inquisitive tonight."

I squared my shoulders. "I sort of have to be. My life depends on it."

He nodded. "So it does." Looking off into the forest again, obviously reluctant to answer, he sighed. "I understand your concern, but there's no need for it."

"It's just that…I really don't know anything about you and less about the Booke. All I know about *it* and demons, I've gotten from you. And demons have a tendency—at least from what I've read—they have a tendency to lie."

"So if I am lying to you, what good are my answers at all?"

"Because…I believe…*you* won't lie to me."

His eyes widened. He stood a long moment simply gazing at me. "Humans are foolish," he said quietly. "And female humans are more foolish by far."

I countered the weight of his gaze with my weary sigh. "Misogyny? Really?"

"Miss Strange…"

"I thought we'd moved on to 'Kylie.'"

"Very well…*Kylie*…it is best to concentrate on the task ahead. There is much to do."

And that was the best answer I was likely to get. I perched the butt of the crossbow on my hip. "Fine. Let's go." I moved forward, shouldering him out of the way.

Splashing sounded ahead. Must be a pond. Or as the locals called it, a *bogan*. I pushed past the bracken and found the ground squishy with mud and cattails. There was that distinctive stinky, marshy smell in the air. And the mist was suddenly thick, surrounding us in undulating waves.

They weren't kidding when they named this place Moody *Bog*. There were lots of them. When the bog or *bogan* revealed itself beyond the thick trees, I saw something white in the distance. My heart stuttered, and fumbling with the crossbow, I got it into a position where I could aim. It had armed itself. Now my heart was trying to beat its way out of my chest.

I snuck a peek at the thing through the brambles…and saw it was only a horse. And the poor thing was stuck in the mud.

I lowered the crossbow but kept it ready, just in case whatever it was attacked the small, stocky pony.

I escaped the foliage and cooed toward the creature. "Hey, boy. Are you okay? We'll get you out of this. Hey, Erasmus!"

Now where was he? Summon him, my ass. He was never around when I called him, despite what he said. Yup, Seraphina was right. Demons lie.

I approached the horse cautiously. After all, I was no horse person. The closest I ever got was those pony rides when I was a kid. I reached my hand out as if offering him something. Did I have anything to give? I plunged my hand into my pocket and found a butterscotch hard candy. I unwrapped it, stuffed the leftover cellophane back into my pocket, and held the candy in the palm of my hand. I seemed to remember that you should keep your palm flat so that their big teeth couldn't nip at the soft skin of your cupped hand. I shuffled forward, one hand stretched out and the other holding a crossbow and awkwardly aiming it into the surrounding woods.

The horse nickered, lowering its head. It shuffled and splashed in the water. He'd obviously gotten loose from a barn or fenced field. He had no bridle. I could grab his mane to lead him around. Would a horse let you do that? I couldn't leave it here. It might fall in and drown.

"Hey, boy." I got closer. His mane was already soaked. He had probably struggled a long time in that bog trying to get out. "Poor thing." I was close enough to almost give him the treat when he raised his head, looking interested, wide nostrils flaring and sniffing.

"Kylie! Stop at once and carefully step away."

I looked back. Erasmus stood at some distance at the edge of the wood, like a shadow.

"It's only a pony. He needs help. Something out here might be hunting it. My crossbow is armed."

"Shoot it!"

"What? No! Are you crazy? This poor horse needs help. He's stuck in the mud."

"Kylie…listen very carefully. Listen to the sound of my voice. Step away from the beast."

"Erasmus, he's a poor dumb creature…Much like you," I muttered the last. I lowered the crossbow and turned back toward the pony.

My jaw dropped. It was not a pony. Its mouth had opened to unnatural proportion. Instead of flat, square teeth, there was a mouth full of jagged canines. Its gentle eyes had morphed into red, glowing lava, and it reared up and issued an unholy shriek. I startled back and fell.

"Shoot it!"

I heard the words distantly, but I couldn't move. Instead of drawing the crossbow up to my shoulder and firing, I couldn't look away from the transformed pony or the water that churned under its feet.

I felt myself rise, felt my feet walk closer to that mesmerizing water—water was cool and tranquil and offered a quiet, quiet peace, didn't it?

A sound, almost something in the back of my mind, was chanting something like *Shoot it! Shoot it!* but it was nothing like the water, the peaceful, deep water. I dropped the heavy thing from my right hand and stretched out my arm. All I needed to do was touch that snowy hide, that wet mane. I just needed to touch it…

A dark shape swooped and knocked me down, and then rose up, crying out in a howl before the pony. The pony screamed again and dove into the bog. I didn't think the bog was deep enough, but it disappeared under the churning waves, until all was still again. There were no howls and shrieks. Only the sound of dripping water, popping bubbles, and the quiet plop of a frog jumping into the pond.

It was like a mist had risen off my eyesight and brain. I had felt a little foggy, a little out of it. And then my senses returned with full force. I gasped and covered my mouth at what I had almost done, what had almost happened to me.

Erasmus's arms suddenly surrounded me and I fell against him, sobbing. He held me tightly, brushing my hair away from my face. Soft murmurings of reassurance rumbled deep in his chest, and I melted into him, wiping at my cheek. Finally, with great effort, I pushed away and used my coat sleeve to clean the rest of my tears. I picked up the discarded crossbow. It had disarmed itself.

"W-what was that?" I rasped, still unable to catch my breath.

"A kelpie. A water demon taking on the appearance of a horse to lure his victims to a watery death. Had you touched him, you would have been stuck fast and unable to escape. You would have drowned, and there would have been nothing I could have done."

"Oh my God. Do you suppose that's what happened to those women?"

"In all likelihood. Young women are particularly attracted to the charms of the kelpie. There is a…visceral connection between women and horses anyway, and the kelpie's powers accentuate that."

"It was the water too. I was attracted to the water." I let my mind remember the sensations. I had wanted nothing more than to let that water enclose me, take me down. I shivered.

"Yes. The doom is complete and inescapable. You will have to fight its call with all of your strength."

"I didn't know before. Now I do. I thought it was just a lost pony."

"Yes, now you know better, but it won't make it any easier."

"And you saved me."

"Yes, the dreadful demon saved your life."

"You're not as dreadful as you'd like people to think."

He stared at me for a full minute before he turned away in a swirl of dark leather. "Don't make it into more than it is."

He was right. He *had* to save me. Not only was it his job, but I still had his amulet. It gave me power over him. Just not the kind I would have liked.

I had to tell my Wiccans…and find a solution.

CHAPTER FOUR

The coven said they'd come the next day after the shop closed. I had customers making good purchases, but I was afraid I sleepwalked through most of it. My mind was on so many other things.

Every now and then, I thought I saw a shadow pass by my window. I knew it was Erasmus.

Once the shop was closed, they arrived. Nick had brought homemade spaghetti and we all ate silently around the farmhouse table in the kitchen. My appetite was off. I spun my fork in the pasta but never managed to bring it up to my mouth. Finally, I just pushed the plate away.

"It's all very distressing," said Doc to break the silence. "A kelpie. I wonder if there is any rhyme or reason as to the monsters the book chooses to expel."

I shook my head. "It's not alphabetical. Who knows?"

"Would, uh, Mr. Dark know?"

"I don't think so. He doesn't seem to know all the finer details of how the Booke works."

"I was reading about kelpies," said Jolene with her mouth full. No one was surprised by her pronouncement. Setting down her fork, she reached into the backpack lying at her feet. The Hello Kitty skull patch on the front pocket was also wearing a witch hat. She pulled out her tablet and started swiping until the page she wanted came up. "It's like Mr. Dark said. Kelpies pose as horses or ponies to lure their prey—usually younger people and women—who get stuck and then pulled underwater. Some legends say that kelpies eat their victims. Everything but the liver, and that's what ends up floating to the surface and washing ashore."

"Eww," said Nick. "That's gross."

"I *know*," said Jolene eagerly.

"Look," said Doc, "let's not dwell on the more prurient aspects of this. Let's just learn all we can so that Kylie can dispatch it as quickly as possible. Before anyone else is snatched up."

"But this is awful." I dropped my forehead to my hand. "We know what it does. Can't we somehow warn the public?"

"And say what?" said Nick. "'There's a demon horse out there. Stay away!'"

"You can't say that," said Seraphina thoughtfully. "But maybe we can say something similar. Doc, can we issue some sort of health alert? Like a rabies warning? If anyone sees a white pony on the loose, don't get close or touch it because it has some deadly contagious disease?"

"That's an excellent idea, Seraphina. I'll have to consult with some veterinarians I know down in Connecticut and see what they might suggest. In fact, let me call one of them now." He took out his phone and got up from the table, scrolling down his list of contacts.

I sat up. Warning people. It was too late for the two missing women, but stopping more deaths would definitely be a win for a change.

Nick was standing and leaning against the table. "So…is Mr. Dark out there right now? I sorta…sense something."

"Yup."

He shook his head. "I know I shouldn't say this, but…he is wicked hot."

Nick had an envious look in his eye. I wondered which fellow in town usually tickled his fancy. Someone dark and brooding?

"I don't think it's all that it's cracked up to be, to tell you the truth. Stick to mortals."

"Yeah. Well…I plan on it. He's, uh, a little scary, really. And that Baphomet stuff—"

"He said we shouldn't use that name. So now I'm referring to him as Goat Guy."

"Goat Guy. I like that."

"That's true," said Seraphina, not looking up from her notepad. "Names have power. And we don't want to summon anything we have no control over."

I tried to tilt my head to see what she was doing. "What's that you're working on, Seraphina?" Looked like my name and some graphs and numbers.

She stopped and stared down at it. "Oh dear."

"What is it?"

She pressed her lips together and blinked her teal-shaded lids. "I was doing some numerology. To see where you stood."

"Oh." Another thing I never used to believe in. Could that be true, too? "What does it say?"

She closed her notebook and rested her hands on it. Each long fingernail was painted a pearlized pink. "Well, some of these things are less than precise," she said nervously.

"It seems precise enough for you to worry. Come on. What does it say?"

"You shouldn't mess with that," Jolene scolded, clearing the dishes. "I don't believe in it."

Seraphina huffed. "How can you not?"

Jolene stopped, the stack of dishes in her hand leaning precariously. "Because it's a quirk of fate. What you're named, what spelling is used, if it's spelled right on your birth certificate. And all sorts of factors go into your date of birth: international time zones, Caesarean sections, incompetent doctors, overeager midwives…"

"Can't you see that all that is taken into account? All those factors come together in the universe to make you who you are."

"But Kylie could have spelled her name with a 'C.' It makes no sense."

"*What does it say?*"

Everyone looked at me. I hadn't meant to yell, but it was all making me nervous.

Seraphina dropped her eyes and slowly opened the notebook again. "I use the Chaldean method of numerology. The total for each of the letters of your name comes to thirty-five. No matter how many ways I try to configure it, it always comes out the same. It is full of serious warnings for the future. Disasters will be brought about by…certain associations. Bad partnerships, bad unions, bad situations. And this combination advises that you should carefully reconsider the path you are following."

Everyone was still, looking at me. After embarrassing myself only seconds ago by yelling, I tried to make light of it. "Oh, is that all? So far so good then. I'd hate to naysay my numbers."

Seraphina laid a hand on mine. "This is serious, Kylie. You must be very careful. This path…"

"I don't seem to have much of a choice about this path. I mean, if I did, I certainly wouldn't be following any of it. I don't have a choice." And then that old engraving came to mind. The one I found on the internet that led me directly to Karl Waters and his museum. The one that maybe led the creature following me to his doorstep. It depicted eighteenth-century Constance Howland—the last Chosen Host we knew of—running for her life right before she was supposedly chased off Falcon's Point. The person chasing her was Erasmus. He told me he hadn't had any physical interest in her, but was that just to appease me?

"Demons lie," I muttered.

"I've got it!" said Doc, coming back into the room and waving his phone. "Hendra Virus Disease causes severe respiratory illness that can lead to death in horses *and* humans and is highly contagious. I'm going to call the sheriff now so he can put out the alert. I hope to goddess this does the trick." He put the phone to his ear and wandered away to tell Ed all about it.

"I wonder if I'm making a mistake." I hadn't meant to say that aloud, but there it was. Freud was really racking up the points, it seemed.

"What mistake?" asked Nick.

"Sheriff Ed. I don't know if it's right to start something with him. According to numerology, my number might be up soon."

He slumped back into his seat sideways, his arm resting on the seat back and his legs dangling over the chair arm. "I don't know, Kylie. I don't mean to be fatalistic or anything, but isn't it a good idea to snatch love where you can get it before something happens? Not that anything is going to happen." He shot Seraphina an angry glare.

"It does say that love and affection will be prominent in your life," offered Seraphina.

Yes, but was that with Ed...or Erasmus?

"Do Sheriff Ed's numbers," said Jolene, coming back from the sink. She peered over Seraphina's shoulder.

"Very well." She scribbled and I found myself biting my nail. When she looked to be finished, she sat back with a frown line creasing her brow.

"It's a very ominous number. Hidden dangers, trials; this is a person who will face an uphill battle..."

Jolene snorted. "It's like a horoscope. It's vague enough to describe anyone. I wouldn't put much stock in it, Kylie."

"Do Mr. Dark's," said Nick.

"Oh, come on, Nick!" Jolene said.

"She did Sheriff Ed's. She has to do Mr. Dark's. Does it even count if he's a demon?"

Seraphina frowned further and wrote it out. My teeth were certainly getting a workout biting my nails. Instead of frowning when she was done, she raised her brows. "It's a...a very fortunate number. It promises the assistance of those of high position. It also has a strong connection to love and is an auspicious number for future events."

"Well that proves it," said Nick. "It's all bullshit."

Seraphina seemed to be recounting.

"How can that be?" I asked. "Ed is all trials and uphill battles, and Erasmus is love and rainbows? That's completely messed up and backwards."

Jolene nodded. "You can't believe in those ancient arts. They aren't worth the clay they're cuneiformed on."

"So how do you pick and choose? Witchcraft is okay but numerology isn't? Horoscopes are hooey but pentagrams are fine?" My chair skidded back as I rose. "None of it makes sense. None of it!"

I fled upstairs. I would have flung myself to the bed, but I just didn't feel up to the theatrics. Instead I sat. What had my life become? I had really hopeful days when it was just me and my shop, and then I had days like this, when everything seemed like a useless exercise. Not for the first time, I wondered if I would end up like Constance Howland. Or would one of the creatures get me? Just because I had the crossbow didn't mean I would always win. Because Erasmus might *not* always get there on time. Nothing was guaranteed. Even my numbers didn't add up.

A rap on the door. When I got up to open it, I wasn't expecting who was on the other side.

Jolene stood awkwardly in the doorway. "Can I come in?"

"Sure." I drifted back toward the bed and sat. She hesitated in the doorway for a moment and then stepped in. After another brief pause, she sat beside me. "You really can't listen to all of Seraphina's wackiness. I've never held any store in numerology. It isn't precise at all, any more than a horoscope."

"What about tarot?"

"Well that's different."

I stared at her incredulously. "How?"

"Have you ever heard of Schrödinger's cat?"

"Yes. The cat in the box. Is it living or dead? We only know when we observe."

"It's a little more complicated than that. It's actually both dead *and* alive until someone observes what it really is. It's always dead and it's always alive while it's in that box."

"So? What does that have to do with tarot cards? That's just as random as numbers and birthdates, isn't it?"

She was getting excited now. Jolene liked puzzles and thrived on their intricacies. "But it *isn't* random. The person who wants the reading shuffles the cards. And until those cards are turned over and observed, they are anything and everything all at the same time. It's the person shuffling that opens the box and allows us to observe."

"Are you saying that the cards can magically *change* until they're turned over?"

"Sort of. The person's life force makes those cards shuffle the way they do, and land where they need to be."

"You know what? I'd rather not have my cards read either."

"Probably a good idea," she muttered.

My fingers were restless in my lap. "It's not what Seraphina said. It's not even the warnings of gloom and doom. I'm already living through that. It's just...everything. The uncertainty. I mean, no one can be certain of their future. I get it. But mine seems wrought with death and injury no matter where I look. So why am I even worrying about Ed or Erasmus? I should just be concentrating on getting this all over with."

"'Cause life is more than just doing your job nine to five."

I stared down at my teenage philosopher.

She shrugged. "My dad is always saying that. He always encouraged a rounded education in the arts as well as the basics. That's why he and Mom never discouraged my interest in Wicca. They wanted more for me than just reading, writing, and arithmetic. I suppose they thought that might mean music or art. But...love is also part of the equation, I guess. You can't just put off love because it isn't convenient. It's a part of life. Not like I can give great advice on that."

"I appreciate you trying to."

"Look, Kylie. I'm your friend...as well as your employee. But as a friend, if you had asked me—which I realize you didn't—but if you *had* asked me, I'd tell you to weigh the pros and cons. Right now, Sheriff Ed would probably be tipping the scales on the con side. Am I right?"

I nodded. But I really didn't want to think about any of that right now. Mostly I wanted to take a nice long, hot bath and forget everything for at least an hour.

A crash sounded from downstairs. We looked at each other for a split second before we both sprinted for the door.

I scrambled down the stairs with Jolene on my heels and stopped at the bottom. Something slammed against the front door again.

My Wiccans were all assembled and frozen in place, staring at the door. The crossbow wasn't making an appearance, and all was silent from the Booke. I figured it was okay enough to see what was going on.

No one else moved as I made quickly for the door and yanked it open. Erasmus was there and he was scowling. He held fast to the scruff of someone he had obviously tackled to the ground. The man was covered in wet leaves and mud.

"I found *this* lurking about, trying to peer into the windows," he said, shaking the man. Erasmus heaved him through the open doorway that he couldn't cross himself. The man fell forward onto my woven rag rug.

"Kylie," the man said. "What the *hell* is going *on*?" He raised his bruised face toward me.

My blood ran cold and just as quickly boiled over. "Dammit! What are *you* doing here, Jeff?"

CHAPTER FIVE

"Kylie baby, I'm here for you. To win you back." Jeff slowly got to his feet. Nick put out a hand to help him. There was the beginning of a bruise on one side of his face and his dirty blond hair had been made dirtier with leaves, twigs, and mud. Erasmus had given him a thrashing. I kind of wished I'd seen it.

"First of all, I'm not your 'Kylie baby' anymore, and second of all, you are *never* going to win me back. How dare you come all the way across the country expecting…expecting…argh!" I stomped away from him to the other side of the room, clutching my arms. I could *not* believe it. The absolute last person I ever wanted to see again, standing here in my new place, *my* sanctuary. "I thought this place was warded against *evil*."

"Kylie baby…" Jeff implored.

Erasmus leaned in as far as the magic would allow him, wearing a hungry smile. "Toss him back out. *I'll* deal with him."

Tempting.

Jeff thumbed back at the demon at the door. "Who the hell is this?" He slowly looked around at each of my Wiccans, the burning sage, and the pentagram on the floor. "And what the hell is going on? Have you gone pagan or something?"

"Jeff, just get out."

"Get out? I came clear across the country to talk to you."

"That's *your* problem. Out."

He looked at the Wiccans again, and by their scowls, he saw no help there. "I don't have a place to stay, babygirl. I thought…" He sauntered forward. Even bruised and muddy, his beguiling smile was on full wattage. His voice softened. "I thought I'd stay here. On a couch or something. Just so we could talk."

"There is absolutely nothing to talk about. I'm here now, this is my new place, and you aren't part of it."

He looked around, nodding. "Yeah. It's nice. Lots of nice touches. You learned a lot from me."

"Yes I did. Mostly I learned what an asshole you are."

"Name calling? Really?"

"I believe in telling it like it is. Now if you wouldn't mind…" I gestured toward the door.

Erasmus was still standing in the doorway, and his duster had begun to smolder.

Jeff lost his smile. "I can't even crash on your sofa?"

"What part of 'no' is so hard to understand?"

"You heard the lady," said Doc.

"Excuse me, Grandpa, but this isn't any of your business."

"Excuse *me*, sonny, but I'm not your grandpa." Doc flicked his wrist and suddenly Jeff was stumbling toward the door.

"Whoa! Wait! How are you doing that?"

He was sent sailing right into Erasmus's waiting arms. "I believe the lady told you to leave." He grinned. Though his face was mostly in shadow, I caught a glimpse of a mouth full of teeth far sharper than a human should have. Jeff must have seen it too, because he was scrambling to get away. And once free, he took off down the street at full bore.

I hadn't realized I was shaking until Seraphina wrapped her arm around my shoulders.

Erasmus seemed torn between giving chase and comforting me. He braced himself forlornly against the jamb, unable to come through. His eyes were too intense, too full of raw emotion. I had to turn away.

"You do realize," said Nick, "that the nearest motel is in Hansen Mills."

"And how do *you* know that?" asked Jolene.

"Shut up, is how," he said, turning red.

I shook my head. "Doug won't know who he is. And with any luck, he'll leave in the morning." But knowing Jeff, how likely was that?

Doc patted my hand. "I can see why you left California."

"It wasn't just him. It was a combination of things. My mom, a new start. I wanted my inheritance to count for something."

"We understand, Kylie," he said. "You don't have to explain. And with Mr. Dark out there, I doubt he'll come around harassing you again."

"You've got your very own watchdog," said Jolene with a weak smile.

Lovely. Just what I wanted. An ex-lover to guard me from another ex-lover. How had this become my life?

"Look, everyone, I think I want to call it a night."

They said nothing and gathered their things. I watched them depart, each giving me their own version of an encouraging smile. I locked the door after them and then began shutting the drapes. I saw Erasmus out there standing in the middle of the street. His eyes were on me as I pulled the curtains together.

I flicked off lights as I trudged upstairs. The Booke had been below before, but I scarcely needed to cast a glance to see that it had suddenly appeared on my bedroom desk. I was exhausted in heart and soul. A bath really did sound good.

My bathroom was cheerful. It had been built sometime in the Victorian era, with more modern additions over the years. It had plenty of tile and charming light fixtures. The sink was a pedestal, the toilet and shower were modern, but the bathtub was a clawfoot. I turned on the water, dumped in some aromatic bath salts, and started shedding my clothes.

The sound of the water was mesmerizing and I seemed to fall into slow motion as I slipped out of my shoes and peeled off the socks. Sweater, jeans. I was down to bra and panties when I went to check on the water level. The aromatics had filled the bathroom with forest-scented steam. I inhaled, gazing into the deepening water, swirling and bubbling. The salts made it a darker blue-green, like the ocean. The water churned, more so than seemed logical for the faucet's stream. Was there something wrong with the drain? I leaned forward to look…

Without warning, something burst forth from the tub in a great blast of water. I screamed. The horsehead of the kelpie snarled and howled at me, clacking its teeth, trying to get a chunk of me. The head lunged and I slipped on the wet tiles, landing hard on my backside. The kelpie shrieked and thrashed impossibly in the tub; there was no way it could fit, and yet it snarled and bared its sharp teeth, red eyes narrowed to slits.

I scrambled on my back away from the tub. One hoof, then another, came up over the side.

Something clattered against the closed bathroom door. The crossbow! I rolled over and stretched toward the door, but a wave from the tub scooped under me and tossed me back, and I was facing the beast again. Its shriek was like fingernails on a chalkboard. I wanted to cover my ears, but I was reaching for anything to get away from it.

The door burst open. I expected the crossbow. But it was Erasmus, his face darkening in fury. He raised his arms toward the beast and howled back at it. He was more beast than man, the demon showing his true self at last. His body stretched and twisted like some giant vicious snake, his duster dark, slick, and unnaturally elongating right along with his suddenly elastic body. He lunged and his whole body curled weirdly around the kelpie's neck, doubling on himself like a python. The monster thrashed, trying to dislodge him, but Erasmus seemed stuck on there, good and tight. The kelpie slammed against the walls, sending a large chunk of plaster shattering to the floor. When it happened again, Erasmus couldn't seem to hold on, so he turned his head and clamped his mouth to the kelpie's neck, biting down, until a hoof came up and knocked him free.

Snarling, eyes blazing red, Erasmus shrieked a horrific sound that sent me scrambling away from him across the wet tiles. He wasn't a man at all anymore, but a monster, just as fearsome as the creature trying to climb out of my bathtub.

The kelpie lunged with its head, snapping its oversized mouth and sharp teeth. Erasmus dodged it. I feared he'd slip and the monster would get him for sure, but quick as any serpent, Erasmus grabbed the kelpie's muzzle.

It arched its neck and wailed, and Erasmus had no choice but to hold on or be shredded. The kelpie whipped him from side to side and a flailing hoof finally smacked him away.

Erasmus skidded across the wet floor, slammed against the wall, and cracked the plaster on that side too.

I heard the sound, and I instinctively lifted my hand. The crossbow slapped into my palm and I took no time to think, just jammed the butt into my hip and fired. The bolt hit the tiles behind the beast, and the kelpie suddenly sank beneath the waves and plunged down the drain with a loud sucking sound.

Erasmus hunched over the tub, searching, but found nothing.

I collapsed onto my back on the wet floor and breathed my relief. My fingers curled tightly around the crossbow's hilt.

Footsteps. When I looked up, he was looking down at me. He couldn't seem to help a smoldering perusal. Lacy magenta bra-and-panty sets did that to men, I guess.

"How did you get in?" I rasped breathlessly.

"Your Wiccans are less than thorough. They have yet to learn how literal the gods and demons are. I'll wager they asked their gods to ward the windows and the doors. But they neglected to mention the chimney."

Even as jacked as I felt from the fight, I couldn't help but smile at the image. "You came down the chimney? I wonder if Santa Claus is just a demon in a red suit."

"I have no idea what you're talking about. But yes. I was able to access the chimney. And I daresay the kelpie was able to come in through your pipes."

I sat up onto my elbows. "Erasmus, I've got to get rid of that thing. And soon!"

"Agreed."

I put out a hand for him to help me up. He reached down and clasped my hand with his warm one. He yanked me up and I fell against him. We were nose to nose. His mouth, those shapely lips, so close to mine…

His duster began to smolder again.

"Erasmus," I whispered. "Don't…catch my house on fire."

The smoke wisped away. But he still held me. He neither moved in to take the kiss we both seemed so desperate for, nor did he pull away.

It was my shiver that finally seemed to snap him out of it. His eyes shifted away at last. "Go put something on. You must be cold."

I ran from the bathroom. My face was flushed and hot as I snatched the bathrobe from the bed and slipped it on. He strode out of the bathroom, looking grim as always.

"Can we ward the house again?" I asked. "Make sure the drains are covered this time?"

"And the chimney."

"I...never mentioned the chimney." When he looked at me, I raised my chin defiantly.

I saw the lopsided grin before he turned away. "Yes. I suggest you do it sooner rather than later."

"I can call the coven back. Tonight."

His eyes roved over me. It didn't seem to matter that I was now covered with a robe. Did demons have X-ray vision? "As you will."

I grabbed my cell and called Doc. And as I talked, I walked to the bed and took the enchanted stone out from under the mattress.

It was a long night. The Wiccans reassembled. Nick had to pick up Jolene, whose parents had inquired but still let her go. The coven threw suspicious glares at Erasmus, but he held firm...and so did I. I wanted him to be able to come into the house for my own protection. That's what I told myself, anyway. Just for my protection. Nothing else. And yet there was something thrumming in the back of my mind, something that thrilled at his presence.

Though all the while, I kept hearing Seraphina's voice intoning, "Demons lie."

Jolene had her tablet and Doc had his book. Seraphina and Nick argued over their shoulders about what spell to tackle while I sat by myself, watching them. A warm hand closed over my shoulder and squeezed. I didn't look up, but keeping an eye on my Wiccans, I slowly drew my hand up and laid it over his.

His touch disappeared suddenly when Doc looked up. "I think we've got one."

He looked tired. I had gotten him up from bed, no doubt, but I was grateful that they all came without complaint. It must have been the most exciting thing to ever happen to Moody Bog since Constance Howland's day...but that wasn't fair. I knew they weren't in it for the excitement, but to keep their village safe from an unspeakable evil. Their generosity humbled me.

"Let's do it," I said, summoning energy from somewhere.

They used the pentagram and the other star for their preparation. "We'll hold hands," said Doc. I looked back at Erasmus with his arms folded and a closed expression. "He won't be joining us," Doc stage-whispered.

"Indeed not," Erasmus snorted. But his eyes took it all in curiously anyway.

This time, Doc's pleas and admonitions were more specific, including windows, doors, drains, vents, faucets, and pipes. I listened carefully to make sure he couldn't sneak in anything that might be interpreted as a chimney flue and joined in the "energy circle" with as much power as I could summon.

The Booke made an appearance, but before it could threaten me, Erasmus grabbed it out of the air and held it fast to his chest, obviously struggling with it.

The chanting was over. The glow throbbed for a moment in the pentagram, and all was still again.

Doc shuffled to his book, snapped it shut, and tucked it under his arm. "I hope that does it." He laid a hand on my shoulder. "You'll be all right. Call us if you need anything."

They offered their weary farewells and left the shop. Once the slam of car doors and the sounds of engines carried away down the road, the shop fell silent again, except for the natural creak and settling of a three-hundred-year-old house.

I glanced at Erasmus. He seemed to be staring at the Booke, which he still clutched in his hands. He seemed puzzled. No. More than puzzled. Confused. And he finally set the Booke down on a side table with a decided thump. "What mischief are you up to now?"

"What's wrong?"

His eyes found mine for a second before he returned his gaze to the Booke. "I'm not certain." He strode toward the window and pushed the curtains aside, glaring into the night.

My heart started pounding. "Do you see the kelpie?"

"No. But…"

Very faintly, I heard a dog howl. It was off in the distance. Usually, a dog barking somewhere in the night was one of those comforting sounds of neighbors and humanity nearby. But this time—maybe it was because of Erasmus's worried expression or maybe just the current circumstances of Moody Bog—I shivered at the sound. There was nothing friendly or homey about it. In fact, it was a bit…terrifying. I hugged myself.

"What…is that?"

Erasmus cocked his head, listening. "I don't know." He opened the sash and sniffed. When the cold air reached me, I shivered harder.

"That's just a dog, right?" But even as I said it, a sense of foreboding stole over me. It could very well have been just a dog. Except for the look on Erasmus's face.

"Kylie, I don't want you to panic."

"I'm not panicked. Who's panicking? I'm not panicking."

He was suddenly in front of me, holding my forearms. "I said 'don't panic.' But…I think…" He looked back with condemnation at the Booke. "I think that the book may have released…*another* creature."

CHAPTER SIX

That was not good news. That wasn't anywhere in the neighborhood of good news.

"Another…*thing* is out there? Wait. That's not fair. The Booke isn't supposed to do that. Is it supposed to do that?"

He shook his head. "I…I don't know. This has never happened before."

"Oh great! Just peachy! Now the Booke is acting out and we don't know what it's doing?" I turned to glare at it. "Talk to it! Tell it to stop that."

"I beg your pardon, but it is simply not done that way."

"I don't care. If it's changing the rules midstream, then it needs a stern talking to."

"It may not be changing the rules. It might simply be…er…"

"You don't know. You're the freaking guardian of the Booke and *you* don't know, do you?"

He frowned. "It opens every few hundred years. How can I be expected to know everything?"

"Great. Just great. So…any idea what it *might* be?"

He leaned toward the open window and sniffed again. His eyes searched, a hopeful look on his face, but he soon sagged. "No."

"So now we have to look for two creatures. And we don't know what this one is. What a great night this is turning out to be."

"I'm sorry."

His contrition took me completely off guard. "It's not your fault…Is it?"

"No. But I am sorry nonetheless. Your burden is already heavy enough."

It certainly was. And I should tell the Wiccans. But I just couldn't face calling them right now. It could wait. Bad news could always wait. Instead, wearily, I closed the window and trudged toward the stairs. Silence engulfed the house again.

Erasmus stood off in the shadows. I supposed he was used to that. I wondered briefly what it would be like always being apart, staying in the shadows. I couldn't tell if he minded.

"What are you going to do now?" I asked. My quiet voice almost seemed too loud for the time of night.

His voice was equally quiet, though it had a gravelly edge to it. "I'm going to stay here. Keep you safe."

I nodded. I didn't give him a backward glance as I shuffled up to my room.

I slept fitfully, dreaming of water, ponds, brooks, and a distant menacing howl. My shower the next morning was the fastest on record. I kept staring warily at the showerhead, but even that wasn't enough to keep me fully awake. And now there was this other *thing* out there. I had to call Doc and explain it.

I was groggy all morning. Lack of sleep and disturbing dreams could do that. But I was more determined than ever that I was going to make a go of it. I had a shop to decorate for Halloween, after all. And I had a kelpie to hunt and this other thing out there too. Maybe they'd both be easier than the succubus. Maybe I could lure them to me. Open the pipes again for the kelpie by nulling the spell and waiting for it. But what about this other creature? We didn't know what it was. I'd have to consult Erasmus...and even as that thought passed through my mind, there was Jeff, banging on my door.

"I do not need this." With a cleansing breath, I strode up to the door and threw it open. "What do you want, Jeff?"

"Look, Kylie. Can I just come in and talk to you? I came an awfully long way."

My gaze darted, looking for that dark shape in a duster, but since I didn't see him, I gave Jeff a jerk of my head in assent and retreated to the kitchen and to coffee.

He followed me and I actually offered him a cup, because I guess my mother hadn't raised a rude child. But I put myself on the other side of my huge farmhouse table. We stared at each other across the expanse of nicked wood.

Clenching his hands, he shook his head. "I don't understand why you felt you had to run away..."

"I didn't run away."

He gestured to the shop, to Maine. "What do you call this? I mean, okay. You wanted to put some distance between us. I get it. But California is a big state. Why go to the other side of the freakin' country?"

"My grandfather lived in Maine." It just came out. It was in the back of my mind anyway. "And it seemed a good fit. And I could afford it. I'd never find anything that I could possibly afford like this with living accommodations in Southern California, and you know it."

"I didn't know your grandfather lived here. Is he...is he..."

"He died a long time ago."

There was a pause and he lowered his head. "I'm sorry about your mom, Kylie. You didn't tell me."

"It didn't matter. We were done by then."

"But I still care."

I studied his face. He wasn't trying to put it on. He had a sorrowful and sincere expression, and I took it in the spirit in which it was given. "Thanks, Jeff. I…I know you do."

"And I'm…sorry for…the other stuff. I really am. You know the kind of guy I am."

"I thought I did."

"I was going to pay you back. It was a loan. I brought a check." He set down the mug and reached into his back pocket. He pulled out a worn leather wallet and fished out a wrinkled check. Slapping it on the table between us, he slid it forward until I could reach it.

It was for a big amount.

"There's a little more in there for, uh, punitive damages, I guess. See? I'm not an entirely bad guy."

"Believe me, I've seen worse," I muttered.

"So Old Jeff isn't the worst of the bunch, huh?"

I chuckled a little. "If you only knew."

"That creepy guy last night? With the long coat? Is he one of the worst?"

I sipped my coffee and thought about it. "I really can't say."

"And what about all those people last night? What the heck was that?"

"That's my coven. Local Wiccans. And they're my friends. I allow them to meet at my shop."

"Maybe it's good for business to have a pentagram on your floor. Makes tourists think they're in Salem or something."

"Something like that."

He shook his head and scratched at his hair. "Damn, Kylie. Everything is so different. And I didn't lie. I do miss you."

"Sometimes…I miss you too, Jeff."

He cracked a smile, and there it was. The smile to melt many a surfer girl's heart. And mine too, once. "Well, all right."

"I'm pretty happy here, Jeff. I've gotten to know a lot of the locals and they've been pretty generous."

"Yeah, they seem to know a lot about you, all right. I went to a bar last night, trying to drown my sorrows and complain a little. They seemed to know you up there."

"Up...where?"

"In the town I'm staying at. Hansen something? They wanted to know all about you. They were real friendly. Bought me a few rounds."

Shit. "Who was real friendly?"

"This biker gang. Said they were friends of yours. Doug was the guy's name. You and bikers."

Double shit. "And...what did you tell them?"

"So I might have had a little too much to drink. You know how I like to talk once I get a few beers in me. And a shot or two. I just told them about California and stuff. Nothing personal. You know. Only that I was your boyfriend."

I set down my coffee. "Jeff, it would be a real good idea to just pack your bags and go home."

"Babygirl, I thought...I thought we were doing okay."

"We're all squared away, Jeff. I harbor no ill will. So you can just...go with a clear conscience."

"Wait. I didn't come here to clear my conscience. I came to win you back."

"And that is not going to happen. So don't waste your time. Who's running the shop while you're gone anyway?"

"Marlene."

"Marlene?" Marlene was less of an employee and more of a hippie maiden aunt. She added great atmosphere to the place, but she couldn't use the register, handle emergencies, or keep track of her key. "Are you out of your mind?"

"This was an emergency!"

The kitchen door opened and my heart sucked up into my throat. But instead of a kelpie or an angry Erasmus, Ed poked his head in. "Hey. I heard voices."

"Hi, Ed!" I scrambled around the table and grabbed him by the arm, holding myself close. "How are you?" I kissed his cheek.

The puzzled look on his face could have been comical under other circumstances. "I'm…fine. What's, uh, going on?"

"Ed, this is an old friend from California. Jeff Chase."

"Another one? Is he staying here too?"

He'd already met Erasmus. I'd had to tell him something.

Jeff plainly saw how the cards lay and didn't put out his hand to shake.

"And this is Sheriff Ed Bradbury. He's the sheriff here. Which…I already said."

"I see," was all Jeff said.

"And what's your business here, Mr. Chase?" asked Ed in a formal tone.

"What is this? An interrogation? I came to talk to Kylie. Talk her out of this crazy move and into coming back to me."

"Yeah, I suspected that's who you were." Ed turned to me. "Do you want me to get him out of here?"

"Hey, whoa, whoa!" Jeff put his hands out. "I'm not doing anything illegal. You have no right—"

"Has she asked you to leave?" He rested his hand on his belt… the one holding his holstered gun.

"Yeah, but—"

"And *did* you leave?"

"No, but—"

"Then I call that harassment." He grabbed Jeff's arm. I was afraid a tussle would ensue.

"No, Ed. It's okay."

"Kylie, you don't have to put up with him." Ed's nostrils flared like an angry bull's. I knew I was in the middle of a pissing match, and though a little comeuppance might be nice, I wasn't ordinarily the vindictive type.

"We're working it out. Look, why don't you call me later. You said you wanted to cook for me. How about tonight?"

He frowned but backed off. When he gazed at me, his face softened. "Tonight? Okay. I'll call you."

"Okay." I reached up and kissed him, but I could tell he was looking at Jeff. And boy, could I ever feel the anger reeling off my ex.

Ed kept looking back, narrowing his eyes at Jeff as he walked out and finally closed the door behind him.

Jeff leaned dejectedly against the table. "You're seeing someone."

"Yes. If you'd bothered to ask…"

"Okay." He smacked his thighs and got up. "I guess I made a real idiot of myself then."

"It's just…" I hugged my arms. "I think it's a really good idea that you go home…before Marlene bankrupts you."

"Sure. I guess so. Well…there's nothing left to say except…" He put his hand out to me. "Have a nice life, Kylie. I hope…it all works out."

"Me too," I said quietly. We shook on it.

He walked to the door without saying anything more. He had pulled it open and just about closed it behind him when he stopped. "You know…if it doesn't work out, the business I mean…you can come back. No strings attached, okay? Just…if you need a place to crash. 'Cause I know you probably sunk your last dime into this shop."

"Thanks, Jeff. That's…that's really nice of you."

He nodded. "Sometimes I can be a dick. But most of the time… I'm a nice guy."

"I remember."

He smiled, nodded, and finally left. Once the shop was silent again, Erasmus abruptly appeared behind me. I gasped.

"You should have let me eviscerate him."

"Wow. Thanks for the offer. But no."

He opened his mouth to say something when the bell over the door jangled again. Hoping for a customer, I was bound to be disappointed. Ruth Russell in the flesh. Erasmus stood behind me, glaring at her.

No greeting. No "nice day for it." She got right to the point.

"You keep telling people we're related. I want you to stop."

I rubbed my palms into my eyes. I really wasn't awake enough for any of this. "If I did so, it's because there is a possibility…"

"No, there isn't. I don't know what you're playing at, young lady, but you aren't going to get away with it."

"Excuse me? You seem to be laboring under the misapprehension that I have to kowtow to you. Now, other people in this village may feel the need to be under your thumb, but I am not one of them."

She pruned her lips and lowered her brows. "The Stranges have nothing to do with my family."

"That's not what your archives say."

"Which you looked at without my permission."

"Yes, you're right. And I apologize for that. But to be fair, if I had asked to see them, would you have let me?"

"Absolutely not."

"Well, there you go. If you had been more neighborly…"

"They are *my* family archives. I don't have to let anyone look at them."

"And is that really fair? I mean, shouldn't those be in a library or a museum? They're founder history, after all."

She stepped close and pointed a finger in my face. I wanted to bite it just to see what she would do. "You are an outsider. You don't get to tell people whose families have lived in this village since the seventeenth century what to do. And you don't get to rummage through my family papers, and you most certainly do not get to tell people we are related when it is patently untrue."

Erasmus was suddenly beside her. "You're a Howland, aren't you?"

We both seemed to have forgotten the demon's presence. "Who are you?" she asked sharply.

"Someone...who knew the Howlands. And the Stranges. I can attest to their being present in the years of the founding. And further, to you having a common ancestor."

"What do you mean you knew the Howlands? I don't recognize you."

"Don't you?" He stood his ground and raised his chin.

Ruth looked him up and down and suddenly her eyes bulged. Her hand flew to her throat. "I have to go," she said curtly, marching out the door before I could ask anything further.

"What happened here?" I said to the empty space she had left. Then I glared at Erasmus. "What did you do?"

"Nothing. I merely reminded her of her own history."

"Wait a second. Does she have that engraving in her collection too? The one where Constance Howland is being chased to her doom by...you?"

"I don't believe so. But perhaps something similar."

"Wow. You get around."

"I must follow the book."

"Well..." I grabbed my coat. "Do me a favor and hang with the Booke and watch the shop."

"What?"

I shrugged on the coat and opened the door. "I have to do some research. Will you watch the shop?"

He looked around incredulously. "Absolutely not!"

"Come on, Erasmus. I need someone to keep the doors open till Jolene gets here at three thirty. Can't you do me a solid?"

"Just what part of 'absolutely not' don't you understand?"

"I know you're allergic to the tea, but can't you help anyway?" I couldn't help myself. I chuckled at it and, of course, he got indignant.

"I have no intention of becoming a shopkeeper for you or anyone else. Book or no book."

"All right, all right. Stupid demon," I muttered. I turned the sign to "closed" and locked the door with him inside.

I got into my Jeep and slammed the door. I don't know why I was startled again when he appeared sitting in the passenger seat. "I'm going with you."

"I don't need you to go with me."

"You might encounter the kelpie."

"I won't. I promise not to go near any ponds."

"Nevertheless. I am going with you."

Starting the car, I sighed. "Suit yourself."

I pulled out and headed for the highway. Erasmus said nothing, just sat with his hands on his thighs. He had buckled himself in as per the last time I instructed him. It was strange having him sit there but oddly comforting too.

I drove along the highway until I saw the library sign hidden behind a large sweeping pine. I made a U-turn into the parking lot.

It was a hundred-year-old stone building, with concrete lions at either side of the steps. Forest surrounded the library grounds, as it seemed to do for most of the area. As I approached the stone lions, Erasmus put his hand on my arm to stop me.

"What is this place? A temple?"

"No. Well, of a sort, I guess. It's a library."

"A library?" He studied its Grecian pillars and pediment. "Are you certain?"

"Very. Come on."

"If it is a temple, I will not be allowed to…"

"It's not a temple. Just chill, Erasmus."

"I feel neither heat nor cold."

I eyed him as we climbed the steps. I wanted to ask. He'd seemed mighty warm to me that one time when we were…

Don't think about that, Kylie. Not when I was planning on another date with Ed.

"How…how is it *not* to feel those things?"

He gave me another one of his you-are-so-stupid looks. "I don't know. I have no point of reference."

"Oh. I guess not." I pushed open the double doors. As I walked over the marble floors, I couldn't help but look up into the high vaulted ceilings, the rococo, and the many rows of dark shelves.

He stopped and looked around him, marveling at the sight. "How is it *you* have access to this?"

"It's a public library." Quieter, I got up close to him. "You see, in this country, we give access to all, this free knowledge of the ages. Pretty good for humans, huh?"

"Yes, indeed," he breathed. I had a feeling he hadn't meant to compliment me or my race.

I went straight to the information desk. The librarian looked up with a smile. "May I help you?"

"Yes. I was looking for genealogy information. Particularly as it pertains to the founders of Moody Bog."

"Unfortunately, most of it is in private archives, but the Waters collection has an awful lot in it."

"Waters?"

"Karl Waters donated it some years ago. It's such a shame what happened to him."

"Yeah," I muttered.

The librarian got a map of the library and wrote down the call numbers. "Just go to this room and ask for the collection. You can't check any of it out, but you're free to look at it for as long as you want. Some are actual eighteenth-century papers but the majority are photographs of documents."

"Thanks. Um, is it possible somehow to look up someone who died but who used to live around here? An address?"

"You could try the census. We have them on microfiche."

"Wow, really? I'm not quite sure what year he died."

"Do you know what year he was alive, then? I'll warn you that the most recent census that will give us any real data, like an address, is from 1940. That one is digital."

"I think he was born around 1928. So if he was born in Moody Bog, I suppose he'd be living here in 1940."

She glanced once at the silent and stoic Erasmus and tapped her keyboard. "And his name?"

"Robert Stephen Strange."

"'Strange' as in 'peculiar'?"

"You got it."

She typed. Erasmus watched her, rapt. He had no idea about twenty-first-century conveniences, like the internet and databases. He was definitely a man out of his time.

As the screen filled with information, the librarian clicked, opening window after window. She scrolled and then slowed. "Robert Stephen Strange," she read aloud. "Married to Josephine Strange?"

"Yeah. That's it." I leaned in, peering over her shoulder. I felt Erasmus's warmth as he drew closer behind me.

"One son, Rupert..."

"That's my dad."

I felt Erasmus looking at me. I wondered what he was thinking. It must have been a huge curiosity to him, these human emotions.

"Looks like the address listed here is at the very edge of Moody Bog, pretty close to Hansen Mills. 1428 Alderbrook Lane."

I released a held breath from my lips. I'd almost thought it was just a dream, the memory was so sparse, but here it was in black and white. My grandfather *had* lived in Maine. And not just Maine, but in Moody Bog. How was it possible that I'd ended up here? Had there been some sort of subliminal message in my brain when I saw the real estate listing? Or was there something else at work? Why had my father left? Had he hoped to escape our family curse? After all, I was now tied to the Howlands and the Booke. I'd have to find the genealogy to see if we truly were related, but I was now in residence in a Howland house and inexorably tied to the Booke's curse. Maybe it was the Powers That Be playing a joke. If so, I wasn't laughing.

Erasmus pointed to the screen. "And you found out all that through this portal?"

The librarian stared at him.

I grabbed the library map and took Erasmus by the shoulders. "He's such a clown," I said, pushing him away toward the other room where we needed to be.

He shook his head and kept looking back. "What sort of magic is that? It is unfamiliar to me."

"I'm not surprised. Because it isn't magic at all. It's science. The ingenuity of human beings."

"That cannot be. You are little better than cattle..."

"You know, another crack like that and I'll let you walk home."

"I don't need to walk. I didn't need to use your conveyance at all. I'm surprised you don't recall that."

"I do recall it. I'm just being snarky. Look, you need to be quiet. We're going to see some old-fashioned paper archives. I think. And then you can help me."

I found the Dutch doors and knocked on the closed lower one. The top door stood wide open and I could see stacks beyond it.

A bespectacled man approached from the other side and looked us up and down. "Can I help you?"

"I'm trying to locate some ancestors. I think I might be related to the founders."

"Founders, eh? Ay-yuh. Not a day goes by where someone don't come up here thinking they're a founder descendant."

"Well, chalk up another one. Can I see what you might have for 1720?"

"Going for it, then? Okay. Be back in a moment."

He disappeared and Erasmus stepped over to examine the digital thermostat.

"What is this contrivance?"

"It regulates the temperature in the room. Makes it warm or cool, depending on what one needs."

"*This* device? *Without* magic?"

"Well, it controls the furnace or air conditioner elsewhere in the building. Mechanical devices. Electricity. You set this arrow up or down depending on the temperature you want. See?"

He got up close, his nose nearly touching the digital screen. "Remarkable."

High praise indeed. The archive man returned and handed me a box.

"Do I need gloves?"

"Just be careful. And don't leave this room."

I found an empty table and opened the box. "Okay, Erasmus. You know what we're looking for."

He seemed on firmer ground with parchment and sat on one of the wooden chairs to carefully go through the pages.

Absorbed in searching, I felt the slight prickle of someone watching me. When I looked up, I just barely caught Erasmus looking away. He cleared his throat. "Kylie...there's something...I need to say..."

"Aha!" I whispered. Proudly, I tossed a photograph in front of him, his pensive face forgotten. It looked to be a reproduction from a page of a family Bible. In faded ink, there it was. The link between Hosea Strange and the Howlands. A cousin of the main line that led to Ruth had married my relative. The Bible had obviously belonged to the Strange family. I wondered where it was. With a pang of regret, I realized I had never seen it before.

The Stranges flowed one generation after another. The last male child was my father, who had no siblings. That only left me. And I had no heirs. Was that significant?

"It appears you are a direct descendant. As is that unpleasant Russell woman."

"Is it significant, Erasmus? Does this prove I have some sort of destiny to fulfill?"

"It seems very likely."

"Erasmus, are all the Chosen Hosts women?"

He hesitated. "Yes."

"What's the significance of that?"

"Women appear to be more resilient and more…stubborn."

"I'm not buying that."

"And yet, regardless of your feelings on the matter, it is true." And before I could round on him, he touched me lightly on the shoulder. "It *is* true. I am not obfuscating this time."

"Meaning you've obfuscated before?"

Caught! He wore an amusingly guilty look.

"Never mind." I hesitated again before I asked, "Erasmus, did you know I was related to Constance Howland?"

He shuffled his papers and wouldn't look at me.

"Well?"

"No, I didn't *know*."

"Have…have they all been related to me?"

"I don't know."

I thought about that as I took a picture of the photo with my phone. "Are there any more parchments we should look at?"

He pulled out a few more showing more of the tree of descendants, all carefully written out with a quill. "By the way, did you see *any* reference at all to the Booke?"

"There was one." He shuffled a parchment from the stack and laid it out. "Mistress Howland's immediate relatives were concerned about the 'devil's booke' that seemed to be distressing her. One kinsman tried to burn it but ended up immolating himself in the process." He chuckled. If it were anyone else, it would have been inappropriate.

I glanced over my shoulder for any signs of the archivist before quietly asking, "Did *you* do that?"

He blinked slowly. "As amusing as it would have been, no. It was the book, protecting itself."

"Then strike off trying to destroy it."

"That would prove as foolish as bricking it up inside a wall, and just as futile."

"Where did it come from? I mean, how did Constance get a hold of it?"

"I don't know. She never mentioned it. I suppose it followed her family from the Old World."

"Did she…" I bit my lip and felt the warmth of the amulet heating my skin beneath the sweater. "Did she wear your amulet too?"

His eyes were suddenly ablaze. Anger, fear? I couldn't read him. "No. Only *you* had the audacity for that."

"The Wiccans. It was their suggestion. I wouldn't have known to do that. It was a good idea, as it turns out."

He clammed up and I took that to mean Sharing Time was over. I spread out a few more parchments, including the one he'd read to me, took pictures, and then carefully packed it all away again.

I handed the box back to the man behind the door. "Find what you were lookin' for?"

"Ay-yuh," I said with a quirked smile. "Looks like you're looking at a founder descendant. The Strange line."

"Strange? I never heard of them."

"Maybe you need to study your own archive."

But as I walked away with Erasmus in tow, I wondered why the Stranges were cut out of history. It was plainly there for anyone to see, yet no one remembered. Though as I recalled, it seemed to me that Karl Waters had. As soon as I had mentioned my name, it flicked on a light switch in his brain.

I wanted to see the place I spent my early summers. Maybe there were answers there. Maybe not. But it was a good place to start. I was just reaching for my phone to switch on the GPS when it rang. Walking quickly across the marble lobby to the porch outside, I looked at the screen but didn't recognize the number. "Hello?"

"Hey, Kylie."

"Who is this?"

"I'm wounded. You don't recognize your old pal Doug?"

I squared my shoulders. "What do *you* want?"

"Oh, not very polite. I mean, after all, we might be in-laws someday, you dating my brother and all."

I hadn't thought about that. And it wasn't a pleasant thought. "I'm hanging up."

"I wouldn't do that if I were you. We've got your, uh, *friend* here."

"What friend?"

"Guy named Jeff. He's going to be our guest for a bit."

I fumbled, nearly dropping the phone. "W-what? If you've hurt him…"

"Nah, nothing like that. Not yet. But we'd like to talk to you. Why don't you come on down to Hansen Mills?"

"No, I'm not going there."

"Ah come on, Kylie..."

"I'm hanging up and calling your brother."

"Well, Jeffy won't like that. Won't like it a bit. We have these *rituals*, you see..."

"Okay, stop." I bit my nail and turned to Erasmus, who was wearing a concerned expression. Covering the mic, I whispered to him, "The Ordo kidnapped Jeff."

Erasmus smiled. "Good."

"No. It is *not* good. They want me to come talk to them. They said something about rituals."

His smiled vanished. "You're right. That *isn't* good. I don't think you should go."

"No shit. But I think I'll have to."

"Then I am going with you, of course."

"Hello?" said Doug. "You still there, Kylie?"

I took a deep, bracing breath of cold Maine air and spoke into the phone. "Where do you want to meet?"

CHAPTER SEVEN

"I don't think you should go with me."

"Of course I shall. I can vanish at will."

Erasmus and I had been arguing since reaching the highway. Navigating the curving country road, I shook my head at my demon companion. "It's risky."

"Shabiri will be there."

How could I have forgotten? The Ordo had their own demon. A sexy lady in a catsuit who seemed to know Erasmus a little too well. I didn't like her for a lot of reasons, but the biggest one might have had to do with their longtime acquaintance. *Jealous much, Kylie?*

"All right. Do your vanishing thing right before we get there."

"As you wish. Ah. I see why they chose this area."

We had just managed a hairpin turn I had taken a little too fast and passed a sign that read "Hansen Mills."

"Oh? Why is that?"

"Can't you see them?"

"See what?"

He sighed wearily. "I keep forgetting you are a mere mortal. The lines. The ley lines. They converge in this area."

I frowned, continuing to steer into the curves of the road. "What exactly are ley lines?"

"Lines of ancient power. Confluences of magical energy. They're rather thick around here."

"What about Moody Bog? I would think all ley lines met there."

"Oddly enough, they don't. They do surround the village, however, in a very curious pattern. But they converge in Hansen Mills."

"I wonder if that was why..." I began thinking of my dream—or memory, I guess. "Erasmus, is there a reason why someone wouldn't go to Hansen Mills in the fall, but only in the summer?"

"Of course. The solstice."

As if everyone knew this but me. I turned to him with an exasperated expression. "And what does *that* mean?"

"Have your Wiccans taught you nothing? The solstices have great power. For good, for protection. But it fades the farther away from the solstice you go. Fall is a very dangerous time for certain mages. They tend to lay low. Except during Samhain, which seems to collect its own form of magical power, concentrating it, waiting for the winter solstice."

"Samhain. You mean Halloween?"

"Your quaint names notwithstanding, that is what I mean."

"Halloween is two weeks away."

"You love stating the obvious."

"No, I mean all this concentrated power is moving toward us. How does that affect the Booke and all the creatures coming out of it?"

"It would accelerate it, I should think."

"Like two creatures emerging instead of one?"

"Or more," he said thoughtfully.

"Great. Just great."

I pulled into the parking lot of Mike's Roadhouse, favorite bar of local bikers. "You'd better disappear," I told him.

He gave me an intense gaze. "I will not be visible, but I will be here."

"Thanks, Erasmus." He seemed to be waiting. I would have happily given him a kiss for good luck, but I knew better than to start something like that. Instead, he merely vanished with startling ease.

I took a breath and suddenly wished I had thought to bring my crossbow with me.

Getting out of the car, I scanned the bar with its old barnwood sides and corrugated steel roof. Across the highway, the forest was thick and dark under a deeply cloudy sky. The smell of pine was strong, with the occasional breath of salt off of the distant sea. Even with Erasmus somewhere close by, I felt vulnerable. What would I be walking into? And why did they care so much about what I did?

I stuffed my chilled hands in my jacket pockets, even though they were feeling a bit clammy. When I pulled the doors open, a blast of warmth hit me, along with the sound of loud rock 'n' roll and the smell of sweat and beer. Just the kind of place Jeff liked, actually. No wonder he'd gravitated here. I wished he would have listened to me and left when I told him to.

Standing on the threshold, I looked around. It didn't take me long to spot the Ordo in all their grunting glory. There was the tall skinhead, Dean Fitch. The upside-down pentagram tattooed on the side of his head looked like a brand on his pale flesh.

Red-headed Charise had tats on her chest and arms, a ring in her nostril, a scar on her face, and a thing for Doug, though I got the feeling it was a one-way street.

And then there was Bob Willis, who looked like a farm boy, with floppy blond hair and a bulky frame. They were all in their leathers, sporting Goat Guy in a pentagram on the backs of their jackets.

But no Jeff.

"What is this? Where's Jeff?"

Doug whipped around, looked me up and down with a leer, and smiled. He was a younger, bearded version of Sheriff Ed, with, unfortunately, the same sort of sparkle in his eyes.

"Kylie! Good to see you. Come on, sit down. Have a beer with us."

Charise didn't seem to think too much of this invitation, but she kept silent except for her sneer.

"Where's Jeff?"

Doug laughed. "Now *this* lady likes to get down to the point," he said to his fellows. "That's what I like about you, Kylie."

"*Doug*," whined Charise. "Just get it over with already."

"Relax, Charise. We're all friends here. We've got loads of time. Sit down, Kylie."

Bob scooted over, making room for me. I looked around, grabbed an empty chair from another table, and slammed it down at the end of their booth. Stepping nimbly around it, I sat. I guess I was too angry to be nervous.

"No crossbow this time, Kylie?" asked Doug.

I folded my arms and said nothing.

"That's okay. I'm not really after that anymore." He took a slug of his beer and set it down again in a pool of water rings. "I'm after something else."

I don't know who liked his leer less, me or Charise.

"How about a beer, Kylie?"

Losing patience, I finally snapped. "Just get to the point, Doug."

"Everyone's in such a hurry," he muttered. "Okay. It's like this. Old boyfriend Jeffy for the book."

I hoped my poker face hadn't slipped. "What book?"

He chuckled and angled to face me square on. "Don't play games. I don't think Jeffy can wait that long. You *know* which book. Our friend Shabiri told me about it."

I laughed. I couldn't help it. Threw back my head and let it rip. "Oh, Doug. If you had any idea how funny that was...If you really had any idea, you wouldn't want it, believe me."

"But I do, darlin'. I do."

"The Booke. Just what did Catsuit Lady tell you about it?"

He grinned. "Well, she told me it's powerful and that it brings creatures to command."

"And just what did she call this book? *Alice's Adventures in Wonderland*?"

He got in close and whispered, "It's called Booke of the Hidden, so don't fuck with me."

I leaned away. "Then she doesn't know shit about it."

"Well, you're right about that. She is a wiseass. Do you have that much trouble with your demon?" He gestured toward my amulet, which I quickly stuffed back in my sweater.

Smirking, I sat back a little less stiffly. "It's a permanent condition of demons apparently."

"I thought as much. I only saw your guy for a few minutes, but that scowl looked like a fixture."

"You know, we could swap stories about this demon stuff all day long, but I'd rather get on with it. I can't give you the Booke and *that* is really *that*. So you have to release Jeff because there's nothing left to negotiate with. And I really am dying to tell your brother about your further shenanigans so you can go back to a cell again. For much longer this time, I hope."

His amiable smile faded. "Well, look who turned into a bitch."

"I *told* you," said Charise with some amount of glee.

"Can you blame me?" I swept over them with a contemptuous gaze. "I gave you a chance, Doug. I didn't press charges like Ed wanted me to do because I thought maybe we could work together. You really have no idea what you're dealing with here. There is no controlling these creatures. They get to do *what* they want, to *whom* they want. And gods like your Goat Guy? They don't do anything for you without a price. Are you really *that* ignorant?"

"That's not what Shabiri says…"

"Demons lie, idiot. It's what they do. They manipulate and trick to get what they want from you. They aren't genies."

Bob shuffled in his seat. "Shabiri doesn't want anything..."

"Oh, do some freakin' research, Bob!"

Their table fell silent. I felt like dusting my hands at a job well done, but since I still didn't know where Jeff was, I waited.

This did not appear to be good news to the Ordo, but Doug plowed on anyway. "Doesn't matter. We want the book anyway. We want control of it."

"Do you think *I* have control of it? Do you have any idea what it really is?"

"Shabiri says—"

"Haven't we already established that demons lie?" This was ridiculous. I stood. "Where's Jeff?"

Doug stood, too, and then the others clumsily followed him out of the booth. They all stood around me, and soon the chatter of the place quieted as the patrons became aware of our little one-act play. "I want the book. It's important to have it. That's what I've been told and that's what I'm gonna do. And you don't get Jeff back until I have it in my hands."

Glancing around, I could tell there were no knights in shining armor ready to come to the rescue. Just curious, bleary-eyed men who had nothing better to do than drink in the middle of the day.

Quietly, I said, "Look, even if I *could* give it to you, it won't do you any good. *I'm* tied to it. I could hand it over right now and it would still come back to *me*."

"So what does it do?"

I postured. "Ask Shabiri."

"I'm asking you."

"Where's Jeff?"

The front door opened and Jeff stumbled in. Bruised, bloody, and a bit out of it. "Jeff!"

He blinked and cast a glance toward us. He seemed to recognize me and staggered forward, but then pushed me out of the way to point a finger at Doug. "You son of a bitch! Someone call a cop!"

"Jeff, are you all right?"

He spared me a glance and shrugged. "I guess. No thanks to your *friends* here."

"They aren't my friends."

"I untied myself and got free. You bastards." And then he suddenly turned to me. "What are you doing here? You gotta get out of here."

"I'm rescuing you."

"What?"

Looking around, it didn't seem that anyone was stepping forward to defend the Ordo. I pointed a sharp finger in Doug's face. "I'm leaving and you'd better leave us alone. You aren't getting the Booke or anything else from me. You need to chill on this stuff. It's too dangerous. More dangerous than you can imagine. You're screwing around with things you don't understand. Hell, *I* don't understand it and I'm stuck in the middle of it."

"Is there a problem here?" The bartender had finally decided to come over and see what was going on. He gestured toward Jeff. "You okay? You want me to call the sheriff?"

"No!" I said at the same time Jeff said, "Yes!"

Jeff glared at me. "Kylie!"

"It's all settled," I said to the bartender. "A bet gone bad, but it's okay now."

"It's *not* settled," said Jeff, getting increasingly louder and more hysterical. "These bastards kidnapped me, beat me up, threatened me…"

"Jeff." I grabbed him and yanked him to face me. "It's over, okay. We're leaving now." I gave Doug a significant look and turned my back on him, shoving a protesting Jeff toward the door.

A waitress carrying a heavy mop bucket across the barroom stumbled, dumping muddied water across the floor. She swore and stomped off to the back room as patrons laughed and applauded, apparently forgetting the drama before them.

The water spread. Even as I was almost at the door, its odd behavior caught my attention. It had stopped spreading and instead rippled and churned, as if wind was blowing over its surface.

I'd seen something like it before. In my own tub.

Before I could shout a warning, the kelpie burst up through the puddle.

Everyone screamed and fell back. Instinctually, I shoved Jeff behind me and backed away as it began climbing out of the puddle toward me.

The patrons slammed the bar door open and poured out. I half-expected the crossbow to appear, but it was probably too far away to travel. I'd have to improvise.

I grabbed a chair to fend off the kelpie. I was holding it more or less at bay until Jeff grabbed my arm to pull me back. The kelpie lunged.

"Jeff! Let go of me!"

I struggled in his grip. The kelpie reared up. I elbowed Jeff in the face. He fell back with a yelp. With one hand, I swung the chair and smacked the kelpie in the muzzle. It fell backward, howling and shrieking, legs in the air, mane flying all around its face.

Out of nowhere, Doug brandished a spear with a glowing head and jabbed it toward the beast. It snarled and lashed its head but slowly backed into the puddle. It flashed its red eyes at me once more before it dropped like an anchor into the water and disappeared.

I stared at Doug and his spear. He glanced back at me, tightening his grip on the shaft and panting.

"Maybe I *don't* want your book," he said.

CHAPTER EIGHT

Doug and I calmed everyone down. We managed to convince the crowd it was a magic trick. In their drunken state, they seemed to buy it—though the waitress and bartender took a little more convincing. I discovered that people are more willing to believe any explanation rather than the possibility that a monster could be real. The bartender was shaken and wanted us to leave, but Doug bought a round for what was left of the house and asked to use the private room in the back. We all retreated there, the Ordo on one side of the small room and me and Jeff on the other.

Jeff was shaking. "There is no way that was a magic trick. Jesus, Kylie, I felt that thing's breath! What the hell is going on?"

Where was Erasmus? He had promised...shit. Demons lie. I really had to take that one to heart.

Should I tell everyone about the Booke? I didn't feel I had a choice anymore.

"Okay. This is what happened. A week ago, I found this Booke bricked up in the wall of my shop. It's old, about so big..." I framed my hands to about ten by thirteen inches. "And as soon as I opened it, I set off a chain of events, and weird demon creatures started coming out of it."

"The succubus," said Doug.

"Yeah, and now this kelpie, the horse thing in the water. I had no idea it could come from a puddle. I thought it needed a pond or a bog or something. The kelpie pretends to be stuck in a bog and lures people toward it. Once you touch it, you're stuck and get dragged down to drown. But it's particularly after me."

"Why?" wailed Jeff.

"Because *I* opened the Booke. I'm…called the Chosen Host. It's my job to kill these things, capture them. They go back in the Booke, and when they do, I write in the Booke's pages with my blood what they are and what happened, and it keeps them there. The demon, Erasmus, is the guardian of the Booke or something. This amulet controls him." I lifted the chain to bring out the warm demon face from my sweater and showed Jeff.

He looked like he was about to have an aneurysm.

"Kylie," he gasped. "Why don't you just leave?" He kept eyeing Doug's spear.

"I can't. It's my fault."

Jeff was sputtering. "How many creatures are there?"

"I have no idea. Something else came out of the Booke too, but we don't know what it is yet. Erasmus thinks that their numbers will accelerate as we approach Halloween. So it's a lot worse than I thought."

"You have to leave. Come home with me."

"No, Jeff. This is my life now. Not *this*, but my shop. But this is also part of it, I guess. The Booke acts like a gateway, like the vortex you guys made," I said to Doug. "Only I have no control over what comes out. So Shabiri is full of shit if she thinks it's useful to you at all. That's why I want your help."

Doug chuffed a laugh. "For the good of Old Moody Bog? I couldn't care less about the people there."

"Then care about yourself. Care about Charise, because women are particularly attracted to kelpies. Just be careful the next time you take a bath."

Charise cringed and grabbed Doug's arm. "Make her kill it, Doug."

He rolled his eyes. "I'm sure that's her plan, sweetheart."

I gestured toward his spear. "Where'd you get that?"

"I decided I needed a weapon too. Something to match your crossbow. Shabiri got it for me. Convenient, these amulets."

"Yes, very."

Doug looked at the spear, whose head no longer glowed. "It's called Gáe Bulg." Sounded like he called it *guy bul-ag.* "It was the mythical spear of the Irish king Cú Chulainn. It means 'Spear of Mortal Pain.' Neat name, huh?" He pressed a button on the shaft and it telescoped like a car antenna. He tucked the now ruler-sized spear neatly inside his jacket. My crossbow didn't stow so conveniently, but I still wished I had it in my hand.

"Why did Shabiri tell you to get the Booke?"

"She mentioned something about whoever controls the book controls the other demon."

Now it was becoming clearer. Miss Catsuit wanted Erasmus. "It's nontransferable. Believe me, if it were, I'd give it up in a second."

"So you're doing this out of the goodness of your heart? Or because you feel guilty?"

"I know this is a tough concept for you, but yeah. I just want to be left alone to run my business. I have absolutely no ulterior motives."

"So how does my dear brother the sheriff fit in?"

I shrugged. "I like him. We're dating."

He laughed. "Well I'll be damned. Seriously?"

"Yes, seriously. Why don't you reconnect with him? He's not a bad guy."

"Oh, no, he's not a bad guy. Perfect Ed. My parents loved him. He could do no wrong. He got straight A's while I struggled for every B and C. He won awards while I just dropped out. Ed became the sheriff and I became a humble grease monkey."

"Oh boo-freakin'-hoo. Get over it. You each have talents the other doesn't have. That's what siblings are all about. It's not his fault that your parents were idiots."

"You know what? You don't know shit about it."

"Kylie." Jeff clawed at my sleeve. "Don't make him mad. He's got that spear thingy."

"And I've got a crossbow. And no chip on *my* shoulder."

"That's not what Jeffy here says."

"Jeff needs to learn to keep his mouth shut."

"They beat me up!"

"Yeah, that's right," I said. "So the question is now, do I tell Ed or not?"

Doug scowled. No, he didn't like that. *Didn't think it through, did you, Dougy*?

"So wait a minute," said Jeff in a stretched voice. "That creepy guy outside your shop...was a demon?"

"Yes, Jeff. He's the guardian of the Booke. He sort of protects me. Though where exactly he is right now is a mystery. He was supposed to keep an eye on me, the jerk."

"Looks like you're pretty good at protecting yourself," said Doug.

I thrust my hands into my jacket pockets. "We're gonna go, Doug. Don't contact me again unless you want to help. I'm going to have to think about whether I tell the sheriff about this."

Jeff whined indignantly. "What about me? Don't I get a say?"

I grabbed Jeff's arm, manhandling him out of the room and across the bar before he could say anything else.

He let me push him all the way out the door. When we came to the Jeep, he shook me off. "I don't know where all this is coming from," he said shakily. "You weren't like this in California. It's those Wiccans, I bet. And why aren't we calling the police?"

"Weren't you listening in there?" I unlocked the door. "Is your car here?"

"Yeah."

"Then get in it. I'm following you to the motel and then you're checking out and leaving."

"You can't tell me what to do! Christ, Kylie. This isn't like you at all."

"I was never in mortal peril before. Didn't know there were vortexes or different planes of existence, or gods or demons. So it *is* different now, okay? And I can't have you getting in the way. Someone might get hurt."

"But what about the police?"

"We don't have time for that now. And it's my only leverage over them."

He stumbled back and fell against the Jeep, staring at me. "Leverage? What about what *I* want?"

"That ship sailed…a long time ago. You're going to pack up and get out of here."

He looked back at the roadhouse. "Those guys don't scare me."

"Well they scare *me*! They're Wiccans too, Jeff, only not the friendly kind that come to my shop. They're the kind that do animal sacrifices. And you were gonna be next."

He touched his throat and swallowed hard. "Jesus. You gotta get out of here."

"I…I just have to finish this job…and then life will go back to normal…I hope." I leaned an arm against the car. "But you have to go."

"Kylie, I want to stay to help."

"You can't."

"Kylie…"

"Dammit, Jeff! Just go!"

"Maybe the lady wasn't being clear," said Erasmus, suddenly at Jeff's elbow. He grasped it and squeezed. Jeff collapsed on one knee, grimacing with pain.

"Erasmus! Stop it!"

He let Jeff go, but it seemed to annoy him to do it.

Jeff rubbed his elbow and used the car to lever himself up again. "Fucking freak!"

Erasmus got up into his face and flashed his rows and rows of sharp teeth. "Oh, I am far more than that."

"Erasmus," I warned.

He smoldered for a moment. The wisps of smoke curled off his shoulders and dissipated. He was coiled to spring. And Jeff, as much as he wanted to put on a good face, was cringing back against the car.

"Jeff," I said gently. "You need to check out of your motel. I'm going to follow you and I recommend you do it."

He looked from me to Erasmus, who was still grinning like he was thinking Jeff would be a good dinner. Jeff swallowed, fumbled for his car keys, and backed away toward his rented blue Toyota.

He started it up as I got into my Jeep. Erasmus chose to go his own way, and I followed Jeff up the road into the ever-darkening shadows of the woods.

He pulled into an old-fashioned motel from the forties, painted red with white trim. Aunt Emma's Motor Court. I pulled into the space beside Jeff's car.

He got out his room key, the old kind with a fob, and stomped to his room. I got out and followed him up to the painted red door. "You don't have to shadow me like this," he said through gritted teeth.

"I don't trust you to do as I say."

"You were never like this before," he muttered, opening the door.

It was an average motel room with two beds. Jeff's duffle bag had been thrown into a corner. He picked it up and began stuffing strewn-about clothes back into it. I grabbed his toiletries from the sink counter and dropped them into his dopp kit.

“I can handle it myself,” he said, snatching his toothbrush out of my hand. “You could at least let me stay long enough to call the airport.”

“There isn’t time. It’s too dangerous.”

He glanced back toward Erasmus, who was standing outside, pacing back and forth across the damp parking lot.

“Is he really a demon?” he whispered, thumbing back toward Erasmus.

“What do *you* think?”

“And you control him…with that?” He pointed toward the amulet.

“Yes, apparently. I know this is really hard to take in, but…”

He ran his hand through his hair. “It’s like a nightmare.”

“You’re telling me. I’ve seen some really weird stuff in the last week. I never believed in any of this either. But now…”

“You should run away. You should come with me. Come on, Kylie. You don’t owe these people anything. Just get out.”

“I don’t know that it works that way.”

“Have you tried? Just hop on the plane with me and let’s escape.”

“I…I can’t. Maybe I do owe them something. Turns out… it’s not just my grandpa who was from here. My ancestors helped found this place.”

“What? Someone’s giving you a load of bull.”

“No. I found it out myself. It’s all true. I think I was…fated to come here. I don’t think I can just run away and leave it all behind. At worst, I think it would just follow me.” Even as I said it, I felt the calling from the Booke. It was far away, back at my shop, but I could hear it like a shuddering in my bones. It would never let me go. But Jeff’s expression and bruised face were getting to me. “Should I… should I help you…with your…” I gestured to his cuts and bruises.

He looked in the mirror and sagged against the counter. “Jesus.” He grabbed a washcloth and ran it under the hot water. Dabbing at his face, he winced from the pain as he cleaned most of it off. The swelling was going to take some days to go down. "Are we at least going to call the police?"

"I…I don't think that's a good idea."

He spun around. "Not a good idea? Dammit, Kylie. Those assholes kidnapped me, beat me up. Shouldn't they go to jail?"

"Yes, they should, but…" I pulled away and looked at the shabby curtains. "Jeff, the sheriff doesn't know about the supernatural stuff. How would I ever explain it?"

"And you like him. You don't want to make waves."

Was that the reason? I shrugged.

He snorted and packed…until we both heard it. He rushed to the window beside me and looked out. That weird howl. It rippled gooseflesh over my neck and arms, but I couldn't see anything in the dense woods across the highway.

"What *is* that?" he whispered. "I heard it yesterday. Are there wolves here?"

"I don't know. Just hurry up and pack, okay?"

He returned to it, packing a little faster. I walked with him to the office but didn't go in. Instead, I stood in the parking lot, waiting, listening for a sound that didn't come again. I happened to glance back at the motel and saw Deputy George, mustache and all, leaving a room, tucking in his uniform shirt, and looking furtively around.

Oh, ho! A little afternoon delight for Deputy Mustache. As he drove away, lights blaring on his sheriff's Interceptor, I kept watch on his motel door, wondering what bimbo might…

"Holy shit."

Nick Riley, goth Wiccan, closed the door after him and sprinted to his junker as it started to rain. "Nick? Oh my God." Nick and Deputy George? No wonder Nick played it close to the vest. Was it love…or the only game in town? I started planning the good-natured ribbing I was going to give him when Jeff nearly bumped into me.

He dropped his bag into the trunk of his rental. "What now? I just leave you here? It doesn't seem to be a very chivalrous thing to do."

"Have you ever *been* chivalrous?"

He lowered his face but said nothing.

"I'll follow you to the highway."

"So this is really goodbye."

I shook my head. "It was goodbye two months ago."

Jeff got into his car and pulled out of the space. I followed behind him until we were well and truly out of Hansen Mills. We hit the highway and I followed for a few miles before pulling over near the verge and watching his car vanish around a bend in the road.

A rush of wind told me Erasmus had decided to join me. "He's gone?" he said.

"Yeah." It felt strange, stranger than when I left him the first time. I wondered why I was filled with foreboding, even as he was fleeing from here and out of harm's way.

Erasmus was staring at me.

"What?"

"Nothing," he said softly.

I got out my phone to escape those eyes of his and punched in Grandpa's address on the GPS.

"What are you doing now?"

"I'm looking for my grandfather's house. It's around here somewhere and I want to see it."

"Do you think there's time for this?"

I checked the car clock. I'd been gone from the shop a long time. But Jolene would arrive soon and she had a key. "I'm here. I might as well. You don't have to go with me."

"I'm here," he said coolly. "I might as well."

"You think you're funny, don't you?"

"A riot," he deadpanned.

I followed the GPS, making a U-turn. It said to take a left onto a dirt road that quickly became muddy and then graveled. My Jeep was doing all right with four-wheel drive, though.

Another right onto a smaller road led me up a hill. My neck hairs began to stand up. This *was* familiar. That bent tree. I remembered it. I slowed as we passed it, looking through the rain-streaked glass, mesmerized by seeing the thing in the flesh, those only half-remembered bits and pieces that turned out to be true.

"Over the hill," I whispered, "there will be a rusty windmill."

Erasmus leaned toward me. "What did you say?"

Before I could answer, there it was. It had lost many of its blades now, but the rusty windmill that had creaked and turned in the summer breezes was still there. And then the house. So much smaller than I remembered. Dingy, gray. The wide porch was still there. The upper window in the lone dormer was dark. There were no lights. The place seemed abandoned.

I pulled up and shut off the engine, expecting my grandfather to come striding out the front door with a pitcher of lemonade or a wrench to fix his tractor. But the view was all wrong. The sky should have been blue and sunny. The trees around it should have been full and green, not twiggy and dead from the fall. I looked back down the hill and could just make out the dark gray Atlantic through the mist between the trees.

I hadn't realized I'd gotten out of the car until Erasmus grabbed my arm.

"You mustn't," he said urgently.

I turned my head to look at him. "Why not? There's no one here. Nothing but faded memories."

"There's more than that."

I didn't want to listen. Striding up to the porch, I peered through the window in the door. Torn and faded lace curtains hung in the shadowy room beyond. Everything seemed covered in dust. A settee, a lamp, a table, an empty rocker. I knocked anyway, which frightened a dove nesting up inside the porch roof. I tried the door but it was locked or stuck.

"Come away from there, Kylie!" he hissed. He had stayed out on the brown lawn, rain beating down on his dark hair.

I couldn't help going from window to window, trying to catch a glimpse of my lost childhood. But that was ridiculous. After Grandpa died, not too long after my last memory of him, someone else *had* to have occupied this house. It couldn't have lain idle since 1994, could it?

"Kylie!"

His voice was so plaintive that I left the porch to join him, blinking through the rain and looking back at the old place. "I wonder if it's for sale."

"We must get back to your conveyance."

"Why? What's your problem?"

He took my arm and dragged me back to the car, nearly shoving me inside. "Drive," he ordered.

"Erasmus?"

But I started the car anyway and pulled slowly around back to the road. "What's got your pointy tail in a knot?"

"The ley lines. They converge…right here."

"But…isn't that a good thing?" I maneuvered the car back to the gravel road and headed toward the highway.

"Only in the summer. After the solstice, it becomes very dangerous. And it is most dangerous nearest Samhain."

"*My* grandpa's house?"

"Do you think it is a coincidence?"

"Well...no. I guess not. I wonder why I didn't remember it for all these years."

"No doubt a very strong protection spell of some kind has been cast on your memory."

"No way!"

He folded his arms, staring straight ahead through the windshield. "Do you question me? Of course you do. 'Demons lie,' so you said. 'It's what they do. They manipulate and trick to get whatever it is they want from you.' Correct?"

So he *had* been there, listening, smoldering. Apparently, I'd hurt his feelings. "I'm sorry. But that does seem to be true..."

"Have I ever lied to you?"

"I don't know."

"You don't know? I see."

"Look, Erasmus, don't get all offended..."

"Oh, why should I be offended? You simply impugned an entire race of beings with no more evidence than hearsay. Why should I be offended?"

I tried not to smile. "You're right. That wasn't very nice of me."

"Not nice at all. And here I am protecting you."

"And just where were you when the kelpie attacked back at the roadhouse?"

"I was searching for Shabiri," he said. "I'm not the only one who can turn invisible."

"Oh. Did you find her?"

"No."

"I believe you." His gaze darted toward me. I glanced back at him only once. "I do. Sometimes."

He sighed and said under his breath, "I suppose I don't blame you."

I smiled. That was quite an admission for him. I wondered how many Chosen Hosts there were before me, and how many had ever taken him to task. It suddenly made me frown. Maybe I didn't want to know how many there were and how many of them he'd...

Shut it down, Kylie. Change the subject.

"That spear. Did you see that spear that Doug had? He called it 'Guy Bullfrog' or something."

"Gáe Bulg," he said. "Spear of Mortal Pain. Shabiri." He growled the last.

"Is it like my crossbow? Can it also kill the creatures?"

"Yes. But..."

"But what? I think we should try to get it from him. Or is it just as tied to him as the crossbow is tied to me?"

"Those objects are not as bound to the person who possesses them as you might think. Because a demon fetched it for you, they can switch their allegiance and assign it to someone else."

"So we just have to convince Shabiri to let us have it? And what are the chances of that?"

"Nil, I should think." But he sat thoughtfully, running his thumb over the stubble on his chin.

"Hey, Erasmus, what was it you were trying to tell me earlier?"

He blinked, seeming almost to awaken.

"You know," I went on. "Back at the library. Looked like you were going to confess something." My stomach did a little flip. It could have been something pleasant to hear...but who was I kidding?

He not-so-subtly turned away. "Er...nothing. Nothing that can't wait."

Struck oddly with disappointment, I feigned a disinterested shrug and left him to it. No use in wheedling it out of him until he was ready to tell me. It was probably more bad news anyway.

I turned the car off the main highway onto Lyndon Road and into Moody Bog. My shop was the first thing we encountered. It did look inviting and quaint, just the place a tourist might want to stop in and look around.

When I parked and got out, I saw Jolene inside, dusting, bless her. Erasmus disappeared in silent retreat.

Jolene looked up when I came in, bell jingling above the door. "Hey, where have you been?"

I doffed my jacket and hung it on the hall tree. "The Ordo wants the Booke and they tricked me into meeting them in Hansen Mills." I relayed the whole thing, including the kelpie's appearance.

Jolene seemed more excited about tales of my grandfather's house.

"Did you go inside? What was it like?"

"Erasmus wouldn't let me. And it was abandoned. Seems odd. My grandpa died around 1994. That hardly makes it derelict. Yeah, it could use a coat of paint and a board fixed here and there, but I don't understand how it could have been left empty for so long."

She had grabbed her tablet and began swiping for all she was worth. "Mr. Dark said it was at the convergence of ley lines. That could have been keeping people away, but I wonder if there isn't something else causing the trouble."

"Trouble? I don't think it's that. I mean, it is kind of remote from the village."

"But there are a lot of farms outside of town. Something is keeping people away. Or maybe some*one*."

"Like what?" I hated the idea that something—maybe a demon monster or evil spell—was interfering with Grandpa's old place.

Jolene looked up eagerly from her tablet. "Something like… your grandfather."

CHAPTER NINE

I should have enjoyed decorating the shop for Halloween. But my head wasn't in it. What Jolene had said left my nerves on edge: "I think your grandfather is haunting the place."

How could that be? Ghosts were someone else's relatives. Surely not mine. But the Stranges had odd ties to the place and even odder ties to the supernatural. Who was I to say?

When I pulled out of my funk, I looked around the shop. The cornstalks were tied upright to the porch pillars, with bright orange pumpkins sitting below. Inside, Jolene had carefully placed cutouts of witches, pumpkins, and a scarecrow. It looked festive in an autumnal sort of way and gave me the idea to maybe fill one of the samovars with hot apple cider from our own blend of spices, another little bag to make for those impulse buys.

It cheered me a bit. The customers who came cheered me more as tea, tea towels, and several mug sets flew off the shelves. It had been a good day for the register.

My phone rang.

"Kylie." Ed sounded agitated.

"What's up? We're still on for tonight, right?"

"Yeah, but I have to ask you something. Were you by any chance in Hansen Mills today, at a place called Mike's Roadhouse?"

Shoot. Maybe that was why Deputy Mustache was rushing out of Aunt Emma's Motor Court. "Um…yes?"

He paused over the line. "Kylie...I heard some very strange things about that..."

"Doug was working out this magic trick and it went off too well." I cringed because that was the best I could come up with.

"*Doug* was working on a magic trick? And...*you* were helping him?"

"Actually, Erasmus was the one doing it. And Doug was kind of covering for him."

"So now you and my brother are chummy all of a sudden? With your...friend?"

"Well, not exactly but...I was kind of at the wrong place at the wrong time."

"I'm just trying to get my head around this. And I didn't know your...Mr. Dark was still in town."

"He comes and goes. Listen. I'm almost ready to close up. Want to text me your address and we'll talk more tonight?"

"Oh yeah, sure. See you round seven?"

I sighed in relief that my misdirection seemed to work. "Sounds good." I waited only a moment for his text and then saved his address in my phone. Seven o'clock gave me a little over an hour to get ready. And maybe come up with a better cover story.

Jolene tried to tell me that Doc had called her and that we should be getting together tonight. But I ushered her toward the door. "Look, Jolene. I have a date tonight. I'll call Doc in the morning."

She turned to me with a grin. "Oh? You'll be busy *all* night?"

I pulled her knit cap down over her eyes. "Children should be seen and not heard. Good *night*, Jolene."

I closed and locked the door to her laughter, turned abruptly, and nearly screamed.

"Erasmus! You've got to stop sneaking up on me like that."

"I wasn't aware I was doing anything of the kind."

"Right. My ass." I stalked away from him and got the distinct feeling he was staring at said ass, but I didn't bother turning around. "I have a date," I threw over my shoulder. "I have to get ready."

"Will you be taking a bath?" He was right behind me on the stairs.

"No way. A real quick shower."

"Would you like me to guard you?"

I stopped and swiveled toward him. "Um…do you think that's quite appropriate, given the, uh, circumstances?"

"What circumstances?"

I leaned against the railing. "I'm getting ready to go on a *date*."

It took him a moment before the penny fell. "Oh." Though he wasn't mortified, he was certainly unhappy. His fingers tapping on the stair rail telegraphed his discomfort. "Then I'll… wait below."

I didn't say anything more and escaped into the bedroom. A quick shower, a dab of perfume, a tight sweater and equally tight jeans, and I was down the stairs again.

Erasmus was standing in the dark of the shop, but his glittering eyes followed my every movement.

"Okay, it's a little creepy your lurking in the shadows like that. Why don't you…take a night off? Go…do whatever it is demons do in their free time."

"I never understand what you are talking about from one moment to the next."

"Just…go somewhere else, Erasmus. But don't follow me."

"But how can I protect you—?"

"I'll be with the sheriff. I'm sure he can do the protecting tonight."

His eyes seemed to blaze for a moment before he narrowed them. "I see." He stalked dramatically toward the door, and without opening it, filtered through and disappeared.

"The man does know how to make an exit," I muttered, before grabbing my coat.

⁂

Ed's place was just down the road and then down another little road. It was a cheerful Craftsman with shingles on the exterior walls and an outspreading elm in front, golden leaves still grasping at its branches. I parked against the curb out front, which was less curb and more gravel mound. Much of Moody Bog didn't have sidewalks, except for in its downtown center. That made it homey and rural feeling.

There was a gas lamp at the foot of a stone walkway curving up to the front steps, and I smiled at the sheriff's nod to pedestrian safety. I got out one knock on the door before he flung it open. I hoped he had noticed me drive up rather than waited impatiently behind the door for my arrival.

"Kylie." He smiled and my trepidation melted away. "Come in. May I take your coat?" I shrugged it off and handed it over. "You look very nice tonight."

I couldn't help but preen and blush a little. "Thanks." He urged me into the living room, where there were two wine glasses filled halfway sitting on the coffee table. I noticed a lot of dark wood and leather, giving the cottage's cozy outward appearance a more masculine edge, but it was still warm and inviting. Ed's tastes veered toward Craftsman furniture and the same period lamps. I sat on the sofa and he handed me a glass. We clinked and drank. Settling back, I cupped the goblet.

"Nice place. It looks like you."

He smiled again, *his* turn to blush. It was a bit disarming. "I've had a few years to work on it. It's a good place to come home to after a long day. The yard out back goes a long way to the next property.

I've got a vegetable garden and a blueberry patch. Not much now, but in the spring and summer, I get the best tomatoes in town. At least, that's my opinion."

"Idyllic," I murmured into my wine.

He shifted closer. "I don't want to put a damper on the evening, but you said you'd clarify what went on in Hansen Mills today?"

I took another slug of wine and set the glass down. "Look, Ed, it was a huge misunderstanding. Erasmus likes to prank, and he did this thing with projectors and hypnotism, and Doug tried to stop him. That's really it."

"So you and Doug…"

"Are *not* bosom buddies, I can tell you. We may have mutual interests but…"

"That Wiccan stuff."

"Well, to tell you the truth, it isn't *my* interest but more my new friends' interest. And they've been very supportive of the shop. Which I appreciate, being a stranger in town."

"Doc is reliable."

"I'm glad you approve."

I guessed he caught the strain in my tone because he took my hand. "Look, I'm sorry. It's just, with my brother into that stuff, it kind of puts me on edge. When Doc went Wiccan, quit going to church, it was a big deal around here. It's a small town, Kylie, and I'm afraid we do a lot of judging of our neighbors even though we shouldn't. But Doc has always been a trusted friend to this community…and to me…and so we are still friends. I didn't mean anything by it…but I did judge there and I apologize."

Mollified, I grabbed my wine glass again. "I'm used to Wiccans, pagans, that type from California, so I get it. Sometimes it's a lot to get used to. Even bikers. Believe me, I've met all kinds, and most people are just fine. I think Doug…well. I couldn't help but notice the chip he has on his shoulder about you."

"What are you talking about?"

"Seriously? It's about *you.* He's completely envious of you and the attention your parents gave you."

"What? Is that what he told you?"

"Not in so many words, but I could certainly read between the lines."

"That's such horseshit! Excuse me. I didn't mean to swear, but Doug is full of it."

"Not if *he* perceived it that way."

"My parents never favored me over him. He was the baby. If anything, it was the other way around."

Time to change the subject. "Okay. I surrender. I really didn't come here to talk about him anyway. I want to talk instead...about that delicious aroma coming from the kitchen."

The darkness in his eyes faded and he was the host again. "It's my famous spaghetti and meatballs."

"Ah. Another traditional Maine meal, then."

"Yes. The meatball goes way back to colonial days. My lady?" He stood and offered his hand. I took it and followed him to the kitchen.

A pot bubbling on the stove smelled heavenly of meaty tomato sauce, oregano, thyme, and marjoram. He turned off the heat and let me taste a small spoonful. I pronounced it fit for the gods.

We sat at his table with china plates and cloth napkins. Ed served up and we chatted while we ate. Maybe pasta is good date food. It's warm and familiar and nearly impossible to screw up. And it has the tendency to put everything at ease while also allowing for unimpeded conversation.

His cell phone rang. With an apologetic look, he dug it out of his pocket. "Could be police business. I have to answer." Putting the phone to his ear and donning his official demeanor, he said, "Bradbury."

That official demeanor soon turned to concern. "How many? Jeezum rice, this is getting ridiculous. A cow? Okay, George. Well, there's nothing we can do right now. No, just go back to the station and file your report. I'll talk to you in the morning."

He clicked it off and stuffed it back in his pocket. "Darnedest thing," he muttered.

"What?" I was already worried about what that kelpie was up to.

"At first, we thought the animals were just missing, but now they're turning up mutilated. Goats and now a cow. Some folks have been saying it's a wolf, but that's impossible."

"Why? Aren't there any wolves in Maine?"

"No definitive sightings since 1993."

"Oh." The kelpie was foremost in my mind, but I remembered the sound of something howling and Erasmus's words on the matter. What *was* out there? Some kind of wolf-like creature?

A hand covered mine. "Let's not worry over it. Are you done with supper? Come on."

He took my hand and led me back to the living room. With more wine, more conversation, and more laughter, I could put aside my fears of the unknown creature out there.

Before I knew it, Ed had gotten very close indeed.

Lying back against his cushioning sofa, feeling just a little bit buzzed from the wine, it was easy reaching up, trailing my hand through his hair, and bringing his head down for a kiss.

Ed's hand found its way to my waist and gently nudged me toward him. A hard chest, hard biceps, hard…everything. He held me close, turned me so that I was flat against him. His heartbeat was strong and fast. Looking at me steadily, he bent forward and pressed a kiss to my mouth, and then another. His tongue flicked at my lips before sliding inside, kissing deeply, lingering. When he pulled away from my mouth at last, it was only to drop his lips to my neck. As he licked and sucked on that sensitive skin, all thoughts of anything and any*one* left me. His hands hadn't stopped either, traveling down from my waist, over my hips, and to my backside, where he squeezed.

"Kylie," he purred. "You're so beautiful. I know we haven't known each other long, but…"

I took his face in my hands and tilted it up to mine. "Yes. The answer is yes, Ed."

He blinked. "Oh. Good. Shall we…?"

I gently extricated myself and stood, holding his hand. He seemed a little thrown by my poise, but he snapped out of it quick enough to stand, kiss my hand, and lead me down the hall to his bedroom.

The bed was a big, heavy four-poster with a chenille bedspread over a down comforter. He turned one corner of it before facing me again. Large hands cupped my face and he leaned in to kiss again. His soft lips molded over mine, even as his breathing sped up.

Trying to be sly about it, he opened a drawer to his nightstand, took out a condom packet, and dropped it to the bed. A gentleman indeed.

I smiled. His face softened, and he leaned over and bought his mouth to mine again. I opened my lips and welcomed his deep and urgent kiss as I grasped his shoulders and pulled him closer. His hands climbed under my sweater and reached higher until he cupped both breasts, gently kneading them. I moaned, and the sound seemed to encourage him to push the sweater up. He broke his lips away from mine to plant them on a breast. I arched into him, giving him full access. He tore at his own shirt, ripping the buttons, and managed to slip it over his shoulders.

His eyes were still on me when I grabbed the hem of my sweater and dragged it up over my head.

Staring at my lacy bra, he quickly kicked off his shoes and unzipped his fly. We each shed more clothes, but he stopped now and then to bend down to kiss and caress my breasts, especially once I unhooked my bra.

I stared at his hairy, muscled legs and defined torso.

The sheriff's department seemed to have an excellent exercise program.

"As a matter of fact, it does."

Oh damn. I hadn't meant to say that out loud!

He licked his smiling lips, took the condom from the bed, and quickly sheathed himself. Moving toward me, he took my shoulders and pulled me in. Flesh to flesh at last, Ed's fingers eased up and down my waist, mouth caressing my skin at my neck, chin, mouth, eyes. "You're beautiful. Do you know that?"

He pressed against me, hips moving against mine. I swallowed and gazed at him with half-lidded eyes. And then he lowered himself to his knees.

Warm hands covered my backside, squeezing, as equally warm lips moved their way across my belly, the curve of my hip, nuzzling lower…

My hands went to his shoulders for support as I rose up on my toes. His lips, tongue, and fingers worked in concert, and he hummed his satisfaction, sending vibrations through me to all the right places. Ed was good at this. Very good.

The white-hot sensations took me by surprise, and even as I cried out, he gathered me in his arms, shoved me against the wall, and lifted. Impaled on his hardness, we moved together. I wrapped my legs tightly around his waist and dragged my nails over his back. I don't think he minded that, judging by the moan he made. Ed dug his face into the space between my neck and shoulder and sucked. I felt the wall shake as he thrust.

A few more deep thrusts and he groaned his release, a shudder from the last of his arousal coursing up his body.

He expelled harsh breaths in my ear and I held on, feeling both our heartbeats drum until they began to slow. Together, we slid down the wall and sat messily on his floor, side by side.

Ed rolled his head along the wall to look at me. "You are one amazing woman."

I scraped my hair away from my face and smiled.

He rose first and lifted me, carrying me to the bed. We got under the blanket, since it had been a little cold on the floor, and snuggled in. Resting my head on his chest, I was still floating a bit when I suddenly thought of Erasmus and it all came crashing down. What might he be thinking? He knew where I was, after all. And for all I knew, he might be here…invisible…

I sat up, yanking the sheets to cover myself, dislodging Ed, who tumbled away with a yelp. "Hey, warn a guy!" He smiled sleepily, eyes gentle and warm. They tracked over my face before dropping lower in appraisal. "Are you okay? There's nothing to worry about. Just come back down. We're just gonna sleep a little. Spend the night, even. If you want to, that is."

Don't spoil it, Kylie.

I shook my hair out of my face. "Yeah. There's just a lot on my mind…" Slipping down, I scooted toward him and let him enclose me in his arms again.

"Don't think about all that now." He kissed me lazily and twirled a lock of my hair with a finger. "Man, I've been wanting to do that with you since we met. I hope that's okay to say."

"Why wouldn't it be? I was pretty much drooling over you too."

He laughed. "I never met a woman like you. You sure speak your mind, don't you?"

"A Strange family trait, I'm afraid."

"Well, Ms. Strange, suffice it to say, I'm very glad you moved here to Moody Bog."

"You know…" I snuggled down and got my head comfortable on the down pillow. "My family is actually from Moody Bog. As a matter of fact, a Strange is one of the founders."

"You still on about that? Ruth Russell was pretty adamant that you weren't related to her."

"No, seriously. The Stranges were a founding family."

He shook his head and frowned. "No, I don't think so."

I looked at him carefully, but he didn't appear to be kidding. I scooted out from under him and sat up, holding the sheets to my chest. "Now that's the weird thing. Because I just looked it up; even found my grandpa's house. Turns out I used to spend summers here."

Now it was his turn to frown. "You spent summers here? Where?"

"In Moody Bog. Up Alderbrook Lane." I was fairly certain I'd told him all this before, and Ed seemed like a pretty good listener. But looking at his face now, I could tell this was news to him.

"No kidding? Wow. Alderbrook? Where's that?"

"His old house looks abandoned. I'm going to check on it and see if I shouldn't be inheriting the thing."

"That's weird." He lay back, head on his laced hands.

You don't know the half of it. "But seriously. I'm a descendent of a founder. Hosea Strange married a Howland. How about that! My biggest fan *is* a cousin, several hundred times removed."

"Really? She won't like that."

"She already doesn't. Came to my shop and, well, threatened me, for want of a better word. Told me I'd better stop spreading those rumors."

"She did?"

"Yeah. I think the woman's got a screw loose."

"Naw, she's just protective of her own personal fame. No one likes being knocked off their pedestal by an upstart. Not that I'm saying you're an…I'm gonna stop talking right now." He tugged on my arm. "Come on back here. It was pretty nice, you snuggling against me."

"You're a snuggler. I knew it." I complied, sighing at the good feeling.

Out in the living room, a cell phone rang. I thought it might be mine. "I should probably get that."

Ed's slow smile reminded me I didn't have a robe. "Go right ahead. I won't mind."

"You dirty man." I grabbed his shirt and whipped it over my shoulders. The man actually pouted as I padded out to the living room, searching for my coat. I found it in the closet, grabbing the phone just in time.

"Doc?" I whispered. "What is it? This isn't exactly a good time."

"Kylie, there's something going on at your grandpa's house. I think you need to meet us there."

"*Now?* Are you crazy?"

"These things that are happening now in Moody Bog because of the book make it somewhat more urgent than usual. Especially if Mr. Dark's assessment about Halloween is true."

"Well…what exactly is happening?"

"Jolene got an interesting message on her Ouija board."

"Sorry. Say again?"

"Her Ouija board. We met tonight at my place and decided to explore the possibility of a presence at your grandfather's house. There was a message."

"Well…what was it?"

"The message read: 'Kylie, I need you.'"

CHAPTER TEN

I gathered my clothes, slipping on a shirt at the same time I tried to get a leg into my jeans. I hopped a bit but fell back to the bed.

"What was the emergency again?" Ed asked, scrubbing at his hair.

"A leak. A major leak. Water everywhere."

He got up from the bed and began searching for his underwear. I had to admit, it slowed me down watching him. "I'll help you clean it up."

"No, no. That's okay. Erasmus is doing it."

"Erasmus," he grumbled. "What's he doing there?"

"He kind of stays there sometimes. Downstairs. Look, Ed, I've got to take care of this. I really, really hate to leave." I was mostly dressed (having just stuffed my bra into my jeans pocket). I leaned in and kissed him. "I really do hate to leave. I had a really good time tonight. Your spaghetti was delicious. And this was…even better. I'll stay the night next time. Promise."

He looked frustrated, like a big, scruffy disappointed puppy. "One thing I'll say for you. It's never dull."

"I'm sorry. I truly am."

"It's not your fault your pipes are old." He winced. "I didn't mean it to come out that way."

Chuckling, I kissed him one last time and dashed toward the living room. "Good night, Ed! Call me!"

The cold hit me hard, even wrapped in my jacket. I longed to go back to Ed's bed and hunker down with him. The man was ridiculously perfect. Handsome, sexy, a dynamo in bed. He had a good job and truly looked the hero. I couldn't say I was enamored of his family, at least the one member that I'd met, but those things could be overcome.

Yet, as I made my way up the icy road toward Alderbrook Lane, I wondered how long I could keep all this Booke stuff from him. And once he knew, how would he ever look at me the same way again? I was becoming addicted to those shy looks, the glittering of his eyes, that slow smile. He'd see me as just another crazy Wiccan. And I didn't know that I could bear that. Not when I was warming up to him and getting over…

A whoosh in the passenger seat. Speak of the devil.

"Erasmus…what are you doing here?"

"Your warlock friend left a message on one of your devices at the shop."

I couldn't help but picture him brooding alone in the dark. "You were waiting for me?"

"You told me not to follow. But when I heard the message…"

"You came running to the rescue."

We sat in silence for a time until he said quietly, "You smell like rutting."

I felt my face redden. "That's none of your business."

He folded his arms and pressed his lips tightly together.

"And furthermore," I said, tossing my hair back, "women can do what they darned well want to in this century and no one has the right to shame them for it. Got it?"

He mumbled something in the affirmative but kept silent the rest of the way.

I'd be damned if some *demon* told me what *I* could or could not do.

I followed the route I had taken earlier today, sans my trip into Hansen Mills, and drove up the gravel road to the other smaller lane, Alderbrook. If it had been a bit depressing during the day with its clouds and foggy memories, it was downright spooky at night. The brush and woods that enticed when I was a child were now a tangle of spindly fingers, reaching for me in black silhouette against a darker background of hills and sky.

The Jeep's headlights swept over the coven as I reached the front of the house. Their eyes shined in the headlamp's light before I switched it all off.

I got out of the car, but Erasmus simply appeared near Nick, who jumped about ten feet.

The house was dark, the shadows from the surrounding trees only casting darker and darker shades. "Why do people always do this at night?" I asked them. "Can't we ghost hunt during the day?"

"There's always more activity at night," said Nick, watching Erasmus suspiciously. He returned to his phone. His thumbs moved across his screen in a blur.

"That's what I was afraid of," I muttered. This bothered me more than any other creature I had encountered. It wasn't so much ghosts I was worried about. But I *knew* this one. What if Grandpa was dangerous? I didn't want my memory of him tainted. Or worse. I didn't want him attacking me or my friends. I was wishing Ed was with us, and then my thoughts drifted toward our spectacular date...until it was interrupted. All I wanted was something normal in my life. Ed certainly represented that, though his relation to Doug put a minor crack in the "normal" spectrum.

Nick stuffed his phone away long enough to muscle the door open. "Is this trespassing?" I asked anyone.

"Well," said Doc, "if no one has occupied this house since your grandpa died, then technically, this belongs to you."

"You'd think someone would have come calling asking for back taxes."

"And you think a haunting is scary."

He didn't see my withering look in the dark.

Nick clicked on a big flashlight that lit up almost the whole room.

"Oh my God. I remember this." There was the parlor, with the ornate mantel around the tiled fireplace. Small windows peeked above the built-in bookshelves, but the parlor's main window faced the yard. An archway with carved corbels in the upper corners opened to the large dining room, with a swinging door to the kitchen beyond. The stairs clung to the wall on the left and led up to two bedrooms, and another flight led to the dormer room, mine.

My mom had always gotten along with her father-in-law. He'd been good to her when Dad died and didn't leave us with much to survive on. I always begged for us to go live with Grandpa in Maine, and then I'd beg Grandpa to come back to California with us to live when Mom turned down my proposal. But Grandpa was adamant about staying. Just how adamant…well, we were going to find out.

"I'm still not comfortable with this."

Doc's hand eased over my shoulders. "I know, Kylie. But we're here for you. Don't you worry."

I had left the crossbow at home. There wasn't likely anything here that I could kill with it anyway. I hoped.

"So…how do we go about seeing if anyone's home? That scrying stick?"

Nick held up his phone.

"There's an app for that?" I said. "Are you kidding me?"

"No," he said excitedly. "It's a ghost detecting app and it's totally sick. I've been dying to try it…no pun intended."

Jolene giggled as she pulled something from my pocket and dangled it in the air. "Looks like we interrupted something."

It was my bra that I had stashed in my jeans pocket. I snatched it out of her hand.

Seraphina chuckled. "I guess your date with Sheriff Ed went all right."

I was glad for the darkness. My face felt as if it were on fire. "It was…pretty darned good. Until it was interrupted."

"I'm sorry about that," said Doc, watching Nick carefully. "I didn't think we could proceed without you. The message was pretty clear."

"Yes, the message was clear," said Erasmus in an acerbic tone all his own.

I moved away from the demon to look over Nick's shoulder at the phone app. Lots of digital dials and gauges. He glanced at me with a smile. "So. Sheriff Ed."

"I'm not the only one interested in Moody Bog's sheriff's department," I whispered.

He snapped his head to stare at me, worry in his eyes. "What are you talking about?"

I got in close and spoke quietly and concisely. "I was escorting Jeff out of town. And he was staying at Aunt Emma's Motor Court." I gave him a wink. "So. You and Deputy Must—uh, George, huh?"

"Listen. He is so not out. He'd kill me if anyone found out."

"I'm not going to say anything. But, uh, he always seemed a little uptight and not necessarily a friend of your coven. Surely you can do better."

"He's not like that in private. But…he does have a lot of issues. Look, I like him and he seems to like me, so…"

"So get him to take you out proper."

He fiddled nervously with the phone. "It's complicated."

"No kidding. I told Ed my pipes burst at the shop just to be able to get out of there. I do *not* like lying to him."

"Yeah." His shoulders sagged. "Sometimes I wonder if he's worth it."

I laid a hand on his shoulder. "Maybe it will just take some time. If you really like him..."

He offered a weak smile but then focused back on his phone when it emitted squeals and beeps. "Whoa."

The hands on the gauges moved wildly, ticking all the way from one end of the dial to the other. "What's happening?" I asked.

The others gathered closer. Seraphina closed her eyes and crossed her wrists over her heart. "I feel a presence."

Nick shook his head at her and muttered something under his breath. He fiddled with the phone. "I'm switching to EVP mode, see if we can get anything."

"EVP?" I asked.

"Electronic Voice Phenomenon. Sometimes you can pick up the voices of the dead."

Feeling a sudden chill, I hugged myself. I kept my eyes glued to Nick's app. The screen showed something like an oscilloscope with a grid and a green line that seemed to be vibrating. Nick held the phone forward, moving it about the room—trying to capture ghost voices, I presumed. The line jumped. He stopped, raising and lowering the phone. The line jumped again.

"I'm getting something." He scrambled one-handed into his jeans pocket and yanked out a pair of bent and cracked ear buds. He popped them in his ears and plugged them into the phone. Eyes wide, he tilted his head, listening intently.

Doc moved in to look over his shoulder. "Maybe this might be a good place to use the Ouija board again."

Jolene dragged the thing out of her backpack. "I'm on it." She set it on the rickety coffee table, covered in decades of dust. It looked like the typical Ouija board: a beige background with letters, numbers, "Yes" and "No" at each corner. She took out a triangular thingamajig—a planchette—with a magnifying glass cut out of the center. The carpet kicked up dust as she positioned herself on her knees before the board. She gently laid both hands on the triangle and asked, "Is there a presence here?"

Nothing.

"*Is* there a presence here?" she repeated.

The planchette jerked. Slowly, it moved up the board and landed on the "Yes."

"You didn't move that?" I whispered, really hoping she had.

She shook her head, watching the triangle as steadily as everyone else. "Do you have a message for us?"

The planchette moved slowly across the board, heading for the letters. It started on the K and by the time it got to the E my skin was covered in gooseflesh.

K-Y-L-I-E, it began. *I N-E-E-D Y-O-U.*

Jolene brought up eyes full of worry. She didn't look away from me when she asked, "Who are you?"

R-O...The planchette stopped. It jerkily changed direction. *G-R-A-N-D-P-A.*

My eyes stung hot with tears. Someone was playing a not very funny joke. You could throw all the demons you wanted at me, but you just didn't go around throwing my beloved dead relatives in my face.

"Why do you need Kylie's help?"

V-I-L-L-A-G-E I-N D-A-N-G-E-R. D-O-O-R I-S O-P-E-N-I-N-G.

Everyone looked back at the door that we had left wide open. Clearly, he hadn't meant that.

I swallowed back the hot lump in my throat and swiped the back of my hand over the tears on my face. "When he says 'door'...does he mean 'gateway'?"

"Possibly," said Doc in quiet, reverent tones.

Nick yanked the earphones from his ears so violently we all startled. "Oh my God. You have to hear this." He rewound whatever he had recorded, turned up the volume, and held the phone at arm's length toward us.

I listened hard, but all I heard was static and a rushing sound. But as it played again, I could start to discern something...something like a voice.

ssssssssHELPssssssssCAN'TsssHOLDssssssssssOFFssssssssssssssBESILENT!ssssssssssssKYLIEssssssssssssssssssss

I walked closer to the phone, listening again as it looped a fourth time. "What's happening? What is it?"

Nick's eyes were wide and shiny in the darkness. "That was *two* voices."

Yes. They were distinct. The one pleading. The other commanding his silence. What was I going to do? What *could* I do?

Jolene stared at me, eyes rounding. She pointed. "Look!"

I thought she was looking at me, but she pointed past my shoulder. I sure didn't want to, but slowly, I turned around. At first all I could discern was a glow on the far wall of the parlor. Something like a passing headlight from a car, only it wasn't moving. But then it began to brighten. It was a misshapen glowing light that seemed to form into a figure.

"Jesus Christ," I muttered, half exclamation, half prayer.

Arms separated from the glow, lifting, imploring. More details began to form until it was clearly my grandpa. My hand flew to my mouth, covering my gasp.

"*Kylie...*" A wispy voice, like something from the next room, something you weren't certain you heard. "*Kylie...you're so big.*"

"Grandpa?"

"*Not much time. Very sorry...about the...*" His words were garbled. The least little sound—the creaking of the house, a branch scraping against the roof—would drown him out.

"Grandpa." I moved closer. I could see more details. The way his hair was parted, the overalls he liked to wear, the worn buckle on one of the straps. I could almost see the blue of his eyes, almost smell the smoky aroma of his pipe. "Why do you need my help?"

"*The village is in danger. I'm sorry. Only you…only you…*"

"I know. I'm trying."

The apparition shook its head. "*Close the door. You must close the door.*"

"I'm *trying*, Grandpa! I'm really trying."

"*Hansen Mills. Ordo. Stop them. The door…*"

He turned to look at something the rest of us couldn't see. "*Wait!*" he told someone. "*Wait…I'm not done telling…*"

The glowing apparition exploded into shards of light that faded like firework embers and disappeared.

"*No!*" I lurched forward toward the place he had stood.

It was cold there. He was gone.

CHAPTER ELEVEN

"Who was with him?" I hadn't stopped clutching my arms. I was as cold as if I'd been standing in a snow drift. "Who was with him?" My voice was quiet, and if you didn't know me, you'd mistake it for fear. But it wasn't fear. I was enraged, and this was the only way—standing perfectly still, raising my voice barely above a hoarse whisper—that I could prevent myself from tearing the place apart.

Nick furiously fiddled with his phone, checking all his gauges and dials. "There's no way to know...unless. I can download the recording to my laptop at home and see if I can separate the layers of sound. I might get some clues that way. If I can really analyze it, maybe I can detect exactly what it was."

"Erasmus!"

He was instantly beside me. His expression of concern soon faded under my steady gaze. "Was that really my grandfather?"

"It was a true spirit, if that is what you are asking."

"I'm asking if *that* was my grandfather."

He shook his head. "I have no way of knowing exactly who that was."

I turned away from him. "Jolene, why did he change what he was saying when you asked who it was?"

She looked meek and chastened, packing away her things. "What's your grandfather's name?"

"Robert Stephen Strange."

"Well, it seemed like he started to spell 'Robert,' I think. But I suspect when he saw it was you...he just switched to the familiar. They do that."

"Okay. So he wasn't spelling out what was with him?"

"It could have been another spirit, Kylie," said Doc. "One not as friendly."

"Can we try again?"

Nick swiped on his phone, head shaking. "I'm not getting any more readings. I'm sorry, Kylie."

"Does that mean he's gone?"

"For now. He could be back. But it isn't likely to be tonight."

"Fine." I headed toward the door.

Seraphina, of all people, scrambled after me. "Kylie!"

I didn't stop. I headed for the Jeep and yanked open the door. She slid into the doorway, blocking me from driving off. "Kylie," she said softly. "Please. Wait just a moment. I know what you must be feeling..."

"Really? You know what I must be feeling? All of you?" I scanned them all as they gathered around my car. "You know what I'm feeling? I really don't think you do."

"Kylie..."

"No, seriously." I pointed back toward the house. "That was my *grandfather* back there. My *dead* grandfather. Who went to the trouble of manifesting himself to warn me about...whatever! And in the meantime, there is still this kelpie out there trying to kill me, the Ordo kidnapped my ex-boyfriend to try to get the Booke, which, by the way, I would gladly give them if only I could, and I can't have one freakin' night where I can have a decent date with a really nice guy! So no. I don't think you know how I feel right now."

I shouldered her out of the way, slammed the door, and started the car.

My tires kicked up gravel and spun as I backed up and tried to punch it out of there. I jostled all over the place down that winding road, bruising my shoulder against the window.

So what? I thought, as I hit the main road and headed home. *So what if I was being overly dramatic.* These were dramatic times.

And goddammit! I was having a good time with Ed. All I wanted was one measly night…

Erasmus appeared abruptly beside me. I didn't so much as blink. "What do *you* want?"

"Nothing," he said, and kept silent for the whole ride back.

I pulled in front of the shop, shut off the engine, and simply sat in the dark. The headlamps went out when the engine was killed. Outside the Jeep, the night was quiet. Only the engine clicked and chattered as hot metal cooled in the frigid darkness. My hands rested loosely on the steering wheel.

"What's it all for?"

He turned to me. His dark eyes glittered in the dim light, but he said nothing.

"What's life for anyway? I guess you don't know. *You* have a purpose. But humans kind of drift a little, trying to find it. But I guess I, too, now have a purpose. And once it's done—I mean really done for good—what then? I just…live my life? Run my shop? Get married? Have kids? That is, *if* I survive at all. What, Erasmus? Why me? Why did the Powers That Be bring *me* here?"

He looked at me steadily, barely breathing. "Perhaps they didn't."

"Oh, I'm pretty sure they did. Of all the people on this planet, they singled *me* out. Or is it one of those things that you're just born to? Fate. Written in the book of life before I was born. Because I have the Strange blood running through my veins."

He was still studying me, eyes roving over my face, but offering no answers.

I leaned my head back against the headrest. "How am I supposed to do this? There's nothing particularly special about me. I have no secret powers. And I'm *so* tired." I closed my eyes, listening to the silence. Until a warm hand covered mine. Snapping open my eyes, I watched as he gingerly took my hand and held it, turning it, examining it.

"You do have special powers," he said hoarsely. "In these hands is an unnatural obduracy that is native to mortals. Only *they* possess it. For mortals do not possess immortality, or the ability to fly, or to breathe through water, or great individual strength…but they do have this."

"I'm special because I'm…stubborn?"

"You would be surprised how valued a thing like that can be."

"*You* seem pretty stubborn to me."

"I can assure you, were I not tied to the book, I would have left some thousand or so years ago."

"Well, that's a testimonial, I guess." I sighed, liking the feeling of my hand in his. "I don't like that my grandfather was brought into this. It was almost like…I don't know."

"You knew nothing of your family history prior to the book's appearance?"

"No. Nothing. I didn't even remember that we used to come here in the summer. And that's a pretty big thing to forget. But you said that maybe there was a spell on me. Or the family. Or everyone, since no one remembers the Stranges."

"Yes. Might your grandfather have left you a clue of some kind? A journal perhaps?"

"I don't know. No. Unless…he left something at the house. I'll have to go back. But not tonight. During the day. I couldn't stand going back at night."

I released the seat belt and rolled out of the car. He followed me in and took up his place in the dark. At the stairs, I paused. "Do you…want to come up?"

What was I asking exactly? I didn't know. I wasn't sure.

I waited.

His eyes registered a kaleidoscope of emotion before he lowered his head and slowly shook it.

The demon was wise. Wiser than the mortal. I nodded and climbed the stairs alone.

⁂

I woke with a start. Confusion. The leftover feeling of dread from a dream I couldn't quite remember. The dark. The pull from the Booke. Ley lines crisscrossing my mind's eye. No, the dream was fading, but something else wakened me, made my heart hammer.

I jumped when the howl seemed to shake the house. It was close. I scrambled out of bed and cast the drapes aside. Looking down the moon-bathed backyard framed by the impenetrable dark of the surrounding woods, I saw nothing stirring. The howl echoed again. My restlessness made me throw on a robe and hurry down the stairs to creep across my shop and peek out the front curtains.

Definitely movement out there. Shadows crossing shadows, and then the sound of cats fighting. Or *was* it cats? Something was out there growling and snapping and rolling over and over. A shout. Was that a human calling out?

The crossbow whirred through the air and landed with a smack into my awaiting hand. It was armed.

Without a second thought, I cast the bolt aside and threw the door open.

A cold blast of arctic air assaulted me as I stood poised on the threshold in my terry robe, crossbow aimed into the gloomy street.

A pause. I held my breath, listening.

"Kylie!"

I jumped. "Jesus, Erasmus!" But then I saw the look on his face. "What's wrong?"

"I heard it but could not find it."

"What is it?"

"I don't know."

In a blink he darted away into the darkness while I aimed recklessly into the scattered shadows. *Just show yourself!* I couldn't stand not knowing. I wanted the suspense over with. The kelpie I knew. It still terrified, but at least I knew what to expect. How could I fight something I didn't even know?

A twig snapped. I almost called out, but I knew it wasn't Erasmus, not with his careful and silent steps. Slowly, I pivoted, the butt of the crossbow in my shoulder, one eye closed as I took aim down the sight.

A rustle, and something staggered onto the moonlit street. It looked like a man with ragged clothes trailing off his arms and legs, like every zombie movie I'd ever seen. My finger closed on the trigger.

"K-Kylie..."

The creature talked. They never talked...as far as I knew. And there was something about that voice...

He got close enough that a splash of moonlight struck his face.

"*Jeff!*"

The crossbow fell from my grip and I moved toward him just as he crumpled to his knees.

"Jeff!" I caught him, or nearly, before he fell all the way. His face was bloody, his clothes shredded. His eyes were dazed as I grabbed his face and looked at him squarely. "Jeff, what happened?" It looked like he was attacked by a bear. Those animal sounds...

"It came at me. There was no time to run."

"What did?" I scoured his face, his body. He was bloody, but he didn't look mortally so. Not mauled. A mountain lion? Did they have them in Maine? "Jeff, what attacked you?"

"I don't know. It…it looked like a wolf. Help me inside. It's still out there."

I got under his arm and braced him, lifting him up and dragging him in. I kicked the door shut and lowered him gently into a chair. The first aid kit was in the kitchen. I grabbed it and rushed back, landing on my knees beside him. He looked worse in the light.

"You're gonna be okay." I wasn't sure if that was more for him or me. My hands were shaking as I reached for my phone. "I'm going to call my friend Doc."

"Call 9-1-1," he said with a groan.

His arm. The most blood was there and I laid it carefully on the chair arm. "Jeff, I'm going to clean things up a bit…"

"Kylie, why aren't you calling 9-1-1?" His eyes were wild and… strange.

"Jeff, I'm pretty sure that that was no ordinary wolf out there. We can't just send you to a hospital. I have to call Doc." But when I leaned over him to look at the wound, he pulled back so violently that I almost fell over. His eyes were focused on my amulet hanging free from my shirt. *Had* it been a wolf…or was it Erasmus?

I punched in Doc's number and waited for him to pick up. "Sorry to wake you," I said when he got on the line, "but Jeff's here and he's been attacked by…something. He's been bitten and scratched, and his clothes are all torn up."

"I'll be right over."

I tossed the phone into the other chair, relieved he didn't waste time on questions. I stood over Jeff, reluctant to do any ministering. Had Erasmus done this? He had a mouth of vicious teeth when he went all demon. But the crossbow…

I glanced around for it and remembered I had left it outside. But I distinctly remembered that it had been armed, and it was never armed around Erasmus.

A breath of air and a pop announced his arrival. Jeff was staring straight ahead, hands clutching the chair arms. He didn't seem to notice Erasmus.

"Did you see it?" the demon asked.

"Did *I* see it? No. I thought you might have."

"No. It was too quick. I see it got him, though."

Jeff suddenly turned toward Erasmus. "It was big and hairy. It *was* a wolf, wasn't it?"

"A wolf..." Erasmus narrowed his eyes, thinking.

"I don't feel so good," said Jeff.

"Let me clean you up..." I came closer again, and again Jeff flinched away.

Headlights swept over us and a car pulled up out front. The Rambler rattled to a stop and Doc hopped out. He pushed through the door in his pajamas and robe, doctor bag in hand. Immediately he went to Jeff. "Now, young man, I'll fix you up. Can you tell us what happened?"

He allowed Doc to minister to him, so I stepped back. Clutching the amulet in my hand, I was almost comforted by its warmth, but when I looked at Erasmus, he was staring at it, just as Jeff had done. He said nothing as he raised his eyes to me.

"I was just coming through the woods to keep an eye on Kylie's place," Jeff was saying.

"What?" Tearing away from my hazy thoughts, I stomped my foot. "You were supposed to be gone. You were supposed to have flown back to California."

"I couldn't. I couldn't leave you here with all this—ow!"

"Sorry about that," said Doc in his soothing doctor voice. "These need stiches. They're pretty deep. A tetanus shot too. Maybe rabies. Now the tetanus I can give you, but I haven't got the rabies shots."

"We don't know what bit him," I reminded. "Maybe those shots would cause a worse reaction."

"I think I know." As usual, Erasmus had been so quiet we forgot about his presence. His hand darted out and captured my wrist, dragging me toward Jeff. He grabbed the amulet and, for a moment, I thought he was trying to take it back. Instead, he shoved it toward Jeff, who shied back with a gruff snarl.

Erasmus released it and me, and I hauled off and smacked him on the shoulder. "What the hell are you doing?"

"The amulet is silver." He hid his hand, but I could see the burn mark on his palm where he'd grabbed it. "Did you see your friend's reaction?"

I shook my head. "I don't understand."

"You're not serious?" asked Doc. His mouth hung open slightly. A roll of gauze bandage hung loose from his hands.

"Of course I am serious. Your friend has an aversion to silver. And a wolf bit him."

In the long pause I got the feeling Erasmus was waiting for me. When I still looked as if I was in the dark—and I was—Doc filled in the blanks.

"Werewolf," he whispered.

"No. That's ridiculous." I turned to Erasmus to confirm, but the demon was stone faced. "This is impossible. I mean, sure, creatures and all, but...a *werewolf*?"

Jeff began to shake. "I don't feel good." He doubled over, moaning. The moaning turned into a whine and the whine morphed into a howl. Dirty blond hair sprouted up from the backs of his hands like some crazy fast-growing Chia Pet. Then his teeth! Oh man! His teeth!

"No!" I cried. "This cannot be happening. Jeff, you stop that right now!"

He turned yellow eyes to me. His ears had elongated to points, and though his teeth had sharpened and there was extra hair on his arms and the backs of his clawed hands, nothing more had changed.

"Kylie." His voice was gruff, a strange combination of a baritone and a growl. "What's happening to me?"

"Oh shit." I couldn't believe it. I mean, I believed a lot of things now—demons, gods, weird Netherworld creatures—but werewolves? I shook my head, willing it all to stop. But there it was in front of my eyes. "Oh, Jeff. I'm so, so sorry."

He stared at his hands and whined like a dog.

"Now, Mr. Chase," said Doc, taking what looked more like paws than hands in his. "You're here with us. The best possible people to help you. So, first things first. You need to calm down."

"Calm *down*?" he growled.

"Jeff," I interjected. "Doc is right. You've got to calm down. We'll…we'll fix this. We promise. Just calm down, relax."

Jeff held tight to Doc as if he were a lifeline, but he locked gazes with me. I breathed for him, taking a deep breath and then letting it out slowly. He followed. The calmer he became, the more his, well, *symptoms* calmed. His ears shrank, his claws receded, the extra hair sloughed off, cascading around him like autumn leaves. Lastly, his teeth and eyes returned to normal.

"His wounds," said Doc. "They've healed up."

"Oh my God," he breathed. "Kylie, please don't say it."

I laid my hand on his now normal hand, still bloody and dirty from his fight. "I don't think I really have to, do I?"

Erasmus stepped forward, subtle as always. "He's obviously been bitten by a werewolf, which means he is now a werewolf and a danger to everyone. It might be better if we just kill him now."

"Erasmus! No killing. Move back, you're getting him nervous again. And when he gets nervous…" I could see that he was morphing again. The eyes and ears were changing. "Breathe, Jeff. Relax. There won't be any killing." His ears receded but not all the way, and his ordinarily blue eyes were caught halfway between blue and yellow, a sickly green with a white outline around the irises.

Jeff glanced desperately between me and Doc. "So…so you can cure me, right? You and your Wiccans?"

Doc sighed. "I don't honestly know, son. We'll have to research it. But in the meantime, it might help matters if you stay with me. I can at least help you control it."

"Why can't I stay here?" There was that dog's whine to his voice, completely unnerving.

"Because as good-hearted as Kylie is—and I sense that she would offer it—she's got enough on her plate. And I'm in a unique position to be able to help you. I have quite a library on lycanthropy."

Jeff lowered his head, scraping back the gauze on his arm, which was now unnecessary. "This is a nightmare. I'm gonna wake up, aren't I? I wish I'd never come."

Hugging myself, I thought the same thing. I didn't hate Jeff, not anymore, but I was upset with him, as anyone would be. And I certainly wouldn't have wished this on him. But Doc was right. I didn't need one more complication on my doorstep. If Doc was willing to take him, then it would be for the best.

After all, I now had a werewolf to kill.

CHAPTER TWELVE

We bundled Jeff into Doc's car. I hugged him, told him it would be all right. But when I did the same for Doc, I whispered to him, "Will you be safe?"

He patted my hand and got in the car. "Don't worry."

I watched them drive away with Jeff's haunted face staring at me through the car window. Doc said he'd tell the others. God knew what they were going to do about it.

I gathered my discarded crossbow and dragged myself back inside.

Erasmus stood before the fire, though he didn't need to warm himself. "I'm sorry this happened." He shifted, staring into the fire. I felt he meant it. "I tried to find the creature…"

"I know you did. It's not your fault."

"Nor yours."

"He followed me to Maine. I told him it was over between us. I tried to convince him to leave."

"Men seem to find it difficult to forget you."

I caught his eye before he turned away.

"It's late. Get some sleep, Kylie. We'll talk in the morning. There is much to discuss."

Trudging up the stairs, I didn't argue. I didn't think I'd sleep, but I did, almost instantly. My dreams were filled with wolf packs running through the wood and arrows flying from a crossbow, chasing them into the night.

I walked through my morning as if in a trance. My mind was on Jeff, my grandfather's house, and Erasmus. Then there were Hansen Mills and the Ordo. Grandpa had mentioned them by name. That was exceptionally bad news. And it looked like the Ordo wasn't messing around anymore. They were goofs to be sure, but they had beaten up Jeff, kidnapped him. That was an escalation. Well, attacking my shop had been an escalation. And I really couldn't tell Ed about any of it. How could I without spilling the beans about the rest of it?

Ley lines. What did those mean? And there was also that vortex in the caves at Falcon's Point, and that voice that had possessed Jolene, if only briefly. And that pentagram at the church.

Whoever said that country life was dull didn't know Moody Bog.

It was eight o'clock before Erasmus made an appearance. He had probably been there all along but invisible. Last night he had said there was much to discuss, but he didn't say anything as he stood there. Just drank the coffee I offered him and became a silent, comforting presence, which I welcomed.

And then I remembered his hand. The amulet had somehow burned him. I darted forward and grabbed his wrist. He glared at me as I turned over his hand. There wasn't a trace of a burn on it.

"This was burned yesterday. You burned it when you touched the amulet."

"Yes."

"What do you mean 'yes'? This is *your* amulet. I took it off of your neck."

"And now *you* are bearing it."

"I don't understand."

"Silver…is anathema to demons."

"So why on earth would you wear a silver necklace?"

"Because I was created with it. Once it left me…it became something…other."

"So if I give it back to you, will it still burn you?"

"Likely not."

"Likely?"

"I don't know. No one has ever…" He fell silent, brooding.

I could get nothing more out of him. I decided to call Doc. "How is he?"

"As well as can be expected." He sighed. "I'm going to need the coven's help. Nick is up on his creature lore and Jolene, well. She's wicked good at filling in the blanks. But it's Seraphina I'll be needing the most. I'm pretty sure we're going to need a potion for this and she's the best where that's concerned. She has that gentle touch."

"So there is a cure?"

"No, Kylie. Unless Nick or Jolene can scare up something else, all the research I've ever done has said there is no cure. But there can be control with the right kind of potion. He'll have to be trained to live with it, I'm afraid."

I felt sick as I sat on the nearest surface—the cobbler's bench in the corner. "That's really horrible," I gasped. Tears stung at my eyes and I wiped at them.

"It is. But I suspect your Jeff is strong and can endure it. Many have before him. What you've got to worry about is the other werewolf out there."

"But wait a minute. Isn't that a person? I mean, all the other things were creatures. I don't mean to be 'creaturist' about it, but I don't exactly feel comfortable killing something…human."

"I'm just speculating here, and perhaps Mr. Dark can confirm this, but the werewolf from the book is likely the first werewolf, and if that is the case, it's been a werewolf for far longer than it's been a man at this point. He may not even be able to shift back into human form anymore."

"But we don't know that."

"No, we don't. I'll be meeting with the coven as soon as possible. Jolene has to go to school, of course, and I don't want Nick to lose his job. Seraphina and I will be putting our heads together before the others can join us."

"Do you need me for anything?"

"Like I said, you've got enough on your plate. And this is a Wicca matter in any case."

"And…are *you* all right?"

"I've spent part of the time teaching him some meditation techniques. I daresay he knew quite a bit already, he just needed reminding."

"Jeff was big into yoga."

"And all that will help him. When Seraphina comes, I'll get a little shut-eye."

"Are you sure you don't want me to come over?"

"Good heavens no. To be honest, I think he might get too excitable when you're around."

Great. Just great.

"If you need anything, Doc…"

"You just run your shop, little lady. And…get that werewolf. Jeff will rest easier when it's gone."

I hung up and found myself staring at Erasmus. He barely moved. The coffee mug in his hand sent up tendrils of steam. How about that? He was his own Thermos.

For some reason, of all the things crowding for dominance, that pentagram at the church was looming large in my mind. Maybe because I didn't want to be blindsided by one more unknown. Maybe it was because focusing on it meant I didn't have to think about creatures or an ex-boyfriend who had turned into a werewolf.

Yeah, that was another one of those sentences I never expected to say.

Maybe I could make myself useful, get over to the church and talk to Reverend Howard. And then still have time to get over to Grandpa's and look around before I opened my doors at…well, realistically ten at this point. I'd never run a successful business this way. But really, I was beginning to wonder if there was any point to it anymore.

We drank our coffee, Erasmus and I, both stealing the occasional glance at each other.

"What did you want to talk with me about?"

He set the mug down and adjusted his coat. "It doesn't matter. We have other things to concentrate on."

"A kelpie and a werewolf."

"Yes. And whatever comes next."

I rubbed my eyes. "The kelpie I understand. The werewolf…I don't. Doc said it's the *first* werewolf, the first person to change. Is it even a person anymore? Please say no."

He smiled grimly. "Not a person you would recognize as human. The first werewolf was the imagination of an angry god. This werewolf is ancient."

"Erasmus, when I shoot these things, are they dead?"

"Not as you understand death. They are returned from whence they came."

"And where is that exactly?"

"It's very difficult to explain."

I waved him off. "You know what? It doesn't matter. As long as they aren't here anymore and can't do anyone any harm, that's good enough for me."

We said nothing more. I sighed, looking at my empty coffee cup. I had to get started. "Listen, I have to go over to the church for something…"

"Beelze's tail, whatever for? There is so much else for you to do."

"But I have to do this. I saw a pentagram over there. I want to find out more about it and alert the pastor."

He frowned.

"And then I'm going to Grandpa's to see if there isn't a journal there."

"I can accompany you. But not to the…the church."

"Oh ho! Hallowed ground, eh? I'll have to remember that."

His disgusted look could wither a mighty oak.

As I grabbed my coat and keys, the Booke was suddenly sitting there before the front door.

"What do *you* want?"

I bent to reach for it and it trembled. Snatching my hands back, I straightened. "Erasmus, what is it doing?"

"You are neglecting your duties. It is agitated."

"Well, tell it to take a chill pill. I'm busy."

"Kylie, the book must be appeased. The kelpie—"

"Is still out there. I know. I really, really do. But these other things must be taken care of too, and I am only one Chosen Host. So the both of you…relax!"

The Booke suddenly stopped its shuddering.

"Oh. Okay then." I picked it up and was a little surprised that it let me carry it to the kitchen and deposit it on the table. "Now you behave yourself. I'll get back to kelpie and werewolf hunting soon. As soon as I can. Coming, Erasmus?" I called over my shoulder.

"Why must you treat me like a footman?"

"Well, you do hover like one."

We got into the Jeep and took Lyndon Road down to the white steeple I could see spearing above houses and shops. I rounded the village green and pulled into the church parking lot. Was eight o'clock too early for a visit? I hoped not. But even now I couldn't get that image of Jeff shifting into an animal out of my mind. Was it a death sentence? Would he, too, change permanently and have to be hunted down? I didn't want to ask Erasmus. I'd wait to see what Nick and Jolene had to say. I trusted their judgment.

The plain white sign in front of the church read, "First Congregational Church of Moody Bog. Rev. Howard Cleveland, Pastor." in gold letters.

There were a few buildings around the back of the church. The church hall, where I saw the pentagram, and another one that looked like a cottage, which I assumed was Reverend Howard's place.

In the far reaches of the green, I saw the janitor trudging his way across, dragging bulging trash bags behind him. I parked, got out, and trotted toward him, sans Erasmus. "Excuse me!"

He kept trudging, oblivious to the crazy woman shouting and running after him.

"Excuse me!" If I only knew his name, I wouldn't have looked so insane.

Finally, he noticed me and stopped, squinting with a doglike head tilt. "Ay-yuh?"

Out of breath (I really needed to work out more), I tried a smile. "Hi. Do you remember me? From last week at the Chamber of Commerce social?"

He looked at me blankly, which was probably just as well. I put out my hand to shake, friendly-like. "I'm Kylie Strange. I own that herb and tea shop near the highway. And you are?"

He stared at my outstretched hand with a measure of skepticism, but never returned the gesture. He sported a full head of white hair, with some of it tufting out of his ears. His nose was round and veined with burst capillaries, and his mouth hung open from hard breathing. He said nothing at first, then licked his lips and muttered, "Mister Parker," as if that was all anyone ever knew about him…which might have been the case. He was, no doubt, one of those indispensable characters no one actually knew well, but who was always working thanklessly in the background.

"Mr. Parker, it's nice to meet you. I wonder if I might pop into the hall for just a quick minute. I don't mean to interrupt your work..."

"Why'd you want to go in there for?"

His Maine accent was thick, the kind one might use for a Maine tourism ad.

"I just need to check on something. I, uh, wanted to give the church something for being kind and hosting the Chamber gatherings, and I, uh, need to check on sizes and stuff." That was vague enough. Lame but vague. But now I'd have to follow through. I wondered if the church needed an additional samovar.

Mr. Parker didn't look any less skeptical. "I don't think I can let you in."

"Oh, it would just be for a minute. Half a minute. Just a poke-my-head-in-the-door kind of thing."

Now he narrowed his eyes. Had he cottoned on to me? After all, if he were a secret Wiccan of the black sort, he wouldn't want me digging around. If he were of the light sort, I figured he'd already be pals with Doc and Company.

"Just a small peek," I said desperately, edging back toward the church hall.

"Young lady, I done said my piece on that. You're gonna have to take it up with the pastor. I don't go letting strange people wander around the hall."

"What's going on here?"

Reverend Howard himself, wrapped up in a parka with his collar peeking out, strode up to the both of us.

"Kylie, how are you? Daniel, what can I help you with?"

Daniel Parker jerked a thumb at me. "This'un wants to go into the hall, sneaking about. Ruth Russell done warned me about the likes of her."

"Now Daniel, that isn't Christian of you at all. Kylie's motivations are entirely honorable. She's the nice young lady that opened that tea shop in town. It's bringing traffic from the highway. We're all grateful for that. And the Lord wants us to greet our neighbors with civility. So what can I do for you, Kylie?"

"Reverend Howard, I wonder if I could walk with you. Have a word?"

"Why, certainly. I'll see you later, Daniel."

The reverend led us away, but Daniel stood where he was, staring. What curses would I be subject to now, I wondered.

"You'll have to excuse Daniel," said Reverend Howard. I had to maintain a brisk pace to keep up with the tall, long-legged man. "He's been at this parish a long time and I daresay he comes with quirks. He's been here far longer than I have."

"Longer than the church maybe," I muttered.

He laughed. "You might be right. But it didn't seem polite to ask. By the way, I was sorry to hear about what happened to your shop. The sheriff has had his hands full with his younger brother."

"Thanks, but it's all mended now. The shop, that is. Ed and Doug have a long way to go to mend their differences."

"People tell me that you and the sheriff are getting mighty tight."

"People do talk, don't they? But we are. We are seeing each other."

"Well, that is nice. Ed is a good friend to the church and a heck of a nice guy. And if you don't mind my saying, you two make a lovely couple."

My face warmed at that. I thought we did too. Of course, my thoughts shot immediately toward Erasmus, who was waiting in the car…or was he? He said he couldn't go on hallowed ground. But how far did hallowed ground extend from the church? Did the hall count?

"Listen, Reverend, I have a rather strange request of you. I would like to take a look in the church hall for only a moment. It won't take long."

"Why? Did you lose something the last time you were here? We do have a lost and found box in the rectory…"

"No, nothing like that. You're going to think it's awfully weird."

"In this town? Even out here in the wilds of Maine, I've seen it and heard it all, I can assure you."

"Well, all right. Um…how well *do* you know Daniel Parker?"

He looked back and so did I. Parker had finally begun heading wherever it was he was heading with his trash bags…full of body parts, no doubt. We veered toward the hall as we walked. "As I said, he was here before I came to the parish, some ten-odd years ago. Daniel's harmless. His only vice, as far as I can tell, is to smoke the worst-smelling pipe tobacco. He doesn't seem to drink, doesn't gamble, doesn't carry on with the ladies. He keeps to himself, does his job, and never complains. Never married and no children. Why?"

We reached the door of the hall and I gestured for him to open it. He took out a full set of keys, found the one he wanted, and fit it in the lock. The door creaked open. Inside was cold and dark, with those same smells of cabbage and spaghetti dinners still lingering within its walls. He flipped a wall switch and the fluorescent lights buzzed and flickered to life.

The parquet floor was open like a school gym, with tables folded and stacked against the far wall. I made a beeline for the kitchen doorway. Its café window was closed and barred with metal rollup doors, but to the right was the custodian's closet. I yanked the door open and flipped on the light. Mops in roll-around buckets, brooms, rolls of butcher paper, boxes of foil and cellophane in industrial sizes, along with cleaning supplies of sponges, sink cleanser, floor cleaner, and ammonia.

But no pentagram.

"It was right here. Right here on the floor."

"What was?" He peered over my shoulder, nose crinkling at the strong smell of cleaner.

"A pentagram."

"What? On *this* floor?"

"Yes. I saw it. I know I did. Of course, it was over a week ago."

"You think our Daniel is practicing Wiccan rituals here in my church?"

"I don't know. But…Look. You're a pastor. You believe in the supernatural, don't you?"

"If you're talking about God and angels, yes."

"And demons."

"To a certain extent." When I gave him a questioning look, he pressed on. "My theology, and that which I preach, is more, well, modern. We profess our love of God and accept His Son, recognize Heaven and sin. But it's a bit murkier when it comes to demons and Hell. Hell, as such, isn't necessarily a place, but the absence of God's divine love. And the demons from the Bible, well. Is anyone ever really possessed by demons anymore? We know that all sorts of chemical and psychological afflictions could have been interpreted as demonic possession in a less enlightened era. So if you're asking if I believe in a Wiccan spirituality, my answer is… to a point. Doc Boone's style of Wicca is about wholeness with nature and one's own spirit or soul, and that I can get behind. But 'summoning' demons and spirits? I leave that sort of thing to Hollywood filmmakers."

"But might certain of these practices cause harm to humans who interact with them?"

"Psychologically. Are you talking about black magic practitioners? That's a slippery slope. It can lead to all sorts of bad behavior. And as far as I know, Doc Boone's coven would never—"

"I'm not talking about them. I'm talking about maybe another group nearby. Doc and his coven are the good guys. What they do protects the village. But there are others out there who are doing it for their own gain. And it's very dangerous."

He got in close. "You aren't talking about…some of these missing people, are you?"

"Not…necessarily."

He seemed taken aback by my vagueness, that I hadn't ruled it out. He rubbed a hand over his face. "What is it you want me to do?"

"I don't know. Some of these people doing black magic…I wasn't a believer before, but I am now."

"People do and say a lot of things, and I have to admit that a lot of it is, well, just in their heads. It's one thing to believe in the higher power of God and His presence, but it's quite another to believe in the power of tarot cards or demonic possession. I'm a practical man, after all. Thoroughly of the twenty-first century."

"Yeah. I can see that. I apologize for this wild-goose chase. I'm normally not like this. But I have to say, I've seen some things lately and…Forget it. I'm sorry to have bothered you."

"No, no, Kylie. Obviously, something has caused you anxiety and I would like to help if I can. I know you've been seeing a lot of Doc Boone's coven. My advice to you? Perhaps…stay away. Try not to fraternize with them quite so much. They are nice people, don't get me wrong, but you might be, well, how should I put this? Impressionable. Being alone here and all. It might not be the best influence on you."

"I see what you're saying, Reverend, and I appreciate it. But if you do see anything here at the church, will you give me a call?" His expression seemed a little uncertain. "Well. I've taken up too much of your time already."

His cell rang. "Would you please excuse me? I have to take all calls. I'm a man with a calling." He grinned and took out his phone. "Yes, Mr. Waterman. No, of course it's not too early." He put his hand over the mouthpiece. "You can let yourself out. And don't fret, Kylie. Everything will be fine."

He walked down the dark hallway toward a distant door, talking in the phone all the while.

I glanced into the closet once more. It was too much to expect the pentagram to still be here after a week. Parker saw me in there, after all. He probably got rid of the evidence as soon as he could. But the question was, what was he up to? I turned to go when I spotted it. Under one of the roll-around buckets. A chalk mark. I moved the bucket and saw clearly not a pentagram but a circle with weird markings in it. It almost looked like a circuit board. I pulled out my phone and took a picture. What sort of hocus pocus was Daniel doing? And right under the pastor's nose!

I wouldn't have noticed the little bag if I hadn't been snooping, but there it was, nailed inside the closet on the top of the door jam. A velvet bag of midnight blue. I yanked it off its nail and pulled on the drawstring. A feather, a sprig of herbs tied with a white string, and a tiny bottle filled with a white powder. I decided to swipe it and show the Wiccans, see if they knew what it was. Stuffing it quickly into my jacket pocket, I turned off the light, closed the door, and hightailed it out of there.

When I got into the car again, Erasmus appeared. "What did you find?"

"Well, this, for one." I showed him the bag.

He frowned and sniffed it. "This is for protection. It keeps people away, creates a barrier. This phial contains crushed bone. Human, presumably."

I took it back gingerly. *Eww.*

"And then there was this." I brought the photo up on my phone and showed it to him.

He paled and grabbed the phone, staring at it.

"What?" I asked. "What is it?"

"Let us leave this place. Now!"

CHAPTER THIRTEEN

"It is the seal of the demon Andras," said Erasmus tightly, staring at my phone as I drove. "His only purpose is to sow discord…and kill when necessary."

I was headed toward Alderbrook Lane without thinking. "Someone is summoning this Andras? Is that what that is, this seal? Why would the janitor be doing that? Who does he work for? Shoot. I forgot to ask where he lived. I bet it's Hansen Mills."

"I am very concerned, Kylie. Andras is in an order higher than mine. I do not know, if tasked, whether I can defeat him."

I glanced at him with an encouraging smile. "If it comes to it, you will."

He gave me a look as if I was out of my mind. "No, I can't."

"Of course you can. You'd be fighting for me, right?"

He didn't reply and kept staring at me as I drove to Alderbrook Lane and made the turn. "Kylie…"

Hesitancy looked strange on him. His hands fidgeted. He looked like he wanted to explain something to me, something unpleasant. And I just wasn't in the mood.

"It doesn't matter, Erasmus."

"But—"

"It doesn't matter. Not now anyway. Let's just do this."

He said nothing more, his hands in his lap.

We traveled up the road, past the tree and the windmill. The house looked far less scary during the day. But it was still a sad sight, abandoned as it was.

I got out of the car. Erasmus was right beside me this time. We walked up to the porch together and the door opened easily for us.

It was just as Grandpa had left it, only under layers of dust and cobwebs. A house that looked like it deserved to be haunted.

"Grandpa?" I called out timidly.

Nothing. I was oddly relieved.

Hands on hips, I took inventory. Quite a mess really. "Now where would Grandpa hide a journal?"

"Look here."

Erasmus pointed to something tucked against the door frame. Another little bag like the one I'd found at the church.

"Another spell for protection?"

He shook his head and I approached, studying it. I reached for it but he grabbed my arm. "I wouldn't do that. I think this is the very spell that prevents anyone from remembering. I think it wise that you do not disturb it. And tell as few people as possible about your grandfather."

So that was why there was never a search for heirs. This spell to forget the Stranges. And it had kept vandals away all these years, too, preserving what was here. Though once mentioned to people, the spell appeared broken, at least to that individual.

"That's probably a good idea." I walked through the archway to the dining room and looked around. "The kitchen jar." I pushed hard on the kitchen doors and the hinges whined in protest. They hadn't been oiled in two decades, after all. I went straight for the shelf above the refrigerator, which looked much like an icebox from days of yore, and reached up to the jar that was still there. It had seemed as high as Everest when I was six. Now I merely had to stretch to grasp the green milk glass jar with its matching top.

Amazing things had come out of that jar; dimes for ice cream, peppermint sticks, stamps, paperclips...it was a most magic jar. Cradling it in my arm, I pulled off the lid...but there was nothing inside. Even the secrets of the green jar would remain secrets.

I set it carefully on the kitchen table and thought. Had to be upstairs in his room.

All the while, Erasmus watched me curiously.

"I'm going to check in his room upstairs. Coming?"

I grasped the banister. It was so familiar. The worn wood, the round finial on the newel post. Erasmus's gentle footsteps followed me, missing every creaking riser. The hallway had an old-fashioned niche for the telephone. There was still a dusty push-button phone in the alcove, sitting on top of an old phone book from 1994. But no other book was there. I moved down the hall, memories pinging in my mind of the sights and sounds of the house: my own running footsteps, my mother calling after me not to run inside, Grandpa laughing and telling her to let me be.

The door to his room was open. The quilt—whatever color it was—lay muted under dust and dirt. There were framed photographs on the side table. I vowed to take all the photos I could find and bring them home. I rummaged in the side table drawers, the dresser...still filled with folded clothes. Nothing.

When I turned, Erasmus stood in the doorway, holding a stiff piece of paper. It was something I had painted as a child for my grandfather. "This is your work," he said, pointing to my uneven signature scrawled at the bottom. "It isn't very good."

I slapped his shoulder, which always seemed to surprise him. "I was only five! A child."

"Oh." He set it aside and gazed at me steadily. "I was created just as you see me now many thousands of years ago," he said quietly. "I never had parents or a childhood. But I can tell...that this is very difficult for you. I am...trying to empathize."

"That's…very good of you." I looked him over. "You really had no parents, no childhood? You were born…fully grown? Like this? Leather duster and all?"

"Yes."

"I'm trying to empathize with *that*. I wonder if *your* existence is kinder, never having to lose those that you love."

"I do not think…it is kinder."

"Hmm." I offered a smile. "I guess you're right. I think I'm still glad I knew them, even for a brief time."

Before sliding by him I reached up and kissed his cheek.

He put a hand to his face and stared after me.

"Something has to be here," I muttered. When I reached the bottom floor and the kitchen again, I leaned against the doorjamb. "Now wait a minute. I remember he used to write his accounts in a little book. And I think he kept it in here somewhere."

Erasmus had recovered from the kiss and was by my side, pulling out drawers. "A book…like this?" He pulled something from a drawer of desiccated towels: a notebook no bigger than his palm.

"That's it!" I snatched it out of his hands and thumbed through it. There were household accounts carefully scrawled in there in pencil on the narrow lines, lists of things that needed repairing, but way in the back, after a…pentagram…were notes written in a strange language.

"Is this Latin? No, Greek. No. I don't know what it is."

Erasmus gently took it from my hands and studied the page. "It is Enochian. The language of angels…and demons."

"How did my grandfather know that?"

"A pity you did not know him better." He read silently for a time.

I tapped my fingers impatiently against my thigh. "Erasmus. What does it say?"

"Much that we already knew. It seems that your grandfather was fully versed on the book. As fully versed as a mortal can be. But he was not a Chosen Host, so much was still a mystery to him. He had never seen it, of course. It says he did not know where it was but only that it was close. Wait. He mentions you. I shall endeavor to translate it as close to English as possible. 'Kylie cannot know, cannot understand, what her role is to be. Even I am not quite certain. But it is clear to me that Rupert never said anything to her mother, and so she doesn't know either. Must keep them away from here in the fall. Not until the proper time.'" He looked up from the notebook. "He never told you?"

I dabbed at the tears in my eyes. "No. He died suddenly of a heart attack. I was six. All I remember is sadness and longing for him. But that was a long time ago."

Erasmus went back to the notebook. "Apparently, the foundations of this house were built long, long before his time, for a much older habitation than this one. The natives of this area once had a lodge of some kind. It sits at the conjunction of several ley lines—but we already knew this. And that it is protecting the village…no." An ironic smile drew up one edge of his mouth. "'Village' in this sense means 'the world.' That it is protecting the world from destruction. And that the curse that has befallen the Strange family is to guard the gate at any cost. The book is one of many gateways, though it also serves as…" He stopped.

"Serves as what?"

"The writing is smudged here." He eyed it closely, bringing it closer to the window to scrutinize it. "Serves as…a key? Hmm. Interesting."

"Wait. The Booke isn't just some stupid parlor trick created by long-dead Ancient Ones? It has a greater purpose than just letting creatures out to wreak havoc?"

"Which makes sense. Most objects created by the ancients had a significant purpose. The releasing of creatures could be incidental to its true motivation."

"Incidental? *Incidental?* Tell that to its victims. Tell that to Jeff. There are people dead because of this stupid Booke."

"I know."

"Oh good. I'm glad."

"Mortals," he muttered with a sneer. "I—who have been intimately intertwined with the book, captured by its covers for thousands of years—*I* don't even know what it does or why. Do you think for one moment *I* like this? That *I* like being yanked about from century to century, listening to the mewling of each Chosen Host as she does her job. Do you think *I* truly enjoy taking my—"

He stopped, shutting his lips as if locking a door.

"Taking your what?"

"Never mind," he growled. "This is *my* lot in life. I was created for *this*. And I shall be part of it until the end of time."

"I don't think so."

"What do you mean you 'don't think so'?"

"I'm stopping this Booke. This is the last generation of crap from it. Its days of taking a Chosen Host are over. My family..." I laughed thinking about it. It's our curse. Did we bring it over to the New World? How long had my ancient ancestors been entrusted with this thing? Cursed by it? "When I close the cover of this Booke, it isn't opening again for anyone else."

He folded his arms. "Oh, how the arrogance of the human race astounds me. Go on. Tell me. Explain exactly how you are going to do that?"

I shrugged. "I don't know. But I've got my Wiccans. We'll figure something out. I'm not alone, you know."

His expression faded and his arms fell away from his chest. "I see. You...you think to succeed where others have failed. Well... the others *were* alone. Perhaps...perhaps there may be something to what you say."

That gave me hope. No, I wasn't alone. If those other Chosen Hosts had struck out on their own without any backup, then of course they had little chance. Ha! I had my little army. There *was* a chance. But then...

"What happens to you?"

He looked toward the floor, his long hair hanging over his face and hiding his eyes. "Then I...cease."

"Cease. What do you mean 'cease'?"

When he raised his head, there was no expression, either on his face or in his usually expressive eyes. "I fail to exist. Or in your parlance, I die."

"What? No. That...can't be right."

"My sole existence is to serve the one who opens the book. There is no other reason for my creation. When the book dies, so, too, do I."

"We'll find a way. We'll find a way to...um...unbind you."

"And why, by Beelze's tail, would you want to do that?"

I breathed. There should have been a lot swirling around in my mind, but there wasn't. Only the aspect of this stupid demon's non-existence. I couldn't fathom it. I didn't want to. Striding forward, I took his face in my hands and kissed him.

His arms were suddenly around me, holding me close. His mouth opened and his lips—so hot, so wet—kissed me urgently, as if this was his last day on earth. I tried not to think about that and just surrendered to simply *feeling*.

He nipped my bottom lip and grazed my chin with his teeth. His mouth was on my neck and I arched toward him. I could feel his hardness through our clothing and I had a flash from about a week ago of my bed, the quilt, the body of a god, and the wildness as we let ourselves go. I had begun vaguely wondering about the kitchen floor when he suddenly drew back. I nearly fell backward when he released me and turned away.

Stumbling, I adjusted my stance and wiped the wet from my mouth.

His back was to me, and his shoulders were heaving with great gusting breaths. "Damn you," he murmured. "We…can't."

"We did once."

"That was my arrogance. And my folly."

I breathed, trying to control the tremors in my body. How he could get me into such a lather, I'd never know. Even harking back to my evening with Ed, it had been good…but it was never like this.

"Okay. All right. Let's focus on what's important. My grandfather's notebook."

"Yes. Yes, all right." He snatched it awkwardly from the counter and opened it again. I couldn't help but watch as he tried to compose himself. It hadn't been my imagination. He had felt it too. Whatever it was that drew us to each other, he felt it like I did.

Erasmus—strong willed, determined—seemed to set his mind back to the problem at hand. "Kylie," he said after a time of thoughtful study. "Do you understand the implications of this?"

"Just assume that I don't."

"Your family is not just responsible for controlling the book, but for keeping the gate from opening, a gate that will destroy the world. But if the book itself is the key to locking that gate for good, then we must find the true answer for the book's existence. It might be the key to understanding how to stop the book for good."

"But don't *you* know?"

"No! Don't you understand? I only awaken when the book is opened. And it is opened very briefly every hundred years or so. My task is to close the book…And wait for it to be opened again."

"So…what do you do in the meantime? Are you like a genie, encased in a lamp?"

"I never understand what you are talking about. No. I simply…go into stasis. Sleep."

"Well that's a horrible existence!"

"It's the only existence I have ever known."

"We've got to get you out of this."

"I applaud your chivalry, but your energy would be better spent on how to capture the creatures and close the book."

"But if I do that, you'll only go to sleep again and wait for the next Princess Charming to open the damned thing. Erasmus, we have to stop it for good."

"Right now we have a kelpie and a werewolf to capture. Each creature will get us that much closer to ending this."

"Erasmus, why was my family never told about this? About the Booke being a key. Grandpa seemed to have had an inkling, but why didn't Constance Howland know?"

He shook his head. "I don't know."

"Did any of them know?"

He thought back and slowly shook his head. "The knowledge seems to have been lost."

Constance Howland's fate was never far from my mind. "Erasmus," I said softly, "what happens to the Chosen Hosts once they're done? We know what happened to Constance Howland. But what of the others before her?"

"What difference does it make? They are long dead."

"From where I'm standing, it makes kind of a big difference."

"Kylie—" He stopped. We both heard it. The sound of a car door slamming. A weird feral expression came over Erasmus—he even crouched a little, as if about to pounce. He moved like a cat with quiet steps toward the kitchen doorway to peer out the front window. Then his coiled muscles suddenly relaxed.

"It's your constable," he said flatly.

CHAPTER FOURTEEN

Ed was on the porch when I came out. He seemed surprised to see me, even though my Jeep was plainly parked in front. "Kylie? What are you doing here?"

"What are *you* doing here?"

He looked puzzled for a moment before he straightened. He was in his sheriff's uniform, Smokey Bear hat and all. "I thought I'd check this out since you talked about it. Aren't you supposed to be in your shop?"

"So…you came to check this out *knowing* I'd be in my shop?"

"What? Wait, this isn't coming out right. Ever since you mentioned it, I've been trying to remember Alderbrook Lane. I've lived here all my life, cruised these streets hundreds, thousands of times, and I've never heard of this street. It isn't on any of my maps. I just stumbled across it. I must have driven by it a million times and never noticed before. Sure, it's overgrown but…" He shook his head. "It's weird."

Before he could think about it too much, I interrupted. "I thought I'd come up here and collect a few of Grandpa's things. Some photos and stuff. It's a little creepy, to tell you the truth."

He stepped up onto the porch to tower over me. "Then maybe you shouldn't be alone."

"She's not alone."

Ed was startled, his hand slipping toward his holster. I covered that hand with mine. "Erasmus came up to help me," I said hurriedly.

"I see. Kylie, can I talk to you for a moment? Alone?"

"I'll be right back, Erasmus."

Erasmus sneered. "I'll be waiting on tenterhooks."

Ed drew me away near his car and spoke softly, eyes flicking occasionally toward Erasmus, who had stubbornly stayed on the porch to glare at us. "I heard a rumor the other day. About your old boyfriend."

"*Ex*-boyfriend." The automatic reply felt uneasy now that Jeff was...well, afflicted.

"Yeah. Him. Well, there was a rumor that my brother and his gang roughed him up. Maybe even abducted him. Would you know anything about that?"

"No...wait. Are you accusing *me* of something?"

"I'm not accusing anyone. I just heard a rumor and I need to follow it up. Where is your ex?"

Shoot. What to say? "He left. I sent him out of town." At least it was the truth. Partly.

"Do you have a phone number where I can reach him?"

"You *are* accusing me. Do you think I hired your brother to knock some sense into him?" When Ed remained tight-lipped, I slapped a hand over my mouth. "Oh my God! You really do! Do you truly think that I would do that? *Me*?"

"Kylie, I just have to check up on rumors, all right? I'd be derelict in my duty if I just ignored this and walked away because of the nature of our relationship."

"Oh, you think there's a relationship after this?"

Ed scowled. "Goddammit, Kylie. You know I'm only doing my job. How would it look if I turned the other way?"

"Call him," I said tightly, rattling off Jeff's phone number. He got out his notebook and took it down. "Are we done here? Did you want to frisk me for deadly weapons?"

He sighed heavily. "I'll call you."

"Doesn't mean I'll answer!" I yelled after him as he turned to get into his car. He winced as he climbed in.

I glared after him as he drove away down the hill. "Can you believe the nerve of that guy?" I asked as Erasmus came up beside me.

"Unbelievable," he agreed.

And then I felt funny about it, wondering if Erasmus had pulled some sort of sorcery. But no. Ed would surely have heard someone squeal about it. Everyone in that bar had seen Jeff all bruised and beaten. Ed *had* to check up on it. And—though I was loath to admit it—I *was* a likely candidate to hire the Ordo to beat him up. It wasn't as if I hadn't thought of something similar before—not seriously, of course. And after all, as far as Ed was concerned, what reason *would* Doug's gang have to rough Jeff up? And now he really was messed up.

I looked back at the house. "It's time to return to the shop. It's already an hour past the time I should have opened up." After I grabbed some photos and the notebook, we secured the front door and got into my Jeep.

As usual, Erasmus was closed-lipped on the ride back, but I got the feeling he was a little too satisfied with himself.

When I pulled up in front of the shop, someone was standing outside, peering in through the window. Erasmus vanished.

I got out of the car. "Reverend Howard."

"Ah, Kylie. I expected that you would be open by now."

"I had an errand that ran a little late. Come on in." I grabbed the photos—the notebook already safely in my pocket—and unlocked the door.

"Looks like it's all repaired." He ticked his head. "Poor Sheriff Bradbury. Those two boys could not be more unlike each other."

"Isn't that the truth?" I set the photos down and was relieved to not see the Booke hovering anywhere. "What can I do for you? Did you remember something?"

"Well, I—" He stopped dead as his eyes obviously swept over the pentagram on the floor.

I hurried forward to…what? Block it? I gave up, letting my arms dangle at my sides. "I can explain that. My Wiccans, I mean, Doc and Company, thought I should have that for protection. I didn't have the heart to get rid of it. And, well, maybe it's working. Who knows?"

"Have you tried a crucifix?" His happy-go-lucky expression changed to a stern one, reminiscent of a fire-and-brimstone Puritan pastor of old.

"I don't really subscribe to any religious belief."

"I can see that," he muttered. So much for all that tolerance he preached at the Chamber of Commerce get-together.

Maybe he realized how stern he was and softened. "I'm sorry. I was caught off guard. I suppose old prejudices die hard, even in an old liberal like me. If this is what works for you…"

"Well, mostly it's to appease Doc," I lied. "I didn't want to hurt his feelings."

"Funnily enough, my visit is about something similar to, uh…" He gestured toward the hearth. "That. After you left I decided to check out the closet myself and I found something chalked on the floor. Wasn't a pentagram, but it might as well have been. Very peculiar and definitely not Christian."

"Oh?" I feigned a curious expression. I clutched my phone, still in my coat pocket, which held in its digital archives a picture of that very seal.

"Yes. I immediately questioned Daniel Parker. He says he knew nothing about it. But he got so agitated that he stomped away. He's worked for the parish for so long. It would be a shame if we had to let him go. Of course, I'll have to discuss this with the church committee of deacons, but…I tell you. I don't know. I wanted you to know that you aren't crazy."

"Oh, thanks. Sometimes I'm never sure."

"Listen, he hasn't been around here harassing you or anything, has he? I would hate for this to become a big deal that we at the church didn't address."

"No. I've never seen him before except at the Chamber of Commerce gathering…and today."

"Well, that's a blessing." He wrung his hands. "I've never seen the like, is all. I mean, he's free to believe what he likes, just not necessarily on church property."

"Maybe I should talk to him. Where does he live?"

"Not too far from the church. On Hawes Stream Road."

"In Moody Bog?"

"Yes. Lived there all his life. That's his parents' house, I'm pretty sure. But maybe you shouldn't, Kylie, if he's got something against you."

"What would he have against me? He doesn't even know me."

"I don't know. Some of these old-timers get notions in their heads. Maybe it's something about this house. Something as mundane as the last owner owing him money and now he's taking it out on you." He gnawed on his lip for a moment. "Do you suppose we should contact Ed Bradbury?"

"No. I mean, I wasn't specifically targeted. I only saw the thing. It's probably harmless."

"But you told me that some of these folks into this black Wicca are harming people. Those missing women. Karl Waters and that bicyclist. We don't really know what's happening, do we?"

"No, we don't. But I hardly think we can blame it on Daniel Parker and a chalked pentagram. What would Ed say if we told him that?"

"Blessed Lord, you're right. I don't know what's gotten into me." He barked a laugh. "Must be going loopy. Look, promise me you won't be going over to Daniel's place. At least not alone."

"I can do that."

"Good. Now...let me get out of your hair so you can open these doors. We want this shop to be successful. All of Moody Bog is pulling for you."

I thanked him for coming over and saw him to the door. What a strange little town this was becoming.

I shouldn't have been startled when Erasmus spoke, but I was. "Perhaps you will allow me to study your grandfather's notebook while you do...whatever it is you do."

I reached into my coat pocket and handed it over. Then I retrieved my phone, hung up my coat, and commenced...doing whatever it was I did.

Customers came. This time I was sure they were Ruth Russell's cohorts, but they didn't seem to mind giving me their custom and ragging on Ruth at the same time. I was beginning to feel a little sorry for her. Everyone appeared to use her and her celebrity, but no one seemed to actually *like* her. Looked like I was going to have to go over there soon with a peace offering.

I called Doc periodically to get Jeff updates. The answer was always the same. He was fine. Trying to cope. Feeling better, stronger. Then, when I wasn't calling Doc, I wondered about my grandfather and what he had said. The Ordo was definitely up to something if his spirit had bothered to warn me. *Stop them*, he'd said. And something about the "door." If it was my destiny to prevent an apocalypse, then I'd obviously have to go back to Hansen Mills and face the Ordo again. And since the Booke was a key of some kind, it stood to reason that I needed to find this "door."

When Jolene arrived, it had started to rain. I pulled her aside. "Did Doc call you?"

By the look on her face, I could tell that he had. "I'm really sorry this happened to Mr. Chase, Kylie. It's pretty crazy, isn't it?"

"That's one word for it."

"I've been researching it all day in class." She motioned toward her backpack, which, no doubt, housed her ever-present tablet. "Found all sorts of useful information. But…" She lowered her head. "As far as I can tell, there is no cure."

My heart gave a lurch. Doc had said it, but it didn't truly feel real until Jolene confirmed it. This was terrible. How was Jeff going to survive this? It was my fault, despite what everyone was saying. "Doc said something about a potion."

"Yes, aconite or the wolf's bane potion."

"I don't have to tell you that aconite is poisonous."

"To you and me. To werewolves, it's like Xanax. It's supposed to keep the werewolf from acting on his wilder, deadlier instincts."

"Doggie downers?"

"Yeah. He'll still turn, but he'll be, well, mellow."

"That's more like Jeff. Then if he takes this potion, he won't, um, kill?"

"That's the idea. In theory anyway. We only have historical documents that say so. No contemporary accounts of anyone in this century actually taking it."

"Oh. Well, keep looking then. I'd rather pay you to do that than work today."

"Are you sure? You don't have to pay me if I'm not gonna work."

"No, it's the least I can do."

She touched my arm. "Kylie, this is *not* your fault."

"Everyone keeps saying that. But I still feel like it is."

She shook her head and moved into the room, suddenly noticing Erasmus sitting on one of the squashy chairs by the fire. She gave him a wide berth as she walked by. "What's *he* doing here?" she stage-whispered, thumbing over her shoulder.

"Studying a book written in Enochian."

She gasped. "No way! I'd really like to see that. I've never seen real Enochian. John Dee's books could never truly be trusted, what with the influence of Edward Kelly. *He* was a complete charlatan."

I didn't know what she was talking about, but I didn't pursue it. I was more concerned with the knowledge that my family had a track record of coming across the Booke over and over again.

"Hey, Erasmus." I leaned on his chairback and he looked up at me. He really was a handsome devil—when he appeared human, that is. But I had seen those sharp shark teeth on rare occasions. Too many teeth for a mortal mouth to contain. "What happens to the Booke if I'm…" I drew my finger across my neck. He squinted at me in confusion. "You know. I'm the last of the Stranges. If I'm killed before it's done and all the beasties are still out there, does it then go on to Ruth Russell's family?"

"That is unknown."

"Isn't she closer to a Howland than I am?"

"You would have to check those genealogy charts to be certain."

"Wait. You knew this and didn't tell me."

"Not…as such. But those particular puzzle pieces have fallen into place. Remember, I am only allowed to be free when the book is opened."

"Kylie!" Jolene hissed. "You shouldn't talk to him."

Erasmus turned a cold gaze on her. "Go away, little girl. The grown-ups are talking."

She snorted at him and threw him a nasty glare. "When the book gets closed, Mr. Demon, you're toast."

He bared his teeth and growled. I had to slap his head and admonish him like a misbehaving dog. "Erasmus! That isn't nice."

"*She* started it!" He sank back down in a huff, but it wasn't long until he was engrossed in my grandfather's faded pencil markings again.

I gave her a shrug. "He knows things I have to know." We both left the demon in peace to gaze forlornly out the window. The rain was coming down harder and the puddles were beginning to form in the street. I watched the puddles as raindrops left rings in their flat surfaces. Jolene and I stood there a long while, mesmerized.

It wasn't until I had reached for the cold doorknob that Erasmus's voice cut through my daze.

I looked down at myself. I was about to go outside, without my coat and without rain gear. Why was I doing that?

He must have read my puzzled expression. "The kelpie is calling to you. You were enthralled by the water, no?"

As I thought back on it, I seemed to have been enthralled by water of some kind—dish water, bath water, rain drops on the window—ever since the kelpie came to town, before I even knew what it was. I rubbed at my face. "Damn. That was weird."

"It isn't just you. I'll wager there are many a young girl wandering about in the rain as we speak."

"This is bad, Erasmus. I could have frozen to death out there."

"Quite."

When I turned and spotted Jolene, she was in no better stead. Her face was nearly planted to the window, staring outside.

"Jolene!"

She snapped to and looked at me. "What?"

"We need to stay away from the window. From all water. We're vulnerable to the kelpie."

"Huh?"

"I almost went outside to meet it and I didn't realize it. Stay away from the windows."

She smartly shut the curtains.

I suddenly didn't feel comfortable in my own house. Everywhere I thought to turn seemed to have water or tea. This was bad. "Erasmus, I've got to go get this creature."

"I know," he said, scrunched down in the chair. "But probably not when it's raining. Water everywhere."

"All the same. The both of us," I said to Jolene, "are going to keep away from running water."

"But the house is warded against the kelpie coming through the plumbing," she reminded.

"Just in case, I think it best we don't."

"What if we have to make more tea?"

"Erasmus can do it."

He spun. "I *beg* your pardon?"

"You *can* turn on a faucet, can't you? Put a kettle on?"

He sprang from the chair. "I am *not* your scullion."

"Whatever that is. I'm just asking you to help out. I'd do it for you."

"Well, I won't do it for you."

"Fine! Be an ass."

"Such abuse is uncalled for."

"I call 'em as I see 'em, buddy."

He raised his chin and stomped back to the chair, where he planted himself purposefully to sulk.

I shared a glance with Jolene. Demons sure were pissy.

We only had a few more customers before the sun set. I decided to close early. The rain had stopped, but there were still puddles outside, so I kept myself far from the windows. Instead, I counted out the till. Another day above water. Between the shop and sales from my website, it was looking like I could make a go of staying in Moody Bog. If I survived with my life, that is.

"Erasmus."

He had long ago set aside the notebook to glare moodily into the fire. He didn't turn or acknowledge that he'd heard me, but I could tell he was listening.

I stuffed the money into a zippered bank bag and placed it under the register. Jolene had settled in at the other chair by the fire with her tablet. "Do you have any idea who might have been with my grandfather's ghost? What creature might have threatened him?"

Jolene perked up.

"There is a Keeper of the spirit world," said Erasmus. "It's possible that he urged your grandfather to hurry his business. The Keeper isn't fond of his spirits getting loose."

I sat on the arm of Erasmus's chair. He scooted just that much away from me. "So…if someone is haunting a house, they have to get back into the spirit world before curfew?"

"Something like that."

"I didn't think the afterlife was supposed to be so complicated."

"Didn't you? Why?"

"Because we all assume we'll, um, 'rest in peace.'"

"Whoever told you that?"

"Culture. Religion…"

"Religion," he scoffed. "The least reliable source of information meted out to mortals. You've no idea at all. Forget all that you have ever heard."

"Doc and his coven seem to know a lot about things like this."

He leaned over his thighs. I almost thought he was warming his hands near the fireplace, but of course, he didn't need to do that. "Yes, but they are the exception rather than the rule."

Jolene preened.

"I hate that Grandpa was being pushed around by someone. Sounded like he might have been in danger himself. But that's crazy…right?"

He shrugged. "I know little about mortals and their afterlife. What I know I got from other demons."

"Swell."

He glanced up at me for a moment before turning back to the fireplace. "I'm sorry I can't tell you more."

"You're doing your best."

Jolene frowned at me but I ignored her.

"I suppose we'll know more when the coven comes."

He rose so abruptly that I nearly fell off the chair arm. "Kylie, may I speak with you?" One glance at Jolene, who stared daggers at him, and he leaned in. "Alone."

I got up and went to the kitchen. He followed. Once I closed the kitchen door, I rounded on him. "Well?"

"It seems to me that you rely too heavily on these Wiccans of yours. You should act."

"And get myself sucked down into a bog by a kelpie? No thanks."

"But there's more you can do. You heard your grandfather's warning. You must go to Hansen Mills and make certain the gateway they have opened is closed."

"I thought we already did that. Didn't we close that vortex, or whatever it was, Goat Guy came through?"

He mouthed "goat guy" again incredulously. "There may be more we don't know about."

"The one in the cave?"

"That we know came from the book."

"Grandpa's spirit was pretty specific, wasn't he? Almost too specific."

"Meaning?"

"I don't know. I'm on edge, you know. Everything's coming at me at once."

"I understand."

"Do you? *Can* you?"

"Yes. My life has been an uneasy journey between the Netherworld and this one. I am perpetually at the mercy of...others."

I thought about what he had said before. "The other Chosen Hosts didn't have a backup crew. My coven. It's probably wiser to wait and find out what they think I should do."

"And in the meantime, you fritter away your hours in this shop instead of taking to the task at hand! More and more time slips away from you."

"Fritter? Excuse me, but this is my livelihood!"

"And do you think that Constance Howland didn't have to worry about *her* livelihood? Or Margaret Strange of Cheshire? Or Ailinor and her three miserable children in Hwicce? Or Elswyth the weaver of Tamworth? Or Aquilina of Carthage? Or—"

"Stop!" I couldn't breathe. How far back did they go? To the Bible? Earlier? To the beginning of writing itself? "Stop." I leaned against the table, unable to hold myself up. The weight of history bore down on me. All those ancestors. And what had happened to them because of the Booke? What was going to happen to me? I swallowed, closed my eyes, trying to recapture my equilibrium.

In the silence between my breaths, I came to the conclusion that Erasmus was right. I had been going about my business as if all of this could be cleared away like yesterday's trash. Maybe the shop was my place to hide from it, not think about it. And I was angry too. I had sold my life in California for a new life here and I had only so much time to make good on it.

But this journey I was now on, this ridiculous duty I was tasked with, wasn't going away no matter how much I wished it would.

Maybe I was hiding behind the Wiccans as well. I was certainly blessed to have them, but they might be a crutch.

Erasmus studied me with a pensive expression. He was probably wondering if he had gone too far. I tried to reassure him with a half-smile. "I hate to admit it...but I think you might be right."

The Booke was suddenly there, vibrating on the table. And the crossbow, too, had appeared within inches of my fingers. I suppose the message was clear. I had to get on with it. There was really no more time to waste on dates and shop business.

"I'll need my coat," I told him.

He seemed happy to play the footman this time and fetch it for me, and without Jolene any the wiser, we snuck out the back door.

I felt a little guilty leaving without seeing Jeff. As much as I owed him a visit, I couldn't face him again without first trying to find this werewolf or that damned kelpie, even in the rain.

Beyond the trees, the windows of distant houses shone warm and golden against the dark blue sky. A sliver of burnt sunset lingered along the ridge of the mountains. The foliage was wet and the trees dripped icy droplets down on me. But Erasmus was beside me, a sure and confident hunter, with eyes that could see clearly in the dark.

Was I being foolish? Had I thrown away my best chance? My coven knew about this stuff, whereas I...I was still such a neophyte. This town. When old janitors could be black magic Wiccans and pompous Mayflower descendants could push people around, there was no telling from where the next bad thing could come. Maybe it wasn't fair, getting others entangled in this. Maybe that was why my ancestors had gone it alone.

Maybe I was making the biggest mistake of my life.

I felt bad abandoning Jolene without even leaving a note. It was rude and possibly dangerous, but there was a little part of me that felt a tiny thrill at going off alone with Erasmus. Yet, as the night closed in on us, my thoughts fell back to the problem at hand. This wasn't going to be an easy trek, especially if he expected me to get to Doug's place in Hansen Mills and look for errant vortexes.

"It's pretty far to Hansen Mills, Erasmus. I don't know if I'll be fit to do anything once I get there."

"You are forgetting you can transport through me."

"Oh, yeah. I had forgotten."

He stopped and grasped my upper arms. Our gazes locked. For a moment, I thought he was going to kiss me. For a moment, I wanted him to. Instead, he closed his eyes and in the next moment I was encompassed by velvety blackness and cold like the cold of outer space. In another blink I was somewhere else.

I didn't recognize this part of the woods, but then a car drove ahead of us, and I realized that the highway was just beyond the trees. Then I realized something else.

I turned to my companion. "I don't know where he lives."

"That gathering place is not his abode?"

"No. That was a bar…a tavern."

"I see."

"Wait." I dug out my phone. "Maybe he's listed. I can find it this way."

He peered over my shoulder and pointed. "This contraption? I thought it was for communication."

"And more." But just then it rang in my hand. It was Doc. Should I answer it? I decided I couldn't afford not to. "Doc."

"Kylie! Thank the goddess. When you weren't here, we thought the worst."

"I'm fine. I'm with Erasmus. Look, Doc, I just felt that maybe…"

"Kylie. Wherever you are, whatever you're doing, we need you to come back to the shop."

"Why? Doc, I'm trying to tell you—"

His voice was breathy and out of sorts. "It's Jolene. We can't find her anywhere. I'm pretty frightened that...well...that the kelpie got her."

CHAPTER FIFTEEN

"Take me back!" I cried.

Erasmus didn't question it. He enclosed me in his arms and I felt the cold of transport again. When I opened my eyes, we were standing in front of my shop. I burst through the door.

"You looked everywhere?"

Nick was ashen and Seraphina seemed less vivid, less colorful. She suddenly looked her age. Doc was sitting with his head in his hands. Jeff sat alone, apart from the others. He didn't look wolfy, but he did seem unusually alert and agitated.

"The door was wide open when we got here," said Nick, voice a bit shaky. "And we couldn't find either of you. We tried calling Jolene but her phone was dead."

"Don't say 'dead,'" Seraphina wailed. She wrung her hands, bracelets clanking.

"I told her to stay away from the windows," I muttered, looking out them myself. "The kelpie has this draw on us. This call. Both she and I were mesmerized. If not for Erasmus, I would have gone out to meet it in the rain."

Doc raised his head. "And do you think that's what she did?"

"Almost certainly. Nick, that scrying thing. Can we use it to find her?"

"Yeah, yeah. I'm sure we can." He grabbed her backpack and rifled through it. We all turned when Doc pulled it from his coat and held it up.

"I've got it here, remember?"

They had used it before to detect our levels of, well, magic, I guess. It seemed to put them all at the level of mage, though I wasn't versed on the different tiers. It was a stick with a crystal bound to one end.

Doc handed it to Nick, who started mumbling an incantation. The scryer began to glow. The brightness pulsed for a few seconds before going back to normal. "Okay," he said determinedly. "Let's go."

Jeff watched the stick with awe. When we all started for the door, he rose. "What about me? Can I—*should* I go? I mean, that werewolf is still out there too. He can't do any more harm to me, but then there's you guys. I'd be all too happy to kill it if I see it." The last was said with a bit of a snarl, and for a moment, his eyes went yellow.

Seraphina laid a hand on his arm. "Remember your mantra, my dear. You mustn't go off thinking of killing. That won't help you."

He shook off her hand. "Maybe I don't want it to help me. Maybe I *want* to kill it."

"Right now, we're thinking of Jolene," she said sternly.

Chastened, Jeff seemed to shrink, his eyes returning to normal. "Yeah. Yeah, sorry."

I pulled Doc aside. "Is he okay to go?"

"He's healthy enough, if that's what you're asking." More quietly, he added, "Mentally, he's thinking like a wolf. That's not to say that's a bad thing. I believe he thinks of us as his pack. He won't harm any of us. For the moment. But that potion is going to be important very soon. It just takes time to make."

I glanced back at Jeff, whose face was red. His wolfy ears could obviously pick up our voices.

"That's a fine conversation to have in front of me," he said sourly. "I promise not to pee on the carpet, okay? Can we go already?"

I nodded. We all went, even Erasmus, whose expression was muted. Nick led with the scryer, which glowed faintly, pulsing in and out. It naturally led us into the woods. All traces of the sunset were gone, leaving us in near blackness. Doc had the presence of mind to bring a flashlight, but that only illuminated the treacherous forest in slim beams and flashes.

I kept looking down at the crossbow. It hadn't armed itself. I guessed that was a good thing, but I still wished it had. I didn't feel safe, even with everyone surrounding me, even with Erasmus nearby sniffing the wind in a disturbingly animal-like way. Jeff was doing it too, seemingly unconsciously.

"Jolene!" I called. Then the others began calling out her name. Nothing.

Whatever path Nick was following led downward. We stumbled and helped each other over the stony trail, through tugging brambles and dried ferns. Even through the noise we made breaking every twig put in our path, I could hear the sound of running water. I hurried, overtaking Seraphina and Doc. I was right next to Nick, scouring the path ahead, listening with sharpened ears.

Trickling and running water. I shook my head. The siren song of the water was strong, but I managed to slough it off. Somewhere below us was a pond or a bog. I could hear the frogs now. Strange. Didn't they go dormant this time of year? The trees thinned to saplings. I nearly slid down the leaf-littered slope, but caught myself, arms outward like a surfer. Rotted logs and rocks surrounded the slow-moving creek, which spilled into a quiet pool. Something was standing in the middle of it. I swung the crossbow up to my shoulder and aimed…but it still hadn't armed itself. What the—?

It wasn't the kelpie. A shadowy figure stood in the middle of the knee-deep pond, just standing there, its back to us. But it wasn't until Doc swung the flashlight's beam that I recognized it.

"Jolene!" I dropped the crossbow and plunged in, splashing water up all around me. Cold seeped in through my jeans and shoes. Another splash behind me and Nick was closing on her too. I got there first and grabbed her, turned her. "Jolene!" I yelled to her blank face.

She blinked slowly, then her lids fluttered, and finally her eyes seemed to register who I was. She looked down, perplexed. "What's going on?"

I led her out of the water, Nick on her other side, helping keep her balance. We rushed up to the mud at the edge of the pond, where she began to shiver. She was only wearing her sweater and had left her coat behind. Nick whipped off his and draped it over her shoulders.

"You're okay, squirt. You're fine."

"But...what am I doing here? And I'm wet."

"The call of the kelpie," I told her. "Maybe you looked out the window."

Her hands came up to her mouth. "Oh my God! I didn't mean to."

"I know. It's okay."

Nick and I helped her up the rest of the way from the pond. Doc took hold of her icy hands.

"We've got to get you back to some warmth. Come on."

Doc led the way back through the woods. Jolene was shivering from more than the wet and cold. That much I could tell. She kept glancing at me. I tried to give her reassuring smiles, but I was worried too. When we got to the highway, I let Doc take her hand while I dropped back to talk to Erasmus.

"What happened? Why didn't it come for her?"

"As with the succubus, the kelpie has become attuned to you. Not that other women and girls are necessarily safe. But it's clear that *you* are now the main target."

"Great. It wasn't anywhere near. The crossbow never armed."

"As I suspected. But you are just as vulnerable as any female. More so, perhaps."

"You'll have to make certain I don't go wandering off at night."

"I will."

It was the last thing he said for most of the night. I dressed Jolene in my old sweats and bundled her in every quilt I had on hand, letting her warm by the fire. I put her clothes, Nick's, and my wet ones in the dryer, and gave her hot tea, before we sat around the pentagram in my shop living room to discuss the problem.

With plans getting kicked around, it also seemed the right time to let them know about the seal in the janitor's closet.

Doc pinched his lip and squinted. "I've known Dan Parker for decades. He's harmless."

I shook my head. "Maybe not so much anymore. I wonder if a demon or god offered him something." I looked to Erasmus and soon everyone was staring at him.

He shuffled. "I do not know. There could be any number of things that a mortal is vulnerable to desiring. If he used a ritual to summon the right demon, he could, theoretically, ask for anything. He may not get it in quite the way he imagines it. The denizens of the Netherworld are notoriously literal."

Doc scratched his head. "But what could Dan Parker possibly want?"

"A girlfriend," said Nick. He shrugged. "Or…boyfriend? Hey, everyone needs love."

"But he didn't summon love," said Erasmus angrily. "He summoned an assassin."

"Maybe he had to," offered Seraphina, "in exchange for his request. I don't think another demon can summon Andras."

Erasmus nodded thoughtfully. "That could be so. Andras would need a human to do the summoning. But why would a demon wish to do so?"

"To get rid of me," I said flatly. It didn't even shock me anymore. "Look, we're all thinking it. If they get rid of me before I close the Booke, then more creatures get out and there's more hell on earth. Isn't that what these Netherworld guys want?"

"This is ridiculous."

We all turned. Jeff was standing the farthest from our group, even farther away than Erasmus. "Are you listening to yourselves? This is insane. Kelpies, demons, assassins...w-werewolves. It's crazy. It's a dream, right?"

Uh-oh. Jeff was losing it. He wasn't adjusting as well as everyone thought.

"Jeff," I said carefully. "You're right. It is crazy. I've had nearly two weeks to adjust to it. And, well, I'm still not adjusted. It's not going to be easy, but—"

He raised his hands to his head, clutching his hair. "You don't know what's going on in my mind. It's like two worlds overlapping, each constantly shifting my attention. There's the man world and the wolf world. And the wolf world wants me to... to...to *run*! To go! It wants the taste of blood, and Kylie...I'm a *vegetarian*!"

I moved toward him but he shied away. The amulet had fallen out of my neckline again, my *silver* necklace.

It was Erasmus who approached him. "I know. You must grasp onto your rational side, Mr. Chase. And when it's time, I will run with you. When you need your wild side, I'll be there."

"Why would *you* do that? You were ready to eat me."

He raised his chin and sniffed. "It's important to Kylie. So I've decided not to hurt you. And I can keep you from hunting others. But for now, you must grasp your humanity. Hold on to it."

Jeff rubbed his arms and leaned against a shelf. "All right. I guess I can try."

I smiled. "Thanks, Erasmus."

"Even though we Netherworld inhabitants would rather wreak havoc?"

He was throwing my words back at me, but I stood my ground. "Well, isn't it true? That's what demons want, right? To run free, cause a ruckus?"

"Not...all."

"But isn't that why my grandpa warned me about the door being opened? Come on, Erasmus. Admit at least that much."

He bristled. "I admit nothing. I am bound to the book. I can do nothing in any case."

Nick folded his arms over his chest and got up close to Erasmus. "But if the book isn't closed, you get to stay out and play. Isn't that right?"

Erasmus scowled and shot a glance at me.

"Yeah, she told us. We're *her* coven, you know. So which is it? Maybe *you* summoned Andras to do your dirty work."

Quicker than a breath, he was in Nick's face. "You whelp! Haven't we just discussed the fact that a demon cannot summon another?"

"So you coerced Dan Parker."

"I cannot enter hallowed ground."

"His house, then."

Gritting his teeth, he glared at me. "Is that what *you* think?"

"Hey," said Nick, tapping Erasmus's shoulder. "I'm the one talking to you."

Lightning fast, Erasmus grabbed Nick's wrist from his shoulder and twisted. The kid yelped.

Both Jeff and I lunged forward. "Erasmus!"

The demon scowled, shooting glares between us. He snarled back at Jeff, who was making warning animal noises.

I raised my hands. "Chill! Jeez, let's all just...step back for a minute. I don't think this has anything to do with Erasmus. He's been helping me. He really has. It's the Ordo we should be concentrating on. After all, isn't it more likely that *they* threatened Parker?"

Seraphina never really turned down her glare at Erasmus. "But the Ordo can summon any demon they want. Why would they need Mr. Parker's help?"

"I don't know. We need to find that out. That's…that's where I was going when you guys called me."

"By yourself?" said Doc, aghast.

"Well…Erasmus was with me."

That didn't turn out to be the most compelling of arguments, judging by Doc's expression.

"Look, it's just that I've gotten all of you mixed up in things that, well, frankly, none of you *should* be involved with. It's deadly. I don't know that I want to risk your lives anymore. I mean…look at Jeff. If he hadn't come looking for me, this wouldn't have happened."

Doc looked ready to pitch a fit. "Don't you think that's up to us to decide?"

"No. I don't. This is all new to you, this level of magic. And though you've all done a bang-up job so far, I don't really know how much worse it's going to get. And the Ordo isn't just a stumbling, bumbling biker gang anymore. They've got real power, just as much as you have, and they aren't afraid to use it. Or more mortal means. They didn't use magic to beat up Jeff. They aren't kidding around."

Jeff growled.

"I'm not afraid of those boys," said Doc, chin high.

"Well I am. I'm afraid of what they might do to you to get to me. I can't do what I have to do if I'm worried about what's going to happen to all of you."

Everyone fell silent. The fire crackled. Someone shifted. Jolene sneezed.

Quietly, I said, "I have to go to Hansen Mills and see what I can find. And I just want it to be me and Erasmus. If something happens to me, then…well. I hope you all will carry on and get that Booke closed."

Nick stepped forward, still rubbing his wrist and staring daggers at Erasmus. "I can't believe you. After all we've been through? You're just upping and leaving? We've been trying to help you."

"I'm not leaving. And I'm not ungrateful. I'm just trying to do my job and not let anyone else get hurt."

"If you're determined to do this," said Nick grumpily, "then you have to at least let us make a charm bag for you."

"*I* want to do it," said Jolene. She looked small and fragile wrapped in her cocoon of quilts, but she seemed earnest as she pushed her glasses up her nose. "It will only take a few minutes. And then Nick will have time to analyze the EVP from last night."

I'd forgotten. Nick was going to break down the sounds around my grandpa, see if he could get a fix on the other voice on the recording. Seemed sensible enough. I lowered the crossbow and sat on the chair arm. "Okay."

Nick hurried to a messenger bag he had left in the corner and dragged out his laptop. He sat it on a small table and knelt before it. Taking a USB cable, he plugged it first into his phone and then into the laptop and commenced typing on his keyboard.

Jeff moved toward me, cautious of the silver. "You're not going to *let* her, are you?" he said to the room.

Nick snorted. "You of all people should know that once she makes up her mind, you can't stop her."

"Then I'm going too."

"No, you're not. Erasmus is. He can do things you can't."

"I can do plenty…now."

"Can you be invisible? Can you detect other demons? Can you teleport me?" He blinked, stunned. "I appreciate it, Jeff. But I'm doing this. With Erasmus and no one else."

Erasmus strutted only a moment before I stared him down.

Jolene shuffled toward her backpack but Seraphina intervened. "I'll help you. Tell me what you want."

"Okay. If you could bring my backpack, most everything is inside. But I will need some of Kylie's herbs."

I nodded. Seraphina already seemed to know what she wanted. I supposed they had done this before. She first dropped the backpack in front of Jolene, who rummaged around, pulling out a large white candle, a square of purple cloth, and a bottle of salt. Seraphina went to my sideboard and opened drawers: sage, lavender, and rosemary.

Jolene lit the candle and laid the cloth flat on the pentagram. Carefully, she took a pinch of the sage and crushed it a bit through her fingers, letting it fall in the center of the square of cloth. She did the same with the lavender, and then the rosemary. "Sage is for purification," she told me. "Lavender for relaxation, and rosemary to repel negative spirits. I'm adding sea salt for an earth element. We've already got plenty of water element around us." She bound it up gently in the cloth, brought up the ends, and twisted the top till it looked like a small sachet. "Kylie, do you have a red ribbon around?"

"Um...I don't think so."

"String?"

"Yeah. In the kitchen. The drawer by the fridge."

"I'll get it," chirped Seraphina.

She soon returned and helped Jolene tie up the tiny pouch with a small length of the white cotton string.

Jolene pulled a marker from her bag and drew a crude triquetra on the side of the small pouch and then held it over the candle flame. "I'm consecrating it," she said in explanation. "Ideally, this should have been done in the middle of a waxing moon, but we don't really have time." She turned it a few times and I could plainly catch a whiff of the blending aromas. The smell of warmed sage, rosemary, and lavender was relaxing and reminded of home.

"There," she said. "Keep this with you."

She passed it to Seraphina, who tried to pass it to Erasmus, but he shied from it like a gardener runs from a hornet. Must be the salt. I remembered that salt was one way to keep demons away.

Exasperated, Seraphina walked it over to me and placed it in my hand. "Wear it, put it in your pocket. Keep it on you."

"Okay. Thanks, you guys."

"Nick," asked Doc, "how is the detecting coming?"

"Almost got it set up. And here we go." He clicked a button on his keyboard and the display showed several vibrating lines. "I'm adjusting the masking element, which should get rid of most of the background noise, but I'll need to fine-tune it as it goes along."

The laptop speakers again played the message: *ssssssHELPssssss ssCAN'TsssHOLDssssssssssOFFssssssssssssBESILENT!sssssssssssKYLIE sssssssssssssssssss*

I hugged myself. The sound gave me chills.

"Let me try this…" The vibrating lines separated and didn't seem as one anymore. They split, growing apart.

……….HELPssssssssCAN'T…..HOLD………OFFssssssssssssBE-SILENT!………KYLIE…….ssssssss

"Better. If I try this…"

…HELP…….CAN'T…..HOLD….OFF…..BESILENT!… KYLIE….

"Okay, so the hiss is gone. Let's concentrate on that other voice."

Over and over on the speakers we heard, "*BESILENT!*" Nick adjusted, elongated, switched more switches. "*BESILENT!… BESILENT!…BESILENT!…BE SILENT! BE SILENT!…BE… SILENT!…*"

He adjusted the pitch and suddenly the growling voice was unmistakably female.

"Wait," said Erasmus. He glanced at me. I was on the verge of understanding and knew it the moment he said it. "Shabiri."

The Ordo's demon, summoned for the purpose of doing their own evil. The yin to Erasmus's yang. Or something like that.

"Wha-what is she doing?" I asked. "Why is she doing that? *How* is she doing that?"

"That is a very good question," he said. "Shall we find out?"

CHAPTER SIXTEEN

Erasmus transported me again to Hansen Mills. It was later now and the highway was a bleak, wet ribbon of black threading into the misty woods. It was quiet except for the sound of raindrops dripping from the trees and the occasional forlorn call of an owl, softly hooting.

I got out my phone and punched in Doug's name. Sure enough, an address *and* a map came up. I turned down the volume on the phone as it read me directions aloud.

"A most unique contraption," murmured Erasmus.

"It's pretty handy." I held the screen forward and followed it. We walked along the highway until I was afraid we'd fall into the ditch full of water. That was the last thing we needed. Instead, we climbed the verge along the road, which raised us up considerably. It gave us a good vantage too. I could clearly see a long way down the stretch of road.

I was so absorbed in watching the highway and my phone that when Erasmus's voice broke the silence, I nearly slipped down the slope.

"What is your plan once we get there?"

"Plan?" Well, shoot. "Um...I don't know. I thought we'd look around a little. I doubt Doug summoned any more vortexes in his living room. He might have an outbuilding, like a barn or a shed."

"I shall be on the lookout for Shabiri."

"What's with the two of you anyway? Have you…known her long?"

I could still feel her breath at my ear. Her arm had wrapped around my neck and squeezed just that little bit. She had warned me. But demons lie. Should I have believed her?

"*You must never, ever give your heart to a demon,*" she had said. "*Oh, I can see it in your eyes, my dear. Erasmus is seductive, I'll give you that. But it only makes the game that much more delicious.*"

I never knew what that had meant. What game everyone was playing. It was the Powers That Be, mostly, and this curse they had put on my family. That was a game to them. But what was Erasmus's part in it besides guarding the Booke and the Chosen Host?

Erasmus took his time answering me. Clearly, he wasn't certain how to parse his answer. "She was created around the same time I was. Yes, I have known her for a very long time indeed."

"As a…friend?"

He snorted. "Demons do not make friends with one another."

"Lover then?"

He kept his eyes steady on the path ahead. "Why are you so curious?"

"Call it a human trait."

"And a demon trait is to keep one's own counsel."

So that answered that. Stupid to assume that he hadn't. He'd already admitted to other human liaisons…and what a little hypocrite I turned out to be. I was supposed to be dating Ed. Although his accusation that I'd hired a hitman to get at my ex kind of put a damper on that. Still. Like he'd said. He was only doing his job and his brother wouldn't have had any other sane reason for beating up Jeff.

I sure focused on the dumbest things when I was nervous.

The GPS told me to make a turn up a dirt road that had turned muddy now after the rain. We slogged upward. When the phone told me it would be the next house on the right, I turned it off and stuffed it back into my pocket. Girding myself, I tightened my grip on the crossbow. It hadn't armed itself. I wondered briefly if it would allow me to shoot people or if its aim was strictly for those of the supernatural variety.

It began to drizzle again, creating mist everywhere. Erasmus's hair glittered with it, and my face felt each cold droplet like an ice pick to my cheeks. Ahead of us on the road, tall pines slanted inward, forming an arch. Beyond that, we turned to find a pond. I might have swayed toward it, but Erasmus's hand gripped my wrist and tugged me back. It took a lot of willpower, but I tore my gaze away and looked instead at the dingy mobile home across the way. Paint peeled from its sides, and a few of the boards that covered the seams were warping away. A rickety stair led to the front door, surrounded by broken latticework. The glow of a TV shone through the window. Nothing stirred.

Beyond that was a barn so ancient it seemed to lean to one side. Its shingled roof sloped in the middle like the spine of a very old, broken-down horse. A faint light shone through the seams of the front doors. I motioned to Erasmus and he nodded, putting out a hand to stop me from going first. It was better if he took the lead. After all, he was the one who could see in the dark.

We crept up to the barn. I kept an eye on the house behind us, but all was still.

I shot a quick glance toward the dark pond and just as quickly turned away. It must have been the same as how an addict feels waiting for their next fix. I was hyperaware that the pond was near. So very near. And I really wanted to go over there, let the water cover me, fill my clothes, spill over my head…

"Kylie…" Erasmus hissed in my ear. "Don't listen to it. Look ahead. Look at me."

His eyes were like glowing beacons in the night. He drew me close. Was it my imagination when he dropped a kiss to my lips? For a moment, I forgot all about the water and the kelpie. Which was his plan. I snapped out of it with a gasp. "Thank you," I whispered.

He didn't glance at me again, but the muscle at his jaw strained. "Look," he said, pointing toward the slit in the door.

I pressed my face to the wet wood and, with one eye, looked through the seam between the doors. At first, I didn't know what I was looking at. A weird glow, a shadowy figure. The glow wasn't like the vortex we had seen before. It was nothing like it, in fact. And then the glow moved and I could clearly see the shape of a person inside it. That person slowly morphed into my grandfather!

I gasped and the shadowy figure turned toward the door.

"Come in, Kylie."

That voice. Yup. She turned so that the glow from my...my grandfather's ghost lit her. Leather catsuit, green streak in her long, dark hair, English accent...It was the other neighborhood demon.

I shoved the doors, and they swung open for me. "Shabiri, you bitch! What are you doing to my grandfather?"

"*Kylie!*" he cried. His voice was soft, distant. "*Get out of here!*"

Shabiri motioned with her hand and he couldn't seem to speak anymore. He clutched at his nearly transparent throat with transparent hands and mouthed something to me.

"So nice to see you again, Kylie. Polite as always."

I looked around. A dark barn, lots of junk. An old sofa probably inhabited by mice, a broken-down tractor beside an old car from the fifties with four flat tires and no windows, furniture tossed into a pile, and other things I couldn't identify through the gloom.

A warm presence came up behind me. "How are you keeping the old man here, Shabiri?" asked Erasmus. "I didn't think it possible to capture a spirit."

"The things I know that you don't could fill volumes...with you stuck in that precious book and all."

He bristled. "Oh, you'd be surprised at the things I know," he said smoothly. We all seemed to be circling one another.

"I *would* be surprised." She smiled. Her sharp teeth suddenly looked normal again. "You being, well…*you*, Erasmus."

"Let him go, Shabiri," he insisted. "What could you possibly want with him?"

She glanced at her nails. "I suppose he has served his purpose."

While they were engaged, I broke and ran for Grandpa.

Erasmus took a step toward me. "Kylie, no!"

As I neared my grandpa, the crossbow was suddenly yanked out of my hands. I twisted toward it, but before I could blink, Shabiri had it in her grip.

"Put it down."

She smiled again, hefting it. "I don't think so."

"Kylie…" Erasmus's voice stretched thin.

I knew I could get the crossbow back. I could feel its tug. I didn't think she could keep it. But I was more worried about my grandfather. I reached out my hands, but there was nothing to touch. My fingers passed through him, ice cold. He still couldn't speak, but up close, I could now discern the words he was mouthing:

It's a trap!

"Erasmus…"

Suddenly, from all sides of the shadows, figures rushed forward. Solid hands closed over my arms. When I struggled, someone hit me across the face.

I shook the stars out of my eyes and stared at Doug. "You bastard!"

He struck me again, and boy! That hurt like a son of a bitch. No one had ever hit me before. The stars were more numerous this time and it took me more than a moment to shake them off.

Erasmus surged forward but stopped dead as if he had hit a wall. He looked down and then glared at Shabiri. I looked too. Salt. They had laid down a circle of salt around me. It didn't affect me, my grandfather's ghost, or the Ordo, but the demons couldn't cross it, and neither, so it seemed, could my crossbow. A trap where Erasmus couldn't save me, where Shabiri couldn't interfere, but where the Ordo could do what they wanted. I was in real trouble.

CHAPTER SEVENTEEN

Doug stood in front of me, fists closed and poised like a boxer. His goons Bob Willis and Dean Fitch each had me by an arm.

"Oh, real brave, Doug," I managed to slur through a fat lip. "Two guys to hold the girl. You're looking real good in front of your boys here."

Nothing like the male ego. I saw it all work itself out on his face. "Let her go."

Farmboy Bob on my right arm squeezed me tighter. "Doug, that wasn't the plan, dude."

"Let her go!"

Skinhead Dean released first and stepped back. He ran into the ghost and shivered. "Back off, old man."

Grandpa didn't seem to like his attitude or what he was doing to his granddaughter. As a ghost, I supposed he couldn't do much, but he did what he could. He stepped right into Dean, which creeped him out good. He sprang away, slapping his body with his hands as if fending off bees.

"Damn, that's nasty!"

Bob let go of my wrist, but he was the only thing holding me up. I sank to my knees. Great. Now what? I was still unarmed, still without demon help.

Doug crouched in front of me. "So here's how it lies, little lady."

"'Little lady'? Really?"

Doug ignored me. "We want the book."

I snorted a laugh. "I *told* you. It isn't transferable. Didn't you learn anything last time?"

"Yeah, well. Shabiri said you were lying."

"And she's Miss Reliable? Demons lie, dipshit. She wants control over Erasmus for some reason."

Erasmus shot her a glare, and Miss Catsuit merely preened. "Hey Doug," she purred. "She's got that amulet. Maybe it would help if you took that from her."

Doug smiled. "That's right." He lifted his own from a chain around his neck. The same sort of demon face as mine, tongue extended, twisting horns, and green eyes instead of the red of mine. "This has certainly come in handy. With your amulet and the book, we can finally get the party started."

"What party? What has she told you? Didn't summoning Baph—Goat Guy get you into enough trouble?"

His smile faded. "You need to zip it. I've got friends in higher places than her." He reached for the chain around my neck. With a cry and the sudden smell of burnt flesh, he leapt back. He looked down at his blistered palm. "What the hell?"

"I guess your guru doesn't know everything." I staggered to my feet. "And the Booke is worse. You aren't its master. If anything, it would master you. And it wouldn't anyway because you aren't part of my family. It's a *family* curse, stupid. So all this planning was useless."

"You think you know," Doug growled, "but you don't."

"I know more than you. We're leaving. And you are releasing my grandfather."

"I don't know," he said, looking the ghost over. "I kind of like gramps hanging around in my barn."

"How are you doing it? How are you keeping him here?"

There was a scramble. Sparks, smoke, growling. I didn't know who leapt first, but Erasmus and Shabiri were rolling around on the floor, biting, scratching. She smashed him in the side of the head with the crossbow and he raised his hands to fend her off.

I was helpless, looking on from the salt circle, trapped in Doug's strong grasp.

Shabiri leapt up and spun. She wound up her arm and a ball of fire with sparks of electricity crackled into existence. She heaved it at Erasmus, who batted it away with a smoldering hand. It exploded against the barn wall, shaking the rafters.

Baring his teeth, he growled, eyes glowing red and wild.

She hissed back, but when he waved his hand, she immediately sputtered and choked. Clutching her throat, she fell to her knees, gasping for air. Erasmus stalked forward and wrapped an arm around her neck. He pressed a single finger firmly to her temple, like it was a weapon. She screamed.

"Look for a charm pouch, Kylie," he said. "They had to have used a spell and the pouch."

Within the blink of an eye, she threw him off. He sailed across the room and landed hard on the floor. She shook off the vestiges of his magic and snarled. "Not so easily done, my dear Erasmus." With one hand still clutching the crossbow, she curled the other into a claw and jabbed it toward him. He was struck with an invisible force that slammed him against the wall.

"Harridan!" he gasped between clenched teeth.

While they fought, I started searching the immediate vicinity for a small pouch.

"What makes you think I'll let you have Grandpa back?" said Doug incredulously. He blew on his scorched hand, shaking it out.

"I'm not asking anymore," I said with a sneer. Before he could stop me, I lunged for the salt circle and swept my hand through it, breaking the line. I held up my hand and the crossbow flew out of Shabiri's grip and into mine. The crossbow armed itself and I swung it toward her.

"Where's the charm pouch? Release my grandfather. Now."

She folded her arms and cast her glance aside. "You haven't got the guts to sh—Ow!"

I fired and the bolt hit her shoulder. I knew it wouldn't kill, or at least *figured* it wouldn't, since I'd also hit Erasmus not too long ago. But if it *did* kill, no tears here.

She stared at her shoulder and smoldered. Thick, sulfurous smoke rose from her. "You little tart." She grabbed the bolt, twisted, and yanked. After she finally pulled it free, she heaved it to the ground. "That's left a hole in my suit," she said between gritted teeth.

"There are plenty more holes where that came from." I aimed. The bolt she had thrown to the ground had appeared again, loaded and ready in the crossbow.

"Wait!"

"Free my grandfather."

Shabiri looked a bit like a spoiled teenager at the mall, rolling her eyes with her hand on her hip. "What makes you think *I* know where the charm pouch is?"

"Lucky guess. Where?"

I felt coldness on my free shoulder and turned slightly. Grandpa smiled at me and pointed upward into the gloomy rafters. A pouch hung from a beam. "Erasmus, can you get that?"

"With pleasure."

He disappeared and Shabiri chuckled. "She *does* have you on a short leash, doesn't she, Erasmus?"

He appeared again beside her with the pouch in hand. "Shut up." He held it aloft and crushed it. It burst into flame, falling to dusky embers between his fingers.

"*Damn. That's a relief.*" Grandpa could speak again and he glided toward me, looking me over. "*My girl. My big, precious girl! How you've grown.*"

"Grandpa. Are you okay?"

"*As good as a dead person can be, I suppose. I'm sorry you were lured here. I tried to tell them the book would do them no good…*"

"She wanted it." I lifted the crossbow toward Shabiri. Even wounded, she didn't shrink from it. Her eyes just glared and glowed with green.

"*A demon might be able to do something with it. I'm…not sure. As long as they aren't the demon of the book. And speaking of…that must be him.*" He was looking at Erasmus like someone examining a lab rat.

"Yes."

Grandpa glided toward him. "*If you touch my granddaughter…*"

Shabiri yawned. "I'm afraid it's far too late for that, old man."

Grandpa looked at me. "*What does she mean?*"

"Oh dear, dear, dear," said Shabiri. "Have I let the cat out of the bag? How careless of me. You've already shagged, haven't you? Erasmus has that guilty look about him. He never could leave humans alone. Disgusting habit, really." Shabiri slunk around Erasmus, almost touching him but not quite. "She's sensitive about it, isn't she? You didn't make her fall in love, did you? Such a cad, Erasmus. I don't suppose you told her about you and how this is going to end."

Now it was Erasmus's turn to smolder. I'd never seen so much smoke come from him.

I don't know why I was defending him, but I hated the way she was speaking. "I know it probably won't end well for me. I'm not stupid." Maybe a few seconds before that, I really had my doubts, but as soon as the words left my mouth, I knew they were true. I was on a long, slow suicide mission. All my dreams were crumbling.

What was the use of continuing the charade of running my shop as if nothing would happen? More than anything else, it pissed me off. *That*, at least, kept overwhelming terror at bay.

"Of course, darling, but did he tell you the rest? I'll wager he hasn't."

Curls of smoke were puffing at regular intervals off Erasmus's shoulders. "Keep your mouth shut, Shabiri, or I will shut it for you."

"But this *is* delightful. You *haven't* told her."

I couldn't help it. "Told me what?"

Erasmus rose up, spreading and widening like a black sail. His voice was ice. "HOLD YOUR TONGUE, CREATURE!"

She rose like him, her shoulders stretching into batwings on either side of her. The Ordo stepped back. "YOU DARE CALL *ME* A CREATURE, FOUL THING?" She laughed tightly. "Look at what you are. You can't even run. You're tied so tightly to the book and that monkey that you have become a laughing stock. I dare not even grace you with the name 'demon.'"

They both hung like that for several heartbeats before Erasmus began to shrink. The fight seemed to have gone out of him. Maybe she was more right than he wanted to admit.

She shrank back more slowly. But before he could react, she slapped her claws to his chest and ripped his shirt open. There was that tattoo again, black and stark against his white skin. "Does she know what this is, what it means?"

"SHABIRI!"

"I know it means 'assassin,'" I said.

"Oh, how charming. That's the *modern* language, my dear. In the oldest of languages, it means—"

Erasmus punched her in the mouth. "I said shut it!"

She fell to the ground on her ass and I almost cheered aloud. But she sprang quickly to her high-heeled feet and postured toward him like a panther, shoulders leading. She wiped black blood from her mouth with the back of her hand. "You're so crass, Erasmus. I'll enjoy destroying you."

"Many have tried. Just as many have failed."

"But why so squeamish about your heritage, darling? Your birthright? Just tell the ugly little monkey. Have the bollocks to do that at least."

"You don't understand the book. You've never understood it."

"I know that once I get it, I get you."

"And you claim *I* don't have the bollocks. Your useless attempts at revenge have led you here, on the leash of…*these*." He waved his arm toward Doug and company.

She spared them a glance. "Everything in its season, my dear."

"I hate to break this up," I interrupted. I made a point of securing my hands on the crossbow, still aimed at Shabiri. "But I have a life to get on with."

"A life!" she said with a laugh. "That's right. We were talking about Erasmus's tattoo. I never finished telling you—" She ducked under Erasmus's swinging fist. "It means 'soul-eater.'" She stepped back from him and smiled. "It's his job, darling. Once you've done yours, he eats your soul. It leaves you not merely dead but…well. A husk. Unable to go to…wherever. Didn't you know?"

I stared at Erasmus. My throat had suddenly gone dry. He wasn't looking at me. He was breathing hard, the flaps of his torn shirt swaying, revealing and shadowing the black tattoo. I'd lost my breath. "Is this true?"

He said nothing. He stood before me, hunched shoulders smoking, and said nothing at all.

I lowered the crossbow, and just like that, Shabiri vanished.

I felt cold. And it wasn't just my grandpa's hands on my shoulders, trying to reassure me. "*Kylie*," he whispered, "*it may not be as she said. I've been studying the book for years. Decades. That may be a lie.*"

"You knew?"

"*I...suspected.*"

"Erasmus..."

"Kylie," he said, voice hoarse. He still wouldn't look at me. "I tried to...to..."

A scream. It sounded like a woman somewhere outside. I looked around. "Where's Charise?"

Doug scanned the barn. "She...she was supposed to be with us."

She screamed again, and I moved first. I ran for the door and was outside in the drizzly wet before the rest of them. I knew instantly where to look. The crossbow had armed itself with a different quarrel. Clutching it to my chest, I ran for the pond.

I stopped myself just at the bank. Charise was submerged up to her hips, the water beginning to bubble all around her.

"Someone help me!"

"Aim carefully," said Erasmus at my ear.

I raised the weapon to my shoulder, closed one eye, and readied myself.

Nothing rose from the pond, yet Charise kept screaming.

There was a splash behind me. I turned too late.

Something swiped at the back of my head. A hoof, probably. The crossbow sailed out of my hand and I went down, stunned with pain. I heard another splash and Erasmus's howl above me. Water churned until it all fell away to silence.

I pushed up from the mud and stayed on all fours before I was sure I could lift my head without getting sick everywhere. "The kelpie," I gasped.

Doug stood over me. "It's gone. I coldcocked it with a rock."

"No, you merely frightened it," said Erasmus, kneeling to help me up. I let him until I remembered, and then I shoved him away. "Don't."

He stepped back. Hurt flickered across his face before he quickly masked it.

I stumbled to my feet, retrieved the crossbow, and looked around. Bob was helping Charise from the pond and the others were standing around uselessly. The dim glow of my grandfather hung back by the woods.

I waved the crossbow at them. "Everyone back in the barn. We're having this out."

Once inside, I kept the crossbow fixed on them. And lo and behold, it was armed. A quarrel it had never used before.

"All right," I said as steadily as I could. "Let me get this into your thick heads. The Booke of the Hidden cannot be loaned out. It's *my* family curse, and lucky me, it's my turn. I didn't know what the Booke was, what it did, and now it's become my job to recapture all the monsters that I let out. To tell you the truth, I don't know what would happen if I was killed and you took it. For all I know, nothing. No one else but me seems to be able to open the damned thing."

"*She's right,*" said Grandpa in that wispy specter voice of his. "*It can only be opened by a descendant of the Stranges. I've never seen it myself, but I damn well knew enough never to touch it if I had.*"

I shook my head. "I sure wish you would have shared that information with me. Or at least told Mom."

"*Your mother did know. I don't know why she never told you.*"

"When you died, she never took me to Maine again. In fact, I forgot all about it. Everyone in town forgot about the Stranges."

"*I put the forget-me spell on the cottage for protection. I thought the book might be there somewhere. I never dreamed it was elsewhere... though I should have known.*"

"It's not your fault."

"*I thought if I could keep the knowledge from you, you might be spared. But ancient magic doesn't work that way. Did you find my notebook?*"

"Yes. I've got someone translating the Enochian now."

He smiled. "*Good girl. It should tell you most of what you need to know. But…*" He looked back at Erasmus. "*I'm…sorry…*"

"My own stupid fault." I choked back a sob. I sniffed, trying to rid myself of the tears threatening to fall. How could I have been so stupid? How could I have allowed myself…I squared my shoulders and fastened my aim on the Ordo again. Charise was shivering and, instead of Doug, Bob had taken over the job of comforting her.

"The Booke won't do you any good," I reiterated.

"But it looks like Shabiri *can* control your demon through it. If she can get her hands on it. And if she controls your demon, then we control him too."

"Didn't you hear my grandfather? No one else can open the Booke."

"How about demons?" He narrowed his eyes at Erasmus. "How 'bout it? Can demons open the book?"

Erasmus scowled.

"Can they?" I asked.

"I…perhaps."

"Great." I sighed. "Doug, I think it's all going to bite you in the ass. And I hope I'm still around to see it."

"I doubt that, sweet thing. Looks like…" He glanced at Erasmus with new admiration. "Looks like your soul is gonna be someone's lunch. I hope I'm around to see *that*."

He flashed by so quickly that I didn't see him move. Suddenly, Erasmus was in front of Doug and had socked him in the face so hard he fell back into the tractor, knocking down the rest of the Ordo like bowling pins. Charise moved first, and much to Bob's chagrin, she threw herself on Doug's still form and wailed.

Doug was out for the count. Dean took a step toward the demon but then thought better of it. "All right," he said. "Now what?"

Good question. How could I control these guys? How was I to contain what they did? They could perform their own rituals anytime, anywhere they wanted. They could still try to get the Booke. How did I know Shabiri wasn't at my shop right now trying to steal it? Something inside me burned hot with jealousy at the thought of her and her association with Erasmus. He would know what she was up to…but I didn't want to talk to him. I was suddenly…frightened of him.

"I don't know. I don't suppose I can get your word that you'll leave us alone."

They looked at each other. Charise surprised me by turning to me. "Why did you save me? You tried to save me."

"Hell if I know. It was the right thing to do, I guess."

That didn't seem to satisfy her. I didn't care. How could I convince them to leave us alone?

The barn suddenly shuddered. Bright light burst all around us. Now what?

Doc's amplified voice, deep and loud, shook the whole building. "Behold the wind, behold the rain! Cursed evil, I bind thee! Release the white, the good!"

The barn shook again and the light faded. The Wiccans stood in the doorway, scrying stick held high, shining brightly. I was pretty darned glad to see them.

"You guys. Thank goodness."

"Thank *goddess*," Doc corrected. "Now Doug…oh. Is he all right?" He switched to doctor mode and almost went over there but Dean Fitch blocked his way.

"He'll be fine."

Doug was already starting to move and moan as Charise ministered to him.

"Well then," said Doc. He seemed relieved, even for all his mage theatrics. "Our people will be going now. I've put a spell on this place to keep you all here. I'm not sure how long it will last. It might be an hour. It might be a few days. But I want you all to take this time to reconsider your ways. Look at what you're doing. I helped all of you into this world, dammit, and I don't want to be the one to kick you out of it. Now either all of you behave yourselves or we're going to have to do something really nasty. And I don't want that either. Doug Bradbury, I'm ashamed of you. I'm ashamed of all of you." The Ordo looked chastened, but Doug, who was just sitting up, didn't seem too repentant to me. "We're going to go now." Doc gestured to me and we backed out the door. The spell released us from the barn and, remarkably, Erasmus too. I thought it was supposed to contain all the evil.

Grandpa glided out and followed us down the road to where they had parked their car. Doc's decrepit Rambler was there and the Wiccans climbed into it while Doc put his arm around my shoulders and led me to the middle seat in front. He gestured to Erasmus. "I trust you can return on your own."

Erasmus stared sourly at his feet. "I…I don't know whether…"

I pushed Jolene aside to scoot out again across the bench seat. "I want to talk to you."

"Kylie…"

"We're going back to my shop. And I'm going to want to talk to you *once*…and then never again." I slid back in the car and didn't look up as I waited for Doc to shut the door.

CHAPTER EIGHTEEN

Once at my shop, we all piled out. Surprisingly, even Grandpa was there. He glided forward and blurred himself through the door as I opened it. Jeff had been waiting and he stood when we entered. He pointed at the glowing specter of my grandfather but no one had time to explain. We gathered in the main room. Nick lit the fire with magic means, and we found our seats.

I paced over the pentagram. Erasmus stood behind the sofa, trying to hide himself in the gloom.

"Okay. I want to have this out, Erasmus. I want you to tell them, tell everyone what Shabiri said. And I want details."

Erasmus wore a stoic expression and grasped one of his wrists, resting it in front of him. His shirt was still hanging open. I supposed he didn't need to bother with hiding the tattoo anymore.

He said nothing for a moment. His frown was deep, his expression pensive. But when he raised his dark eyes, he scanned everyone in the room, as if daring them to say something. Lastly, his gaze fell on me, and it softened a fraction. "This mark," he began, gesturing toward his chest, "means…what I am. 'Soul-eater.' You asked me once if I ever ate, and I told you that you wouldn't want to know. Well. There it is. I eat the souls of the Chosen Hosts."

Everyone burst out with exclamations. Jolene jumped to her feet, looking like she was ready to hurl a curse at him. Seraphina began an incantation. Nick looked ready to punch him. Jeff growled, his hair standing on end, ears growing. Erasmus allowed it for a moment before he raised his hands, palms out like a traffic cop. The effect was immediate. They each fought against it but found themselves seated again, *pushed* into their places, mouths glued shut.

I didn't know he had that kind of power. He'd never used it before. But there was far too much I didn't know about him.

"Kylie has asked for an explanation and I shall give it without interruption." He calmed himself, stopped the smoke that had begun to unfurl from his coat, and took a breath. "It is what I am. It is what I was created for. The Chosen Host was to restore order, to return that which she had unleashed upon the world. And to make certain the book was secure, the demon of the book was charged with...disposing of her, to stop her from ever opening the gateway again." His eyes turned to me then, burning like the last slash of light at sunset, or the flash of a lightning bolt. "I know of no way to destroy the book, and so your ancestors were doomed to open it again and again. The Powers That Be, though they might find the book amusing, hide the fact that they cannot destroy it either, and so they sent me, created me, to guard it." He raised his chin, trying for that arrogance he was so good at, but now I could see that it only served to mask his true emotions, whatever those were. "I eat souls. I devour them. And in between the time the book is opened, for those long hundreds of years, I burn with hunger."

He walked slowly toward me. I held my ground for as long as I could, but then the fear took over and I backed away. "I consume not the body but the spirit and leave behind a shell that soon dies. For without the soul, the body is nothing. A husk. A carapace. It is my singular function. And I do so with delight." I backed against the wall and couldn't move away. His eyes. They were consumed with hunger. How long had it been? Since Constance Howland's day, almost three hundred years? "But hear me, Kylie Strange, before these witnesses. I have eaten the souls of all your ancestors. But I will not eat yours. Do you understand me? I will not."

Breathing hard, trembling, I said, "I…don't…believe…you."

His eyes widened a fraction. "Believe it."

"Demons lie."

"I am not lying. I won't lie to you. I can, but I won't."

I shook my head. I couldn't speak.

"And now I leave you. If you should ever need me, all you need do is call out my name. I *will* come, Kylie. I will help you at this dread task. You only need call me."

"I won't."

He winced. I doubt the others noticed it, but I did. "I make you this vow. I will not harm you. I will not." His eyes were on me a moment more and then they weren't. He'd vanished.

I don't know how long we all stood in silence. But the logs had burnt down to a smoldering gray and glowed red under the ash in the grate.

Doc cleared his throat. "Kylie…I…don't know what to say…"

"Then don't say anything. I knew the moment this began that it wasn't going to be all tickertape parades when I was done. At least now I know the whole truth."

"I hate to say this," said Nick, "but he really sounded sincere."

Seraphina glared at him. "Kylie's right. She can't believe him."

"Way to give her hope, *Esther*!"

"Her numerology said…"

"Oh, not with that crackpot stuff again."

"Guys!" said Jolene. The feuding duo stopped and looked at her. "Her grandfather is trying to say something," she said quietly.

I looked to the shadows where the specter of my grandfather hovered. Maybe he'd been trying to speak for some time but his ghost voice was too quiet. I walked toward him. He smiled kindly.

"*Kylie, I have to go. I've stayed on this plane too long as it is.*" He glanced toward the clock. It was after midnight. "*I want to tell you to be strong. You were always so strong. Just like your father. You make the same facial expressions; did you know that?*" His smile faded. "*You'll have to be strong. I know you can be. I know you'll do what is right. Now…I'm not certain if I can return to you…*"

"No, Grandpa. There…there are so many things I want to ask you." I wanted to hug him, feel his arms around me, but he was only spirit. There were no arms to feel.

"*I know, sweetpea, but things just don't work that way on this plane. I'll try, but I can't promise. I just wanted to say, I don't know much about demons—I did write down what I knew in the notebook—but from what I've learned in these last two decades… that demon of the book, that Erasmus…he doesn't sound like any demon I've ever heard of.*"

"Grandpa…"

"*I'm serious. Serious as a heart attack.*" He grinned. "*Listen, these folks are from Moody Bog.*" He gestured toward the Wiccans. "*I trust them. You can too. You can't do this alone. You're gonna want to, because you're a Strange and we usually go our own way. But this time you don't have to. Listen to them, sweetpea. Do that for me?*"

The tears were salty when they tracked down to my lips. "Okay."

"*I love you, Kylie. Be strong.*"

He faded. He kept looking at me and blinking, until he dispersed completely and the glow was gone.

I lay in bed the next morning, staring at the ceiling. Why get up? Why bother? Why even open the shop? It was all for nothing. I catch a kelpie or it catches me. If I survived this, there was that werewolf, another creature to capture. And then another. How many until I was done? And when I was done…what then? Was Erasmus lying? Why would he promise that? Grandpa thought it was unusual, but it could all just be lies, lies trying to lull me into a false sense of security, and then wham! Soul eaten.

That thought was so awful. I didn't know what it meant. I never really went in for all the religious trappings of Heaven and Hell, souls and demons. But now I needed a crash course.

I dragged my body, heavy with anguish, out of bed, wrapped myself in my terry robe, and sat at my little desk. I opened my laptop and began searching. Souls. Demons. Soul-eaters. I found all the usual things, Judeo-Christian theology. It was all the same information I had heard before as far as I could tell. I looked up Asian religions, read about souls and reincarnation, but there was little there to be had. Maybe Jolene could search deeper. Heck, she probably already was.

Maybe I should talk to Reverend Howard.

It was too early to call him, too early to open the shop. Should I just hunt this kelpie and be done with it?

But as I contemplated calling Reverend Howard, I thought about Daniel Parker and why he had etched the seal of an assassin demon on his janitor closet floor. Maybe it was time to pay him a call.

I took a quick shower on a bed of wet towels. I didn't want any puddles around me where the kelpie could get me unaware. I never even made coffee or boiled water for the samovars. I just grabbed my keys and the crossbow and headed for the car.

As I drove, I wondered how Daniel Parker played into all this. Was he some kind of mastermind? Could it be mild-mannered old Mr. Parker summoning up the apocalypse? I hadn't forgotten that this demon—Andras—was some sort of killer himself. Had Parker already summoned him or was the demon yet to come? I wasn't buying that Doug and his gang were able to do some of the things they were doing on their own. I mean, *I* had Jolene and

Nick. They were the ones who figured out about the amulet and the chthonic crossbow. True, Doug must have asked Shabiri to bring him something *like* my crossbow and she probably came up with the spear, but how the heck did they get themselves Shabiri without help?

And I never had a chance to ask Grandpa about his original message: "The village is in danger; the door is opening." He hadn't said the door was already opened, but that it "*was opening*." Why hadn't I asked him about it? Maybe Jolene could use the Ouija board later.

If only I could ask Erasmus…

I shut that down. No way. A Soul-eater. Well, wasn't that just swell. And I'd slept with him! And I'd wanted to do it again. Doc and Seraphina warned me, but did I listen?

I adjusted my grip on the steering wheel. One thing at a time. Maybe Daniel Parker could enlighten me or maybe it was a dead end. Either way, it meant I could check something off my list.

I must have passed Hawes Stream Road several times before I doubled back and finally found it. It was another one of those little lanes off a regular neighborhood, much like Ed's. Just a street sign and a dirt road. The road sloped downward and followed a stream—Hawes Stream, I presumed—and I took it, keeping a wary eye on the water till I came to a ramshackle house. Reverend Howard said the house had been in Parker's family for years, and he wasn't kidding. Probably for generations. He might have kept the church in good repair, but he seemed to neglect his own property. I couldn't tell if it had ever been painted, but the clapboards were a slate gray that warped and wobbled along the structure. The shingled roof had seen better days, and the stone chimney was leaning a bit away from the house. A steady puff of white smoke emerged from it and rolled down its sides. I guessed he was home and starting his day. The old-fashioned way.

I parked the car in front of his place and got out. It was actually sunny today, though clouds were gathering over the hills. I was hoping it was a good sign.

He had a carelessly laid brick walkway. It was a lawsuit waiting to happen, though I doubted he had many visitors. The yard was overgrown and the large tree out front had dead limbs barely still attached to the trunk. I stepped carefully over the uneven raised brick path and made it to the porch. When I knocked, the door pushed open. In Moody Bog, no one locked their doors, but didn't they at least close them? I poked my head in.

"Hello? Mr. Parker? It's Kylie Strange. Are you here? Your door was open." I stepped in halfway and paused. It wasn't a very big house. I could see a glimpse of the kitchen off the living room and a hallway where the bedroom likely was. "Hello? Mr. Parker?"

And that's when I saw a smudged bloody footprint.

Maybe it's paint, said the optimistic voice in my head.

"M-Mr. Parker?" Why was I going in? The logical part of my brain was saying, *Kylie! Get out of there!* But I couldn't seem to help myself. I was drawn in down the hall. I stepped carefully, wishing my chthonic crossbow was in my hand and that the floor would stop creaking. A bathroom door stood open to my left. No one there. The other door on my right was closed. I gathered my courage and knocked. "Mister…Parker?"

The doorknob was cold when I grasped it. I turned it and pushed the door open. A large pentagram was chalked on the floor and Mr. Parker was sprawled in the middle of it…his insides torn out and spattered around him.

CHAPTER NINETEEN

I waited in the living room by the fire till Ed arrived, which didn't take any time at all. He noted the bloody footprint before he took several strides toward me, yanked me to my feet, and enclosed me in a fierce hug. "Are you all right?"

"Yeah, I think so."

He pushed me back and studied me. "You'll be okay. Wait here."

Ed left to go down the hall. I hadn't even noticed Deputy George standing there. His hands were hooked into his gun belt and he stood feet apart, eyes scanning the room.

"Hi, Deputy," I said weakly.

He touched the brim of his hat. "Ma'am."

He said nothing else, just twisted to look into the kitchen, out the back window—all around him. Ed came stalking back out of the hallway and pushed his hat up his head till the rim tipped back. "Jesus," he said. "I gotta call the coroner. George, can you take some pictures of that footprint and secure it? Then get some shots in the bedroom. Be warned. It's pretty bad."

"On it," he said, his voice more certain than he looked. He left the house, to get a camera I presumed, while Ed got on the phone.

Ed talked a long time with the coroner, Gunther Wilson, and then he looked at me. "Did you see anything? Hear anything?"

"No. Nothing."

"Why are you here?"

"I was coming to talk to Mr. Parker."

"Why?"

"There was…something I needed to talk to him about."

"What?"

"Ed, I'm not a suspect, okay? You don't have to interrogate me."

"I know that. But I'll need it for my report."

Which meant I was a suspect. Not his fault. He was only doing his job. So I lied. "I was going to talk to him about a donation to the church. You know, a coffee urn. They've been really nice to me."

"I see." He stood a moment across the room just staring at me before he took a few steps closer. "I missed you. I'm sorry about… everything."

"Jeff's back in town. Never really left, I guess. You can talk to him personally, see that I had nothing to do with his getting knocked around. He's staying with Doc."

He sure looked as if he wanted to ask about that one, was desperate to even, but all he said was, "Okay. Will do." He was closer now—that safe, imposing presence. "I'm more concerned with you. And me. I don't want this stuff to come between us. I…care about you, Kylie. I want to see you again. I don't want you to…hate me."

I shook my head. "I don't hate you. I know that you're only doing your job. I'm sorry for getting wound up about it."

"You had every right to be. I came on a bit strong. I'm sorry."

"It's fine. Really."

He was right in front of me and I was sure he would have taken me in his arms if Deputy George hadn't come in with a camera and police tape.

"Listen, Kylie. You don't have to stay here. You can go."

"Should I…call Reverend Howard? I'm sure he'll want to know."

"I'll take care of it. You just get yourself out of here. You don't need to see any more of this."

"Okay. Listen, Ed. Call me, okay?"

He smiled. "I will." This time he did step forward and touched a kiss to my lips. "Soon."

Standing on the porch, I took a deep breath of cold, cleansing air. I felt better about Ed. Pretty crappy about Mr. Parker. Whatever happened to him spelled bad news all around. I'm sure the Wiccans would be questioned next. I dug my phone out of my coat pocket and disappeared into the warmth of my car to call Doc.

"Oh dear goddess," said Doc when I told him the whole thing. "Poor Dan."

"Listen, I think this is too important to keep for later. Can you rustle up the coven and come over to the shop now?"

"Jolene will be in school, but we can carry on without her for now. Yes. I'll call everyone."

He hung up before I could say anything else.

I left the closed sign on the shop door and waited in the quiet. The radiator banged and clattered, and the fireplace was warm enough, but I couldn't seem to warm myself. I was wearing a pullover but threw on a cardigan as well. It didn't help.

The Booke took to following me from room to room now. Even the bathroom wasn't sacrosanct. Pervy Booke.

When the Rambler pulled up in front, I jumped to my feet. Didn't realize how jittery I was until I swooped on the door and opened it even before anyone got out of the car. I was a bit relieved Jeff wasn't with them, though Seraphina was. She was supposed to be working on the wolf's bane potion. I was too wound up to even ask about it.

We took our spots before the fire. Seraphina had a haggard and worried expression. I had never seen her other than bubbly and that in itself was a bit disturbing. I supposed the Booke was getting to all of us.

Nick was serious but determined as he laid out his laptop, ready to go. Doc sat on the wingback and stared thoughtfully into the hearth.

"So," I began. "What do we think happened?"

Doc gathered himself. "It could be that Dan was trying to summon something perhaps too strong for him to control. It might also be—dear goddess—that he himself was used as a sacrifice. But without seeing the pentagram, it's hard for me to say."

"I…took a picture."

Nick gasped. "Kylie!"

"What? I thought you guys should see it. Believe me, it's not something I want on my phone." I called up the picture and passed it around. Seraphina shrieked, paled, and passed it quickly to Nick. She fanned herself with her scarf.

Nick stared at it with a horrified grimace. "I can't believe you had the presence of mind to take this."

"The picture doesn't do the scene justice, trust me." I hadn't looked at it since I took the picture. My stomach turned every time I thought about it. The smell of all that blood…

Doc got the phone last and sat with it for some time. "Well, it's not a pentagram, it's some kind of seal. I don't know that I recognize it. Nick, can you do a search?" He handed the phone back to Nick, who seemed disinclined to look at it again, but the man did his best, under the circumstances.

"Could be a seal," he said, typing away. "Could be a mandala."

I wondered what the difference was but didn't have the will to ask. Instead, I watched distractedly over his shoulder as he scrolled through the images that came up.

Sitting on his chair arm, I began to think. "Were you guys close enough last night to hear Doug's rant?"

"We heard some of it," admitted Doc, "but not all."

"Well, when I accused him of doing whatever Shabiri asked, he said something about having friends in higher places than her."

"Maybe he meant Baph—I mean, Goat Guy," said Nick, still typing.

"I didn't get that impression," I said. "After all, I don't think they're smart enough to be able to summon a demon—let alone Goat Guy—on their own."

"Their powers are enhanced by the book," said Doc. "We already established that."

"Their magic powers, maybe, but not their intelligence. No one in the Ordo is a Nick or a Jolene. I mean, they've got enough gray matter to fix their Harleys but that's about it."

Doc nodded. "I see what you're saying. Perhaps there's something to that."

"And maybe this other person whom we don't know is in charge, giving them tips. This mastermind could have been Daniel Parker."

"Then what?" asked Nick. "They got tired of being pushed around and offed him?"

Doc squirmed in his seat. "I've known Dan a long time, and with all due respect to the dead, I never took him for a very great wit. It can't be him. He had to have been a tool."

"That leaves us guessing who. Hey." I pointed to Nick's computer screen. "What are those?"

"These? They're sigils in the form of mandalas, decorative designs. You see them in Muslim and Hindu cultures. They may look just decorative, but each design means something. Protection, or danger, or, well, summoning. Witchcraft in these cultures has been mostly hidden. No one likes a witch, it seems. So they hid their importance in these intricate designs. You just have to know what to look for. There's always a flaw in a witch sign."

"But that one." My finger touched one of the pictures. "I've seen that one before."

Nick clicked on it and looked at the description. "Whoa. That's a powerful mandala. Used sometimes as a sigil or seal. Major protection from nasties. Something you would have seen on a sorcerer's house or even a palace to protect a king or sultan."

"I know where I saw that. At Ruth Russell's house."

"What?" said Doc. He and Seraphina got up and stood behind Nick's chair, looking over his shoulder. "*Where* did you see that, Kylie?"

"On her front porch. In the stone, this glass mosaic tile. It looked *kind of* like this."

"Are you sure?"

"You've been to her house, haven't you?"

"A few times over the years, but I don't remember...wait. She's always had a welcome mat there. Was there a welcome mat when you went?"

"Neither metaphorically nor physically. Just that mandala or whatever you want to call it. Could the previous owner...?"

"She and her husband built that house."

"And where's Mister Russell these days?"

"In Moody Bog Cemetery. He died twelve years ago."

"What if Doug didn't mean supernatural high places...What if he meant something more local? Like *really* local. What do any of us really know about Ruth Russell?"

"Whoa, whoa!" said Nick. "Are you accusing the High and Mighty One? She's a bitch, yeah, but Satan Central? I don't know."

Doc walked to the fire. "I've known Ruth a long time. And her husband. We haven't been close but...that's a far cry from calling her a...what? An intermediary? A sorceress? As far as I know, she's never been a practitioner."

I looked at each of them. "And how many people in town could be a practitioner without you knowing it? Is there some sort of sign? Do they sparkle in the sunlight? Won't go out on a full moon?" I winced. That was nothing to joke about anymore.

"Charm pouches," said Seraphina. "They'd be wearing them, or have them in their pockets, or nailed above their doorways."

"But wait a moment," said Doc. "I can't believe for one minute that she would have killed Dan Parker. Ritual or no ritual."

"I didn't say that."

"But you're putting it in our heads."

"What kind of ritual was it?"

Nick bent back to his computer. "I was looking that up, remember?" Doc returned to Nick's chair, where he and Seraphina hovered while I clung to the chair arm. No one said a word. For the umpteenth time, I wished Erasmus was there to offer some advice... but I just as quickly shut that down.

"Wait," said Nick suddenly. "Does that look like the same seal from Dan Parker's house?" He turned his computer toward Doc.

Doc studied it with care and slowly nodded. "Looks like it."

"Then we are in big trouble."

"Why?" I asked. "What is it?"

"This is big mojo. We thought that other vortex was big. This one is the mother of all vortexes."

Breathless, I looked down again at the photo on my phone, trying to get past the...the viscera. "Do we know if it's opened?"

"I don't think so. It's a multistep ritual anyway. This one sort of puts the key in the lock."

"So when you say 'mother of all vortexes'..."

"The big time. Hell's Gate, that sort of thing. Everything that ever went bump in the night gets to crawl out...including the succubus you already put back in the book."

"Okay, that's not good."

"Understatement," he muttered.

I exchanged glances with Doc. "My grandpa's message? 'Opening the door'?"

"Ay-yuh. That would be it."

"Shit. What are we gonna do?"

We fell quiet again until I blurted out, "I planned on going over to Ruth's to make peace with her. But I guess now it's a reconnaissance mission…with Bundt cake."

"No!" they said all at once. Doc took my hand. "No, Kylie. *I'll* go."

"But I have a perfect excuse. Besides, the more she goes off on me, the more clues I can gather."

"Maybe she should," said Seraphina calmly. Everyone turned toward her. "Now just think about it. If she knows that Kylie is her nemesis, it would behoove her to have Kylie there, to study her. Maybe even take a sample from her."

"A sample?" I wasn't keen on the sound of *that*.

"A hair. A thread from your clothing. You will have to try not to leave anything behind."

"Like DNA? Isn't that impossible?"

"Don't eat or drink anything she offers."

"Just suppose I can't help leaving something behind. What could she do with a…a sample?"

"Oh my," sighed Seraphina, hand to her cheek. "All kinds of voodoo."

"Voodoo? Right. Got it. Don't leave samples."

Doc joined me at the hearth. "I don't want you going alone."

"I'll take…" I had been about to say Erasmus, but I had no intention of calling him. "How about Ed? That's innocuous enough. And not suspicious. It's just a friendly drop by."

Nick closed his laptop. "It's not ideal, but I think it's a good idea, your going over there. Though I wish it was one of us. Maybe Doc."

Doc shook his head. "Ruth isn't enamored with our little coven, or have you forgotten? No, I think Ed is good cover for Kylie. If there is a way you can do any, well, *snooping*, that would be a bonus."

"Ruth is already suspicious of me."

"I'm sure you'll find a way."

I felt better with a plan. Someone had put poor Mr. Parker up to making that seal in the church janitor's closet and then used him in a ritual. That wasn't very cricket. And it was way better to be actively investigating than sitting around as a victim.

So. Now to bake a cake.

CHAPTER TWENTY

"Kylie, it's *so* good to hear from you," said Ed when I called him later. He sounded relieved. "And not in an official capacity for a change," he went on.

I felt terrible that I was about to use him.

My cake was cooling on a baking rack, but I couldn't help but peel a few crumbs from the side and pop them in my mouth. "That was pretty horrible what happened to Daniel Parker."

"Just so you know, in my official capacity as sheriff, I had to talk to Doc and the others. And I found nothing to associate them with the crime."

"As I knew you would."

"So." His voice got all deep and melty. He sounded good even on the phone. "I want to see you again. Maybe get out of the village a little. Take a day trip to Machias. Get to know each other better. And...come back for supper and get to know each other...even better."

That sent a pleasant shiver up my spine. "That sounds spectacular. But I was wondering if you wanted to come over now."

"Now? I'm still on duty."

"Just a quick visit...over to Ruth Russell's."

"What? Uh...why do you want to do that?"

"She and I got on the wrong foot and I'm afraid if we don't patch things up, it's going to get difficult. And it's too small a town for that. So I baked her a cake and thought I'd bring it over."

"What do you need me for?"

"So she doesn't slam the door in my face. Maybe if she sees you, she'll know I'm on the level." How many lies had I just told in that one sentence? I hoped no one was keeping score. "Please, Ed? I could use you as backup."

"Kylie, I'm in the middle of several murder investigations. Not to mention missing persons."

He sounded tired. I felt bad for him. "I know. But all work and no play..."

He sighed. "It won't take too long, will it?"

"Just enough time to hand over the cake, chat a little, patch things up." And in the meantime, I would try to think of an excuse so I could sneak away.

"Okay. For you, anything. I'll be right over."

Ed was such a blessing. I'd be a fool to turn him away. And my mother did not raise a foolish daughter.

When Ed arrived, I was ready to roll. I had to admit, he was pretty sexy in that uniform, with its tight tailored shirt, the gun belt, and even—God help me—the Smokey Bear hat. We went in the sheriff's black and white Ford Interceptor SUV, and I pored over the gadgets on the dashboard. The radio was on, but he turned the volume down and I got to listen in to the chatter from the dispatcher. Her name was Patty and she was apparently a sore loser at poker.

"Sorry about that," said Ed, turning the volume even lower. "Patty isn't supposed to use that kind of language on the job...or talk about off-duty stuff."

"It's a small town. It's kind of—"

"So help me if you say 'quaint'..."

"Uh...amusing?"

He said nothing, but a smile spread wide on his face.

We pulled up in front of the Russell mansion—because it really couldn't be called anything else—and got out of the car. I protected the cake plate from the rain with my arm as we hurried up the path to the front door.

This time a welcome mat with "Russell" emblazoned on it covered the mandala I knew was there. As if there was any doubt as to whose house it was. As surreptitiously as I could, I toed one corner of the mat away and made a mental note: One mandala of protection? Check.

The maid answered the door. She was surprised to see Ed but far more surprised to see me. "Hi!" I said chirpily. "Is Mrs. Russell home?"

She gave Ed the once-over again and left us hanging on the porch as she said, "One moment, please," and took off.

A moment later, Ruth showed up and, as polite as you please, opened the door. "I don't know what Stella was thinking leaving you out here. Won't you please come in?"

She was one of those women who never wore slacks, apparently. A tweed, mid-length skirt and short matching jacket was her preferred country manor look. A gold locket hung over her silk blouse, with simple gold earrings peeking out from a solid Nancy Reagan coif. Her hair was shellacked with so much hairspray that it couldn't move even if you begged it to.

We walked through the foyer and followed her into the living room. Before Ed could say anything, I forged ahead.

"Ruth, I couldn't help but feel we got off on the wrong foot. I would love to start over. I baked you one of my famous chocolate-toffee Bundt cakes as a peace offering."

She took it graciously. "This looks positively delicious." *You don't fool me, you old crone*, I thought. Perhaps that was uncharitable, but she'd never acted this nice when we were alone. "But if you don't mind if I ask, why is Sheriff Bradbury here?"

He'd removed his hat and crushed the rim in his fingers. "Well, Kylie…that is, Ms. Strange…Kylie and I are dating and she just thought…we thought…"

"My goodness," she said with a pasted-on smile. "Stella! Where is that girl when you need her? There you are. Could you take this into the kitchen and put some slices on plates. Bring in the coffee service too."

"Oh, we couldn't impose," I said half-heartedly. *Impose away!* The more distractions the better.

"Don't be silly. Please, sit down. May I take your coats?"

Ruth didn't take them, but Stella balanced the cake plate in one hand, and had us lay our coats over her other arm. We moved into the living room and sat on one of the sofas while Ruth took a chair opposite. She folded her hands primly in her lap and cocked her head at me.

The room was the same from last week, decorated to the nth degree for the fall, with sprays of fall leaves, cattails, and sheaves of wheat. Pumpkins, both real and made of Venetian glass, were dispersed throughout, and the huge fireplace was aglow with birch logs.

"Now Kylie, I do believe you're right about being wrong footed," said Ruth. "I just don't know how it happened."

"Well, Ruth, I did look around in your library without permission, and I do apologize for that. I was just so anxious to learn about Moody Bog, and everyone said you were the person to go to. But I've since been to the library and did some studying on my own."

"Oh?" Her fingers squeezed one another so tightly they whitened.

"Yes." Should I spill the beans? Well, I'd already let the cat out of the bag to her. No use in hiding it now. "It looks like the Stranges *have* lived here since the founding too. And I'd only just recently remembered that my grandfather used to live right here in Moody Bog and *I* used to come here in the summer. Isn't that a weird coincidence?"

"Startling," she said tightly. She was spared further comment when the maid came in with a rolling cart. She placed the plates of cake in front of us with silver dessert forks and laid out the coffee service. She poured it into teacups and saucer, asking if we wanted milk or sugar and actually doing it for us. I wondered where Ruth and Mr. Russell got their money. Wherever it was, she seemed to still have plenty of it.

Ruth complimented the cake and Ed gave an embarrassing moan at the taste. "Sorry," he said, covering his mouth, "but darlin', you know how to bake!"

My cheeks warmed from the compliment, but I hid it by raising the coffee cup to my lips. I remembered at the last moment that I wasn't supposed to eat or drink anything. And now I wished I'd vacuumed myself before I left the house. I didn't want to leave a hair behind. I resisted the urge to straighten or fluff my sweater. I didn't want to shake loose any stray strands. And now that I knew I couldn't, the compulsion to do that very thing was almost overwhelming.

"Sheriff, I'm so happy to see that you've started dating again. Our Miss Strange seems like a good match for you."

Started dating *again*? Who had he dated before? And why was it such a thing that she would mention it?

Ed sensed a change in my energy perhaps and glanced worriedly in my direction. "Uh…I hope you and Kylie can patch up this little tiff between you. I think you both have more in common than you might believe."

"We do?" she and I said at the same time.

"Jinx," I said with a fake chuckle.

Ruth narrowed her eyes just that much.

"This is such a beautiful house," I rushed in. "You built it yourself?"

"My late husband and I designed it, and we watched over its construction."

Well I didn't think your *scrawny hand ever picked up a hammer.* "It must be nice to be able to do that."

"Yes, it is. I'm very glad that my husband got to enjoy it for at least ten years."

"I was sorry to hear about your loss."

"Yes, not a day goes by that I don't miss him."

"What sort of work was he in?" I almost tipped the cup to my lips again, and I set it down to forestall any accidents.

"He was in real estate, investments. And what about your people, Kylie? I thought you said they were from California."

"On my mother's side. Apparently, my father's side is from Maine."

"So you said. I can't say I remember anyone named Strange..."

I know Ed was only being helpful, but there wasn't a thing I could do to stop him when he offered, "Up on Alderbrook Lane. I didn't recall either, but now I seem to remember Robert Strange up there. That's Kylie's grandfather, but he passed some twelve years ago. Same as Gene."

The spell was broken. She blinked and I could see the scales fall away from her eyes. She turned them on me. "Your grandfather was Robert Strange?"

"Guilty as charged." I wanted something to do with my hands, almost picked up the cup and saucer again, but resisted the urge.

She kept staring and I kept feeling fidgety...until she finally turned away. "I remember him well."

Where was a Ouija board when you needed one? I really wanted to talk to Grandpa about the Russells, see if he knew if they were a little less than ordinary folk.

"You're involved in the church, aren't you?" I asked.

She sipped her coffee but never touched the cake. "Why, yes. We have our pew and I daresay we've donated more than our share to keep the roof repaired, that sort of thing."

"Then you should know about the murder of Daniel Parker."

"Kylie!" hissed Ed.

Not protocol, but I wanted to see her reaction. Which surprised me since it didn't look faked. Maybe she was a good actress. "Murder? Dear God." She turned to Ed. "What happened?"

"It's not general knowledge," he said to me with a stern brow, "and I can't go into the details. But it happened sometime last night, at his home."

She was becoming more upset as she sat there. She didn't seem to know where to look, what to do with her hands. "But this is dreadful! Does Reverend Cleveland know?"

"Yes, I informed him." Ed looked like he was about to get up, announce that he had to go and continue his investigation, and I hadn't even looked around yet. I drummed up a sudden coughing fit. Ed pounded me on the back. "You okay?"

I feigned that I couldn't talk, kept coughing, and with hand signals excused myself down the hallway. Once out of sight, I coughed a bit to keep up the pretense of searching for a bathroom. There was the library and I headed toward the door. Locked. Damn! I bet she did that right after Stella told her of her guests. Okay, there were more rooms to explore.

I quickly headed up the stairs for the next likely room, something at the far end that had double doors. Pay dirt! The main suite. A large four-poster with a canopy amid other colonial furniture—the real thing, no doubt. French doors out to a balcony. An eighteenth-century painting of some stern-faced Puritan woman glared down at me from across the room. One of the fabled Howlands, I supposed. I hurried over to it and took a quick look at the little engraved plate on the frame.

Wait. *Constance Howland?*

I stared at her anew, Chosen Host to Chosen Host. The painting was in that flat, primitive style of the eighteenth century, when traveling portrait artists went from town to town, hiring out their services for rich landowners who could afford a portrait, then moving on to the next place. So the Howlands had always had money.

But here she was, in the flesh, if you will. Her face was plain, if the artist's rendering could be believed. Very European looking, with pale skin, long features of face and nose, light brown brows in faint arches, green eyes, and light brown hair, parted in the middle, under a starched white bonnet. She wore a gold necklace, but whatever was on the pendant was cut off by the bottom of the frame. The background was just dark brown, nothing distinguishing it from anywhere else. But it was probably painted in my house, since that's where she lived. Come to think of it, why didn't the Russells live there? I bought the place from a holding company, probably owned by the Russells. I'd have to look at my contract later. But for now, I was busy trying to be stealthy but rushed.

I searched from room to room, but when I felt I'd been gone too long, I finally made my way to a downstairs bathroom, splashed my face with water, and headed back. No charm pouches, no sigils marked anywhere that I could find in my hurried perusal.

I patted my damp face as I returned to the living room. They were both standing. Ed had his coat on and had mine over his arm.

"You okay?"

Ed looked solicitous; Ruth looked suspicious.

"I'm fine. I don't know what came over me. I've had a lot of weird allergies since coming here. Not used to the damp, I guess."

Ed helped me on with my coat and placed his hat on his head. "Thank you for your hospitality, Mrs. Russell."

"Yes, Ruth. It was so nice of you to give me a second chance. Thanks. I appreciate it. Don't worry about the plate. Send it along when you're done with the cake."

A quick glance at our plates revealed that only Ed had eaten his slice.

Ruth walked us to the door. "Please come over any time, Kylie. We really should get to know each other better. Perhaps for tea, just you and I."

"That would be nice." I put out my hand to shake and she took it briefly.

I dug my arm through Ed's as we walked back to the car. "That went all right," I said, even though I had found nothing to incriminate her.

But if Constance Howland was such a sore subject, why did Ruth keep a portrait of her in her bedroom?

Ed had to go and do his sheriffing, but now that I was back in my shop, I felt a little lost. Open the doors, don't open the doors? Was there a point to it anymore?

A knock at the back of my head and I whirled. The damned Booke! It was hovering, trying to knock against me again. "What is your problem!" I yanked it out of the air and slammed it down on the nearest surface. The cover fell open to the page I had written in my own blood about how I secured and captured the succubus. The page flipped over to reveal a blank one. Pages kept flipping, showing me all the other blank pages waiting to be filled.

"I know, all right! I know!"

I slammed the cover closed and kept my hand on it, even as it tried to wriggle away from me. "So you want me to hunt, huh? Is that why the pre-show? Okay. Fine. Why not? I'm doomed if I do, doomed if I don't."

Without even realizing it, I flung my arm up in time to receive the crossbow as it hurtled through the air. A full conspiracy, then, between Booke and crossbow. Lovely. If this was my last day on earth, then so be it. I'd have to leave the Wiccans to figure out

Ruth's plot for the mother of all gates. Maybe I'd be around to help, maybe not.

I didn't bother locking the door. I didn't bother with my car. I just stalked toward the woods, planning on heading down the first path that led to a stream or *bogan.*

I wasn't interested in stealth, and it was a good thing, because my heavy steps mashed crackling leaves and broke the loudest twigs ever. I was a bull in a china shop for sure, but, in a way, I wanted it to know I was coming. Because this was it. No more playing games. I was done. This needed to happen and this was how it should be. Me, alone. No one riding shotgun, no one to worry over. No help at all. I didn't need it. Maybe it was the Booke giving me courage, maybe it was just my natural foolhardiness. But the kelpie, at least, was done…today.

The shadows darkened. When I looked up, I saw gray clouds swiftly moving, covering the sunshine. The wind picked up and leaves from the forest floor took flight in small whirlwinds around my feet. The branches above me groaned and creaked. For once, it wasn't the middle of the night, but it didn't seem to matter to the general creepiness of the situation. I could see, yes, but maybe that made it worse. Every little movement was my creature, and my head swiveled around more than Linda Blair's in *The Exorcist.*

The gathering clouds darkened the forest even more and the ground began to slope downward. I adjusted my grip on the crossbow. It had armed itself. "Here we go."

I followed my own path until I could hear running water. The smell of marshy wet filled my nose as I got closer. "Come out, you Celtic nightmare! Let's get this over with."

A whinny behind me, and I spun.

There it was. That white pony standing in a clear pool of water. The leaves that had sat on the pool seemed to make room for it, scooting to the edges and leaving a wide berth of mirror-smooth surface. The white pony was beautiful, shimmering and majestic as it bobbed its head. Its flowing mane was plastered flat to its neck, and barnacles and shells clung to the wet strands.

It looked perfectly normal, even whinnied again, its dark eyes sad as it gazed at me. So deceptive. So deadly. Standing in such… lovely, clear water. Water that reflected the moss and fern of the woodlands. Such calm water. So smooth.

The pony shook its head, lowered it, coyly watching me.

I walked forward, my feet feeling heavier and heavier. Each time I lifted a foot, it seemed to drag along the duff. Wouldn't I be weightless in the water? Wouldn't I flow smooth and quiet through those waves?

Slowly, I felt the heavy crossbow lower to my side…

CHAPTER TWENTY-ONE

I walked to the edge of the water and the pony took one step back, sinking deeper. Before I realized it, my feet and calves were wet. The water was starkly cold, but for some reason I didn't seem to mind. I lifted my free hand without thinking, stretching it toward the beast. In my mind, all I could think of was how soon it would all be over. I could float free in the depths of those dark, cool waters.

My hand reached. That white coat, that velvety nose—it was all so inviting. Those forlorn eyes were fixed to mine and I was only an arm's length away. I wanted to touch that smooth, white coat.

I looked into those eyes again to see if it was okay. They were dark, like black buttons…until they swirled with color, like a drop of red ink in a black puddle. The red bloomed until the glossy eyes were full of red. A small horizontal pupil expanded, opened, and somehow, glowed, like the beacon on a buoy or street light. Suddenly, the red was all I could see.

A ripple slithered up my back with a sense of wrongness. Something deep in the back of my mind told me to stop.

My fingers were inches from touching that white pelt. But I halted.

"A horse's eyes are not red," I slurred aloud. "Not red." I blinked. If I turned my head, the pony didn't really look much like a pony in my peripheral vision. It was white, yes, but something my mind wouldn't focus on gave me a shiver again. It was squat and hunched over, with what might have been talons, and a rapacious hunger in its red, red eyes.

When I looked at the pony again, something was definitely wrong. The angles, the shapes. It was making me dizzy and nauseated. What I was looking at seemed to be warring with my perception. Wasn't I seeing a pony...or was it something else, something alien?

The pony opened its mouth, and instead of big, square teeth, they were sharp and predatory. Not a whinny, but a wheezing sound in some strange high register. Its breath was foul, like carrion, and the lip pulled back in a snarl.

It was like being shaken awake from a nightmare. My heart jerked, the adrenalin flowed, and I took two steps back.

It screamed. I was fully myself again. Even as I fell backwards into the murky water, I raised the crossbow at hip height and fired.

I was no more than two feet away. The quarrel seemed to fling from the crossbow in slow motion. It speared forward, wobbling as it spun. It easily pierced the snow-white hide of the beast's chest and stuck fast, the feathers protruding.

The kelpie screamed bloody murder. It thrashed in the water, kicking up great waves that soaked me. I scrambled back as it continued to whip about, but even as it did so, beams of bright light burst from its mouth, nostrils, eyes, and from the place where the bolt had entered. And like a piece of newspaper on the fire, holes began to form and burned away the beast.

The Booke snapped into being in front of me with a loud crack and fell open to a blank page. A quill appeared beside it.

I grabbed the quill, jabbed it into the palm that had barely healed from the last time, and gathered the blood like ink in the quill's nib.

Quickly, I scratched into the Booke:

I followed the Kelpie into its pool, and though its call was strong, I shot it with a bolt...

The more details I added about its snow-white hide, its forlorn expression, the more it screamed and disintegrated that much faster.

I dipped and wrote, dipped and wrote. The Booke obligingly stayed open and hovered before me. Until the kelpie exploded into shards of light and disappeared.

The Booke slammed shut and fell to solid ground. The pool had vanished, leaving only mud behind. And, of course, my jeans were soaked in chilling water.

I fell back against the leaf duff and breathed. The forest was quiet. The screaming had stopped. There was only my hard breathing and the occasional one-note call of a bird.

I did it. It was gone. The kelpie was gone. And then I began to cry. I didn't even know why. My throat was hot and thick and I just couldn't help it. I let it go with ugly, gut-deep sobs. I threw my muddy arm over my eyes and lay on that forest floor and let myself have the good cry I'd been needing for a while.

After a few minutes, I inhaled some air, calmed myself, and slowly sat up.

Shivering from the cold, from...everything...I picked up the Booke and the crossbow and trudged toward home.

No fanfare as I made my way back through the woods. But I did feel lighter. Accomplished. I could take that long bath now without worrying about a creature coming through the pipes. But even that bit of euphoria didn't last long. The werewolf was still out there. I could almost feel it stalking me. No, I hadn't yet seen it, but I saw what it did to Jeff, an irreversible curse that would plague him all his days. I'd never seen Jeff so quiet, so pensive. His whole demeanor had changed. His eyes were haunted and I feared for his future. What would his life be like? Could he ever return to California? It made me sick to think that he couldn't really go home, that we—my coven and I—were the only ones who could fully understand his predicament. He'd have to stay, and with that realization, I felt a strange sense of dread. "So much for my escape."

Dragging the crossbow behind me, I shoved open my shop door with my shoulder and let it slam. I turned the deadbolt, left the Booke on a table—where I felt it would stay, at least for a while—and dropped the crossbow into the nearest chair. I trudged up the stairs to the bathroom and filled my giant claw-foot tub with hot water and bath salts.

Once I'd had my long soak and was wrapped in a fluffy terry robe, I called Doc.

"My God, Kylie! You should never have gone alone."

"It's my job," I said blankly. I really had nothing to add. I was still feeling...aimless.

He had no answer to that. But he asked if he could bring the Wiccans over later and I agreed. Jeff needed his potion, after all, and there was a werewolf that needed killing. I knew Jolene would be coming over soon after school and I ensconced myself upstairs to listen for the sound of her.

❧

The front door rattled and finally opened. The bell above the door, oblivious to whatever happened around it, rang merrily.

"Hello?" called Jolene cautiously.

I hadn't realized I'd been sitting in the dark. My damp robe had long ago started to feel uncomfortable and clammy. I pulled myself from my chair and went to my bedroom door without opening it. "I'm up here, Jolene. The coven is coming. Open the doors, don't open them. I'll...be down in a while."

I heard the quiet sounds of Jolene switching on lights, checking the register, doing the mundane things I should have been doing. But I couldn't summon the interest.

Instead, I stood over my dresser wondering if I should dress. It didn't take me long to decide that I should. Jeans, a sweater, socks. I dressed, pushed my damp hair back from my face, and trudged downstairs.

Jolene was helping some customers, but she spared a worried glance my way. She had made tea for the samovars, something I hadn't done in days, it seemed. I got a paper cup and opened the spigot. Cranberry Pomegranate. I inhaled the fragrant aromas and drank, warming my throat and spirit with the herbal and fruit flavors.

I sank into one of the wingbacks, listened to the effusive customer go on about how wonderful the shop was, and watched her leave with her bag of purchases.

Jolene came around the side and stared at me. "Doc told me," she said quietly. "Are you all right?"

"I don't know."

"Should I just…leave you alone?"

"Yeah. That would be good."

She watched me as she walked away. I held the hot paper cup in both my hands, warming my fingers, and then moved to put it down on the side table. The Booke was there. I almost set the cup down on the cover but decided against it. The Booke might decide to launch itself and I didn't need hot tea all over me.

Customers came and went. Their chatter was white noise in the background of my thoughts. I kept seeing the kelpie. But mostly, I kept seeing Erasmus the last time I saw him, when he made his terrible confession. He hadn't shown. I'd half-expected him to. I was glad he hadn't.

My phone rang, and for a strange moment, I thought it might be Erasmus. But looking at the number, I realized it was Doc.

"It's not Doc," said the unexpectedly gruff voice of Jeff. "I, uh, just wanted to…talk, I guess. How are *you* coping?"

"*I'm* fine."

I said nothing and for a long time neither of us did, before he sighed. "Gigantor in a Mountie hat came by to talk to me."

My turn to sigh. "You mean Sheriff Ed?"

"Yeah. He's, uh, kind of imposing."

"What did you tell him? Jeff, I swear, if you told him about all this magic stuff—"

"I didn't. Keep your shirt on. How could I tell him your ex is a werewolf? I told him you had nothing to do with the Doug thing. I didn't know that asshat was his brother."

"You told him about that?"

"Well, I didn't beat *myself* up. He was real mad, and by the time he left, he was steaming. He peeled out of here in that Interceptor like it was a racecar. I think he plans on talking to him. With his fists."

Shoot. I really didn't want Ed anywhere near this garbage. "When was that?"

"A couple of hours ago." He fell silent again. I tried to fill the gap.

"Is Doc there with you?"

"He and that Seraphina chick are working on the potion. I think Doc left to get something. He's a nice guy, but it's pretty boring here. There's no TV and the Wi-Fi is nonexistent. I mean, it was nice of him to let me stay, but I'm going out of my mind."

"Hang in there. You seem to be taking it all well…or are you just putting on a good face?"

He laughed. "That's not what his furniture says. I kind of freaked that first night and tore the place up."

"Oh, Jeff."

"He was nice about that too. I'm going to pay him back. Kylie, I was thinking…I might not be able to go back to California…"

"I know. I was thinking that too."

"Kind of awkward my being here. Cockblocking you and all."

"There's my grandpa's place." The moment I said it, it made sense. "It's a mess now and needs major cleaning, but you're welcome to stay there as long as you like, so you can get back on your feet."

"My *paws*, you mean," he said bitterly.

"Jeff—"

"It's totally all right. I'm getting with the canine sensibility. I've gone off my vegetarian diet big time, though. Almost all meat now."

"I'm sorry."

"It's no biggie. Takes less time to fry up a steak than it does to put together a bean and rice casserole. You can get used to anything if you have to."

I nodded, even though he couldn't see it.

"So what about this kelpie thing," he said, somewhat brighter. "I'm ready to help."

"I already took care of it."

There was a pause. "When you say 'took care of it'..."

"I already killed it. Just this morning. It's gone."

"Killed it?"

I could sense his tension even over the phone. "I mean, I guess. I don't know what really happens to them. They sort of burst into shards of light and become another page in the Booke."

"Just another page."

"That's not going to be you, Jeff."

"But it will be that other werewolf, right? Is it a dude? Do we even know who? Doc says none of you have ever seen it."

"Jeff, I just don't know. A werewolf is a different kind of thing."

"You said it. Did you know that it doesn't even take a full moon for me to change? I can change at any time. Sort of like the Hulk. If I get too emotional, I can 'shift,' as they call it. Seraphina's been teaching me some stuff. So along with my yoga, I'm keeping it under control. But...sometimes, at night, after a bad dream, I kind of…shift a little. The teeth and the eyes. Once it took hours for my ears to go back to normal. I've never fully gone wolf. I want to, though. The feeling is really strong, especially when the moon is out. That's what the wolf's bane potion is for. Seraphina says she'll get it done any day now. Kylie…you trust these people, right?"

I tucked a strand of hair over my ear and resettled the phone against it. "I do, Jeff. With my life. You can too."

"I guess I'll have to." He took in a shaky breath. "You…care about them, don't you?"

"And you. I really do. I want the best for you."

"And that demon guy."

I sucked in a breath. "He's gone. I'm not calling him again."

"Kylie…can I ask you something?"

I had a feeling I knew what it was. "No."

"Kylie…Man, I don't even know what to say."

"Then don't say anything."

"I mean, you and a demon. What's the matter with the sheriff? Not that I'm endorsing that."

"It's none of your business."

"I understand that. None of it is. It doesn't mean I don't want to try and understand."

I rubbed my face. "I don't really understand it either, Jeff. It just happened. He was different—exciting, enticing. I don't know. Why does anyone like anybody? Chemistry."

"Dude, he's a *demon*."

"Yeah, I got that, Jeff."

"Not even our species."

"Yup."

He was breathing hard. "Of course, neither am I anymore."

"*Jeff.*"

"It's okay. Now *I'm* exotic. I guess."

What could I say? I couldn't think of any reply to that.

"I'm really sorry for what I did to you, Kylie. About everything, you know?"

"Yeah, I know."

"Seriously. That was messed up. I know that now."

This was a discussion I could put off indefinitely. I rubbed the ache in my forehead. "Look, Jeff, can I talk to Seraphina?"

"Sure. I'll bring the phone to her." I could hear him walk through the house, his footsteps, the different hollow sounds of the corridor, some fumbling, and then Seraphina's chirpy "Thank you, Jeff" and Jeff's retreating "No problem."

"Kylie?"

"Hi, Seraphina. How's the potion coming?"

"I've had a few false starts. Aconite is very tricky, with its poisonous aspects, but I think I have an excellent recipe now. It just has to boil down. Should be ready to administer by tomorrow."

"Jeff was saying that he could change at any time, not just at a full moon. Is that right?"

"According to all our research, this is correct. To keep him from dangerous shifting, he's going to have to take this potion."

"For how long?"

"Oh my dear, didn't they tell you? For the rest of his life."

I supposed that settled it. Jeff couldn't leave. How else was he to get his potion? He could end up killing someone if he didn't take it. Or infecting someone else.

I swallowed the hot lump in my throat. "I want you to know, Seraphina, that I really appreciate your doing this."

"Kylie, it's—"

I waited for the end of that sentence. When nothing came, I asked, "Seraphina?"

A female voice that wasn't Seraphina's got on the line. "Witchy can't come to the phone right now. She's a little tied up."

"Shabiri. If you've touched her..."

"You'll what? Wave your little amulet at me? Stick me with your crossbow arrows again? And by the way, that fucking *hurt*. But as you can see, it can't kill me. So try again with your empty threats." She paused for dramatic emphasis. She was a real soap opera queen, all right. "This is what I want you to do. Bring the book to Doug's barn. And leave your junior Wiccans at home, for goodness' sake. I'd hate to have to eviscerate them before your eyes. Oh wait. Maybe I *wouldn't* hate that."

The phone clicked off.

CHAPTER TWENTY-TWO

I wasn't stupid. I waited for the coven to assemble and told them everything.

"Well, obviously, we're going with you," said Nick.

"Obviously. But you can't be so close that Shabiri will know you're there."

"I'm not sure how close that is," said Doc.

Jolene perked up. "An invisibility charm. But those are really tricky. And dangerous."

"Dangerous how?" I asked.

Jolene began typing on her tablet. "Because sometimes the caster is so successful they can't make themselves *un*-invisible."

"And," said Nick, "you spread the stuff on your eyelids. If any of it gets in your eyes, not only are you invisible for a very long time, but you also can't see too much—or at all, because everything becomes transparent. Sounds pretty harsh."

"Then maybe you shouldn't—"

"It's not a guarantee," Nick added, "but it's better than being caught by Shabiri. Compared to Erasmus, she is *not* on a leash. I mean, I hate to say it, Kylie, knowing what he is, but he could have killed any one of us at any time. But he didn't. Shabiri doesn't have that kind of incentive."

"What do you mean by 'incentive'?"

"You know." He squirmed a bit, wouldn't look at me. "He didn't seem to want to get you mad."

"What could *I* do to him? The crossbow has no effect."

Doc put his hand on my arm. "I don't think that's what he means."

"Oh, please! The only effect I have on Erasmus is as a dinner bell. And he doesn't have to make nice to me for that outcome."

Nick and Doc exchanged glances but didn't say anything. It annoyed the hell out of me. "Subject closed. Next. Invisibility?"

Doc ticked his head. "It's possible. At least, with our enhanced abilities it is. And I'm pretty sure a demon wouldn't be able to see us."

"'Pretty sure'? Are those good enough odds?"

"I'm willing to take the chance."

"I'm not so willing to let you."

Nick broke in between us. "As Doc said before, that's really up to us, not you. And we aren't going to let you go alone, and that's final."

My heart warmed. I swallowed back the lump in my throat. "Thanks, guys," I said quietly.

Doc was looking at me earnestly. "Have you considered...calling Mr. Dark?"

"No. Absolutely not."

"He could..."

"I said no."

He raised his hands in surrender.

"I'll need some ingredients," said Jolene. "Kylie has some, but I don't know if we can find the rest. I have powdered moonstone," she said, digging into her backpack...which she must have gotten from Mary Poppins because everything was in there. "But I'm a little shy on luna moth wings. I don't like dealing in animal parts."

"My dad has a butterfly collection," said Nick thoughtfully. "But if he ever found out I took them..."

"I don't want you getting into any trouble, Nick," said Doc. "I know you and your pop have a tough enough relationship as it is. But it seems to me there's a fine collection at the library."

"So...stealing from the library is better?" said Nick.

"I'll go. You help the ladies get the spell started."

I went to the hall tree and grabbed my coat. "Look, I've taken enough time already. I've got to get over there. Who knows what they're doing to Seraphina."

Nick was startled. "It's gonna take at least half an hour for Doc to get to the library and back."

I took in all their desperate faces. Jolene had already set up a brass bowl in the middle of the pentagram and was mashing my herbs in a glass mortar.

"How would it look if I delayed too long?"

"Give me a five-minute head start," said Doc. He rushed out the door. His Rambler roared to life and kicked up a spray of gravel as he peeled out.

I grabbed the Booke and sat with it in my lap, watching the clock. Jolene stopped by me and put a cotton bag in my hand. "Salt. You might need it."

"Thanks." I stuffed it into my coat pocket.

Nick and Jolene seemed to work double time, getting the spell ready to go while waiting for that one ingredient. It wasn't long before they, too, were sitting around the hearth, tapping their fingers and squirming impatiently in their seats.

The clock ticked. I kept flicking the lock on the Booke open and closed, the lock only I seemed to be able to tap.

Six minutes had passed. It was time to go. I stood.

"Aren't you going to take your crossbow?" asked Nick, coming with me to the door.

Maybe that was a good idea. I raised my hand and there she came. I gripped it tight for a moment before lowering it to my thigh.

Nick shook his head in admiration. "That is wicked cool."

"Come soon, okay?"

I threw the Booke and the crossbow into the passenger seat and started up the car.

❧

Driving to Hansen Mills in the dark was getting old. But with worry of the kelpie behind me, I was remarkably lighter, surer of myself. And sustained by my anger more than anything else.

It concerned me that Shabiri was so adamant about getting the Booke. And it wasn't just about controlling Erasmus, if she even could. It was more about the Enochian sentiments from my grandfather's notebook that the Booke was more than it appeared to be. That it was a key that could lock the Hell Gate for good. But I wasn't all that stupid—I knew keys could *open* doors as well. What was her plan? And who was the one holding the puppet strings? Was it Ruth Russell? But I hadn't seen anything implicating her in my incredibly hurried visit to her house. Only that sigil or mandala on her front porch. But that was for protection more than anything else. That's what Nick had said, anyway.

What about Baphomet? I had sent him back to wherever with a well-placed arrow, but it didn't mean he couldn't return. If the Booke was a gateway or a key to a larger gateway, he could get a foot…or *hoof*…in the door. Maybe he already had. Maybe Shabiri was helping him. Seemed we needed to do a lot more research on Goat Guy. *If* I made it out of there unscathed.

I made the now familiar run up the road to Hansen Mills and took the turn to Doug's place. But it wasn't until I rounded the curve on the long driveway to the mobile home and the barn that I saw the sheriff's SUV. Shit. Ed had talked to Jeff and left in a hurry to talk to his brother. And he was obviously still here.

Nothing I could do about it now. Maybe Ed could help.

I pulled the car in front of the barn. Lights spilled out from under the doors. I got out and slammed the door since stealth seemed to have gone out the window. With the Booke under one arm and the crossbow in the other, I stalked up to the barn doors. Before I could open them, Miss Catsuit opened them for me.

"And here she is at last," she said with a sneer a mile wide. "I wondered what kept you."

"Had to put on my best party dress," I muttered, shouldering past her, making sure I bumped her good. I scanned the place. Same junk in every corner, except now there was Seraphina tied to a post, a gag in her mouth, with Bob Willis and Dean Fitch standing over her. She was awake and upright at least and looked pretty mad. That was good. Better than scared.

That was more than could be said for Ed. I jolted toward him before stopping myself. He was down, lying on his side with some blood on his face, but he was still breathing.

Doug stood near him, wearing a frown. He didn't bother with his friendly act.

"Did you do that to your own brother?"

He snorted. "Don't worry. I don't think he's got any brain damage. It would be a miracle through that thick skull of his."

"You're a piece of work, you know that?"

"Enough chatter. Is that the book?"

I held it tightly. Who knew I could be so protective of the thing that had made my life a living hell. But if I handed it over, how much more hell was there in store for me?

I sure hoped the Wiccans had gotten their moth wings and were on their way. I guessed stalling was in order.

"So how long were you guys stuck in here? Just as a matter of research."

Doug sighed and folded his brawny arms over his chest. "Too long. Till dawn. I mean, my Ordo is great, but spending that many hours with them…Let's just say they aren't the best conversationalists."

"Like you said, it's *your* group. You're the one who hangs out with them."

"What can you do? Sometimes you gotta make friends where you can."

"Hey!" said Dean, holding out his hands in a "what the hell?" gesture.

Doug merely waved him off. "The book," he said again.

"Okay. But you've got to let Seraphina go."

"Oh yeah. No problem."

"I'm expected to believe that? Like you let Daniel Parker off the hook?"

Doug blinked and shook his head. "I don't know what you're talking about."

"Sure you don't. You killed him. In some kind of sacrifice. A very dangerous one."

"Babe, I just don't know what you're telling me, but we didn't kill anyone. Not yet."

"Are you really going to stand there and—"

"Who's Daniel Parker?" asked Bob.

Doug shrugged. Doug could be lying, but I wondered if Bob was that good an actor.

"The *book*!" said Doug again, patience thinning.

I looked down at the thing. "Doug, honest to God, I don't know what will happen if I try to give it to you."

"Let's just find out, huh?"

With a bone-weary sigh, I hefted it up in my hand and stretched out my arm.

"Wait," said Shabiri behind me. "Where's Erasmus?"

The name was like a shock ripping through me. "He's not here."

"Forgive me if I don't believe you. Why don't you call him?"

"No."

"Oh. The honeymoon is over, is it? Once you found out you were today's blue plate special, the bloom is off the rose, eh?"

"Something like that," I grumbled.

"Call him anyway."

I turned to face her with the nastiest expression I could muster. "No."

"I felt you really meant it that time." She went back to slouching and watching with predatory eyes.

My arm was getting tired holding out the Booke. "Are you going to take it or what, Doug?"

He took a step closer. He was trying for indifference, but I could tell he was afraid to touch it. I took a step toward him, and just as I suspected, he stepped back.

Shabiri scoffed. "Oh, for Baphomet's sake!" She stalked forward and grabbed it.

Two things happened at once.

A flash of light and Shabiri sailed back as if she'd been punched good and hard. And then Doug was flung back in the opposite direction in the same manner. They were both down.

The Booke hovered between them, slowly turning, with a pulsing glow. I didn't know if I should grab it, but I figured it knew how to take care of itself.

Shabiri picked herself up first. She brushed off the straw from her form-fitting leather suit and snarled at the Booke, baring sharp canines. "How did you do that?" she said in a voice dripping with bile.

"*I* didn't do anything."

Out of the corner of my eye, I saw Bob make a move toward me. I swung the crossbow toward him. "Don't do it."

He stopped, casting a glance to Doug, who was finally coming around.

I couldn't keep my eye on them *and* Shabiri, so I grabbed the salt pouch from my coat and made a quick circle for myself.

Shabiri scowled. "Now that's not fair."

"You'd better watch it," I said, "or your face is going to get stuck that way." She scowled on top of her scowl. "Dean," I directed, barely turning my head, "untie her."

"I don't take orders from you."

"Dean," said Shabiri wearily, "untie her."

"I don't take orders from you either, bitch."

She slowly swiveled her head toward him. I couldn't see what sort of face she made, but Dean's horrified expression showed exactly just who the bitch was. With trembling hands, he quickly cut the bindings from Seraphina. The first thing Seraphina did was yank the gag from her mouth and heave it to the ground. Then she turned, cocked back her arm, and punched Dean in the face. Down he went.

Bob lunged toward him but I swiveled my bow in his direction. "I wouldn't, Bob."

He froze when he saw me. My Spidey sense was tingling and I suddenly turned and aimed it at Charise, who was coming at me from behind. "Really?" I said.

She gave a bitchy sneer.

"Both of you over by Dean where I can see you." I urged her with a gesture of the crossbow.

"*Doug*," she whined. "Are you going to let her do this?"

Doug was just getting up, and none too easily. He dragged his feet through the straw, moving sluggishly.

Ed moaned, and I glanced toward him, taking my eyes away from Doug for only an instant.

It was enough. Doug saw his opportunity and scrambled into the hay, snatching up the hidden spear.

He brandished it in both hands and charged me, spearpoint aimed right at my stomach.

Someone screamed. For a moment, I thought it might have been me. But it was Charise.

I stiffened, expecting the sharp pain. I braced for it. There was nowhere for me to go.

Suddenly I was sideways. Erasmus appeared out of nowhere and shoved me aside. The spear that was meant for me plunged deep through him.

"*No!*"

"You idiot!" shrieked Shabiri.

Was she yelling at Doug or Erasmus? I couldn't tell. I didn't care.

Doug yanked the spear out. Black goo dripped from it...as well as from the hole in Erasmus's back.

I staggered forward. "Oh my God!"

Erasmus shuffled back. He looked down at the carnage of his chest. A bright light shone from it, the same that I had seen when Baphomet took an arrow to the breast. He fell to one knee. I threw myself to the floor next to him.

"What did you do?"

"I...protected you," he said huskily, coughing. More inky blackness dribbled from his lips.

"Why did you do that? I didn't call you."

"You should have. You needed my help."

"Don't talk. You're hurt."

"Oh, you *think*?" said Shabiri. She had her hands at her hips and she was spitting mad.

Doug held the spear loosely. Even though he had been ready to spear *me*, now he seemed lost. I guessed this wasn't the plan.

I flung myself toward him, trying to hit him with my crossbow. "Doug, you asshole! You idiot!" Firing at him wasn't personal enough. I wanted to beat him with it. "Were you really trying to *kill* me? Look what you've done!"

Doug seemed to come back to his senses and dipped the end of the spear in a puddle of Erasmus's blood. He quickly scrawled some sort of symbol on the floor and began chanting.

"What are you doing?"

He ignored me and continued. The barn walls began to clatter and tremble.

"Dammit, Doug. What the hell are you doing? Haven't you learned anything?"

The symbol on the ground began to glow. I turned toward Erasmus, still on the floor, holding his chest. I clutched at him. "What's happening?"

"Beelze's tail." I was never so happy to hear that stupid curse. "He's summoning him."

"Summoning…who?"

"Baphomet."

Shabiri glowered down at the two of us. This whole game was thrown out of whack for me. I didn't understand what she wanted, but it didn't look like this was it.

"Erasmus," I rasped. "I need your help. Are you going to be all right?"

"I don't know. I've never been stabbed with the Spear of Mortal *freaking Pain* before! It's living up to its name." He gathered himself, breathing deep, and reached for me. "Help me up."

I took his arm and braced him with my legs. He grunted as he put his weight on me and stood unsteadily, still clutching at his chest, black ooze dribbling over his hand. How much blood could he lose?

Surprisingly, Shabiri tried to take his other arm.

"Haven't you done enough," I spit.

She stepped back, fingers curled into claws. If Erasmus wasn't standing between us, I figured those would be gouging my eyes out about now.

He was breathing heavily in short, jerky breaths. I'd never seen him like that. I'd never seen anyone in that much pain. "We must stop him from conjuring Baphomet," he rasped.

"How?"

"I don't know."

Shabiri pushed me. Not as hard as she could have, but it still sent me sprawling. I guessed the truce was over. I had forgotten and left my salt circle. Erasmus wobbled and doubled over.

"You're *not* going to stop it, meat girl."

"Why's it so important to you, Shabiri? Are you into goats or something?"

"Better than humans," she sneered, glancing disdainfully back at Erasmus.

Erasmus was barely holding himself up. And for some reason I couldn't fathom, I wanted to help him.

But more immediate problems were arising. Like the fact that Goat Guy was making a repeat appearance, climbing up through the floor.

CHAPTER TWENTY-THREE

The god climbed out of his sigil as if ascending from a hole. His goat head bore tall, spiraling horns, and they emerged first. The fur of his head was black but his eyes—those weird horizontal pupils in them—shone yellow. His torso was bare and that of a man, while his hindquarters were goat, complete with shiny cloven hoofs. And when he finally got out of the sigil, he stood some seven feet tall—*not* including the horns.

He made that howl again, neither goat nor man. More like an angry cow being strangled. Not a pleasant sound.

Terrified, I did the only thing I could think to do; I aimed the crossbow at him.

His eyes blazed and his muzzle snapped toward me, teeth gnashing. With surprising speed, he darted his long arm forward, grabbed my weapon, and whipped it out of my hands.

"Wha—?" I stood immobile in shock.

Taking the crossbow in both hands, he snapped it in two, hurling the broken pieces to the ground.

I gasped. "Oh! I didn't know you could do that."

Erasmus staggered forward. "*Run*, Kylie!"

Baphomet wound up his arm and reached for me. I ducked and swerved to the side. But now Erasmus was in his path. I was caught between a no-man's-land of possible escape in one direction and the destruction of Erasmus in the other. I didn't have time to ponder it. Baphomet zeroed his creepy eyes on Erasmus, and with a deep growl, grabbed him by both arms and lifted.

Erasmus yelled and threw his head back. Like he was in agony. Baphomet screamed into his face, blowing his hair back. He was ready to rip him to shreds.

What do I do? I don't have anything...

The crossbow was gone, busted. I'd used my bag of salt, though I doubted that would work against a god. I didn't have a gun...

I whipped my head around. *I* didn't have a gun, but Ed did. I scrambled toward him and skidded on my knees. He was moaning but still effectively out. I should try to get him out of here. But first, the gun. I grabbed it from its holster, looked for something that might be a safety, and clicked it.

Smoke surrounded Baphomet now. The sigil glowed under his hooves.

"Seraphina!" I yelled.

"Kylie, I'm here!" she called. She was inching her way along the walls toward me.

I aimed the gun two-handed at Baphomet. "Get Ed out of here. Drag him if you have to."

"Kylie, I don't know if I can do it."

"You'll have to. I know he's heavy, but you have to try."

The last thing I saw over my shoulder was Seraphina dragging Ed by his arms toward the door, and she was doing a pretty good job of it. The Ordo didn't try to stop her. They were standing around Baphomet, eyes shining with equal parts awe and fear.

I checked my stance, aimed toward the chest, and fired.

The kickback knocked me over. Fire erupted from the barrel. The bullet hit Baphomet on the shoulder, winged him.

It was enough for him to drop Erasmus, who fell like a sack of potatoes and groaned, trying to crawl away, leaving a swath of black blood behind him.

Baphomet turned his eyes on me. He screamed again as I fired a second time. It only seemed to slow him down. I kept pulling the trigger, but it didn't look like mortal means would stop him.

The next time I clicked, the gun was empty. Baphomet bore down on me.

I heaved the heavy gun at his head. It knocked his muzzle to the side, which only seemed to make him angrier.

It was over. This was how it would end. I backed up, but the doors were too far away. In the time it would take me to turn, it would be too late.

Something caught his eye. The Booke was still floating in the air, still pulsating and turning like some cheesy store display. Baphomet's eyes shone with greed as he reached toward it.

The barn door exploded in shards of wood and splinters. A beast's roar shook the rafters.

Now what?

When I turned, I blinked. It was…a wolf, but *not* a wolf. It stood upright on two human-like legs. Its barrel-shaped torso was covered in thick, black fur. Its yellow eyes swept the room and fell on me. The mouth was certainly that of a wolf—with massive fangs and salivating foam. It fell into a crouch and stalked slowly toward me.

Was it Jeff? I wasn't sure, and I backed away.

Baphomet watched it curiously for a moment, before turning back toward the Booke.

I looked around for any help. Doug had been holding his spear, but as I watched, it abruptly jerked out of his hands and hung in midair. He stared at it, not knowing what to do. When his mind kicked in, he tried to snatch it back, but it was already hopping in the air toward me. I had the surprising presence of mind to grab it.

Baphomet snapped his attention away from the Booke. It looked like he'd rather clobber me instead. His steps shook the earth as he lumbered in my direction. His hairy shoulders swiveled with every stride. Just as Baphomet loomed above me, the werewolf flung himself forward and dug his teeth into Baphomet's shoulder.

The god turned and swiped at him with his taloned hand.

It was now or never. I held the spear tightly and shoved hard.

The sharp tip sank into Baphomet.

He screamed and threw the wolf off him. It skidded several feet away and lay there, dazed.

I expected the same white light, the same ripping of the planes, as had happened last time, with Baphy sinking into the ground, angry but gone.

That's not what happened. At all.

He yanked the spear out of his gut and let it clatter to the floor. And then he glared at me, horns tall and sharp.

"I know you now, Kylie Strange," said Baphomet, his voice a combination of a deep baritone and a lowing cow. Enormous batwings snapped out from his back, spreading wide to touch both sides of the barn.

Startled, the awakening wolf whined and fell back.

Baphomet pumped the air and his cloven hooves lifted from the floor. The wind he created knocked everyone off their feet, and he lifted higher till he reached the roof and burst through it. Rafters, beams, roof shingles showered down around us. We all scrambled, looking for shelter. He lifted higher into the night, and I cast about desperately for something, anything, to stop him.

By the time I looked again, he had disappeared into the dark sky…on *our* plane. Even a plebe like me knew this wasn't good.

The werewolf got to its feet, ignoring Baphomet's flight. I backed away. "Jeff? Is that you?"

But I saw no recognition in its eyes. No humanity at all. It roared at me, spittle flying. I cringed back and covered my face as it charged.

Another roar and the werewolf was flung backward. When I opened my eyes, a second werewolf, one with a light down of blond fur, was attacking the first one.

"Jeff?"

The blond werewolf sank his teeth where he could, but the black wolf swiped its immense claws. Jeff whined, cowered back. He took a look at me, seemed to take courage from it, and reared up again to pounce on the black wolf. Fur and blood flew up around them. Jeff opened his jaws and lunged, clamping down on the werewolf's shoulder, tearing and shaking his head. The wolf went down on one knee, but still wouldn't yield. And I began to see the problem. Because it came from the Booke, Jeff couldn't kill it. Only *I* could.

I barely had time to process all that, when the spear rose again and floated toward me. My Wiccans! Their blessed invisible selves had arrived!

Shabiri rushed forward, screaming bloody murder. "I told you what would happen if you interfered again, old man!" she cried. The space flickered and suddenly Grandpa appeared, holding the spear.

"*Don't worry,*" he said to me. "*I'm watching over you, sweetpea.*"

"Grandpa!"

Brandishing a small pouch in her hand, Shabiri charged and flung the pouch at him. Its contents erupted and glittered all around his transparent figure. He flickered. He looked at me, wide-eyed and angry, trying to speak, and suddenly tossed the spear toward me before he disappeared with a flash.

The spear hit the ground.

Shabiri made a grab for it, but I was faster.

"What did you do?"

"What I should have done before. Sent him packing for good."

"God damn you!"

"Much too late for that."

We seemed to both realize at the same time that I had the spear in my hand. I jabbed it at her, but she jumped back. "What are you going to do now, monkey girl? Baphomet is free."

"Not sure. But the first chance I get, I know I'm going to kill *you*."

She seemed surprised by that, and then a little fearful. Before I could do anything, she made a hasty exit and disappeared, leaving Doug and his gang holding the bag once more.

I turned quickly to the fighting werewolves. They were in a clinch now, but it looked to be a stalemate. Except that Jeff would tire and he *could* be killed. It wouldn't be easy getting to the black wolf. And would the spear even work? It was all I had.

Roaring and snarling echoed off the walls. Every instinct was telling me to run. The wolves tumbled over and over each other, fur flying, blood spraying. They came too close, knocking into me, sending me reeling back. Remarkably, I kept hold of the spear and righted myself with ninja-like reflexes that were all Booke. I didn't have time to congratulate myself. I tightened my grip on the spear, got in as close as I could, and jabbed hard.

The black werewolf threw back its head and howled. I'd caught its shoulder—not a mortal wound. Jeff came at him again, clamping down on the same wounded shoulder with his toughened jaws. It distracted the black wolf long enough for me to take a second shot. I cocked back as far as I could and heaved the spear, wrenching my shoulder in the process. Holding on, I followed the spear with my body weight, driving it deep. Both spearpoint and I fell into him, my nose filling with the acrid smell of skunky musk and the metallic scent of blood.

Rolling away, I lost the spear. It was imbedded deep in the werewolf's chest. He screamed, clawing at it. And then the familiar glowing beams tore through him, consuming, ripping ragged holes of light.

The Booke was suddenly at my shoulder, open to a blank page. The quill hovered beside it. I grabbed the quill and jabbed the open wound on my left palm. The blood pooled quickly and I had my ink.

I stabbed the werewolf with the Spear of Mortal Pain in the Ordo's barn, I wrote, relishing the flourish I gave each sentence as the Booke consumed the werewolf that had bitten Jeff. His screams rang out over the roar of the fiery light as the Booke devoured him. When he finally disappeared with a loud crack, I dropped the quill and fell back, all my strength sapped.

The Booke slammed shut and fell at my feet.

Silence. No one spoke. Until…a low growl.

I snapped my head toward Jeff. But he wasn't Jeff. He was a blond werewolf, mouth covered in the gore of the one who had made him, and he was stalking toward me.

"Jeff, it's Kylie. Jeff, I know you're in there. Just stop." I scooted away, but I really had no strength to get up and run if it came down to it. I knew I didn't. "Jeff, you know we can help you. Stop, Jeff. *Stop!*"

His irises dimmed from their striking yellow, and he cocked his head, doglike, looking me over. He whined, looked around desperately, and finally bounded away on all fours, disappearing out the door.

"Jeff!"

But he was gone.

The crossbow lay on the ground in two pieces. Erasmus was still wounded, groaning on the floor, and I only hoped Seraphina had gotten Ed to safety.

I faced Doug, who looked a bit dazed. His Ordo didn't seem as triumphant as I'd expected. Maybe the reality wasn't as great as the fantasy. "That was…Jeff?" he said.

"Yeah. A lot has happened since the last time you beat him up." Doug didn't look happy. "Are we done here, Doug? Do you get it now? You can't touch the Booke. Whatever Shabiri told you was a lie. You've got to leave us alone…or help us. No one's gonna win here. Seriously."

He still seemed a bit distracted. "You have your schemes, we have ours."

"And what happens when Ed wakes up? He'll have this place so surrounded with state troopers. You guys will be Waco-ed for sure."

"Thanks for reminding me, sweetheart." He seemed to have swept this new revelation about Jeff aside. "A simple forget-me spell will clear that right up."

"I wish I could cast one on you to make you idiots leave this crap alone. Why did you summon Goat Guy? And now he's free."

"Just as he planned. He wants the book. Still wants it, I imagine." We all glanced toward it, lying innocently on the floor.

"Forget it. I'm not kidding. Neither you nor your demon can get it. So just put it out of your mind."

"Love to, darlin', but my Lord Baphomet has his heart set on it. So if he wants it, I don't see how you can stand up against a god. Even *with* a pet werewolf."

"So far, I'm three for three, or have you forgotten?"

"I wouldn't count on that forever. He's a *god*, remember?"

I couldn't argue. I didn't know enough.

Where were the Wiccans? I had thought it was them being invisible and bringing me the spear. But obviously it hadn't been. Were they okay? I needed to alert them that Baphomet was alive and on the prowl.

A car roared to life outside. A screech of tires, and suddenly the police Interceptor crashed through what remained of the barn doors, sirens and lights blaring. I jumped aside just in time.

Jeff, normal-faced but still with a heavily hairy torso, leaned out of the driver's side window. "Get in!"

With spear in one hand, I grabbed Erasmus, half-dragging, half-carrying him to the car. Seraphina popped out of the back seat and helped shove him in. She got back in as I leapt on top of him, and without closing the door, I cried, "Go! *Go!*"

Jeff slammed into reverse and executed a perfect J-turn, screeching into drive down the narrow road.

I braced a hand on the ceiling and held Erasmus down with my leg as we jostled over the terrain, sometimes on the road, sometimes not. Ed was strapped into the passenger seat, head flopping this way and that. We made it to the highway and Jeff punched it back toward Moody Bog. But when he passed the turn, I grabbed the headrest of his seat. "Where are you going?"

"I'm taking us directly to the airport."

"No, Jeff. Stop. Take me back to my shop."

"Are you crazy?" he shouted over his shoulder. "That's the first place they'll look."

"I know. They know where I am, I know where they are. We each have protective charms on us…but we should have put one on you. Except I thought you left town like I *told* you to."

He grumbled for a moment. "I didn't know that," he muttered.

"There's a lot you don't know. Turn around."

He drove until he could find a turnout. He pulled off the road and swiveled toward me. "What happens when Romeo here wakes up? Your cover is blown."

"I don't know. Doug said he'd use a forget-me charm. He'd be in a lot of trouble if he didn't."

"A spell? Is that what you mean? A freakin' *spell*?"

"Are you still light on the concept of magic, even now?"

"No. I just…" He ran his hand up through his sandy hair. He stopped when he felt caked blood and looked at his hand. Oh yes. He remembered it all. That answered *that*. "It's freaking me out."

"I know."

"I saw that…that *thing* fly out of the roof. What *was* that? Another demon?"

"No. That was a god. Baphomet."

"A *god*? What the hell, Kylie?"

"What do you want me to say, Jeff? This is all new to me too. I didn't ask for any of it."

"Neither did I," he said softly. He stared at me long and hard. "It's not freaking *you* out though, is it? Look at you. You saved that demon guy *and* your boyfriend. *And* me. Without even breaking a sweat. That's some new life you got yourself, babygirl."

"I know."

"You know. That's it? And, uh, what about that damned book? Those guys still have it."

"Not for long."

"What does that mean?"

No sooner had he said it than it appeared on the back seat beside me with a pop.

"Whoa!" He jolted, bumping into the steering wheel.

"Yeah," I said, sitting back. "It does that."

"So it looks like you got this all sewn up. And now a shiny new spear to add to your collection of crazy. Fine. You wanna go back? Let's go back." He hit the gas and headed back toward Moody Bog, turning at the welcome sign.

He turned on Lyndon Road and headed to my shop. Doc's Rambler was still there. He screeched to a halt in front and shut off the siren and lights. The Wiccans poured out the door and surrounded the car. When Seraphina spilled out, everyone took turns hugging her.

I opened the door and slowly climbed out, body aching. "Doc, Ed's in the front seat, knocked out cold."

Doc hurried to that side of the car, and he and Nick carried him inside. Seraphina and Jolene stared at Erasmus and the black muck smearing the back seat.

"He's hurt," I said. "Can you help him?"

Barely awake, he followed along, saying nothing. Jolene helped, and the two of them managed to get him into the shop too.

Jeff stood by the Interceptor and rubbed his arms. More blond fur fell, shedding off him at a faster rate. What I had taken for baggy pants was really just werewolf fur. I realized he'd soon be naked.

"Uh...Jeff?"

He looked down. "Shit. I'm about to embarrass myself, aren't I?"

I grabbed a coat from the Interceptor and thrust it at him...not a moment too soon. He wrapped it around his waist and suddenly seemed to be standing on a pile of fur.

The Booke floated out from the car. I guess there was no reason to carry it. It hovered beside me as I clutched the spear.

"Are you sure you're staying, Kylie?"

"I have to."

He watched the Booke levitate.

"There's one reason right there," I said.

"And two more inside, huh?" He shook his head. "You're going to have to choose, you know."

"What are you talking about?"

"Those guys. The demon and the sheriff. You'll have to choose one of them."

Jeff didn't know about my fate. He didn't know my soul was forfeit and choosing would be moot. Unless...unless Erasmus meant what he said. That he wouldn't take my soul.

"I don't have time to think about that right now, Jeff. There's a god on the loose and he isn't happy."

"Yeah. Sentences like that...I really wish I'd left that first time. But now...I can't leave."

"I meant what I said. You can live at my grandpa's old house."

"That was him, wasn't it? A ghost." He shook his head. "A ghost, a werewolf, and a demon. This is turning into its own horror franchise."

I laughed. I didn't know I could still do that.

"The wolf," he said, gesturing to himself. "It got out. I didn't mean for it to. But when they took Seraphina and then I smelled... *him*, I couldn't stop it. I went after him. It was a good thing, I guess, because...maybe I helped a little?"

"You helped a lot. And you remember it all."

"Yeah, it's not like in the movies. It's...real."

"I know."

He looked around forlornly, measuring the dark street. He shivered. His chest was bare, after all, no more fur left. "Kylie, I don't like cold weather."

I smiled. "But you'll have a fur coat."

This time, a tiny smile formed on his face. "You made a joke. Maybe...you aren't so mad at me anymore."

"Maybe I'm not."

He hitched up the coat around his waist. "I, uh, gotta get some clothes."

"Go inside. There's sweats in my room. Go on."

He nodded, ducking his head apologetically, and hurried through the door.

⁂

There was a long silence after I told my tale. Ed was sedated this time, lying on the couch. Erasmus was laid out on the kitchen table and patched up as best we could, an herb and honey poultice applied to his wound. He was conscious but just barely. I didn't know what to say to him.

Jeff came down the stairs. He'd thrown on one of my sleep shirts and a pair of sweats. It was actually something he used to do…and I didn't know how I felt about that. At any rate, he looked normal again. Human. I was glad he'd washed off the blood from his face and hands.

I paced from one end of the shop to the other, the Spear of Mortal Pain in my hand. I moved it from palm to palm absently. Baphomet was out there somewhere, and he wanted the Booke. The Booke seemed arrogant about that, freely following me as I paced, seeming to not want to be sneaky anymore.

"I'm sorry we weren't there," said Doc for the umpteenth time. "We just couldn't find the luna moth wings. We were fixing to head out anyway when you came back."

"It's all right. There wasn't much you could have done anyway. But what are we going to do about Baphomet?"

"First things first. I think we need to take care of Ed."

"What do you mean?"

Nick edged Doc out of the way. "We've got it all planned. We'll drive Ed in his SUV up the road, get him into the front seat, and, well…leave him there."

"And let him think he just had a blackout?"

"It's better than the truth. And if Doug keeps his word and puts a spell on him, he won't remember why he was out anyway."

"Oh, Doug will. If he doesn't, it's *his* head, and he knows it."

"Ed will likely come to me for a diagnosis," said Doc. "Even though I'm retired, he and some of the other folks in town still come to me occasionally. I'll just tell him that it might be a side effect of the other fall he took."

"When he was ducking a succubus." I wrung my hands. "The poor guy might take himself out of policing. It's not fair."

"I'll tell him it isn't likely to happen again."

"I don't like messing with him like that."

"We don't really have another choice."

I knew that. Of course I knew that. "Okay." But then something else was plaguing me. "Did Shabiri ghost-kill my grandfather?"

Jolene adjusted her clear-frame glasses. "Sort of sounds like it. I'm sure he's okay though."

"How do you know?"

"Spirits really aren't supposed to be on this plane. It's only when they have unfinished business…or died in a really violent way. And because of you and the book, he had a lot of unfinished business. That's my take, anyway."

"But there was so much I needed to ask him. So much I wanted to say."

"He's just back where he is supposed to be. But…it's not likely he can get back here to communicate with us. Shabiri's a real bitch."

I shook the spear. "I'm going to kill her someday." I think Jolene sensed I wasn't just posturing because she backed up a little. I really did mean it.

It was time to get Ed out of here. Nick, Doc, Jeff, and I muscled Ed into the car and Nick drove it away. He'd leave it in some corner of town and hopefully Ed would be all right. At least that's what Doc assured me. I'd call him sometime in the morning to make sure.

Doc and Seraphina talked quietly about Baphomet while Jolene researched him online. I couldn't concentrate on their conversation. As they talked, I drifted away into the kitchen, starting at the spear I'd left there.

I watched as Erasmus breathed. He seemed so vulnerable. His black hair sprawled on the table around his face. His coat lay open and his shirt was still covered in black blood that was still drying. I just stood over him and looked at him—the heavy dark brows, the beard scruff, the elegant nose and shapely lips.

"You needn't worry over me," he said in a roughened voice, eyes still closed. "I won't die."

"I…I'm worried anyway."

He peeled his eyes open. "You saved me."

"Yes."

"Why would you do that?"

I shrugged.

"You know what I am."

"Stop talking." I didn't want to hear it, to be reminded of it.

"Foolish mortals." He sighed before struggling to rise.

"Hey." I was at his side instantly, trying to press him back to the table. "Maybe you shouldn't get up."

He sat up anyway. Staring at the poultice bundle pressed against his stomach, he slowly stripped it away. We'd cleaned the blood as best we could. Doc wanted to stitch him up but Seraphina insisted on the poultice first. But when he set the bundle aside, there was no wound. Not even a scar. He still looked pale though, slumped as he was, legs dangling over the side of the table.

He raised his face enough to look at me. "I told you I wouldn't take your soul."

"Why should I believe you?"

He raised his brows and shrugged slightly. "I don't know. But you did save me. I owe you for that."

I shook my head. I didn't know what to believe anymore. I was exhausted, physically and emotionally. I didn't know what I wanted, what I could have. "Baphomet is out there."

"Yes. That is a complication."

"Why does he want the Booke?"

"That is puzzling. But he is one of the old gods. He knew the Ancient Ones. The book is at least that old. It's possible he knows how to manipulate it to his will. More than the Powers That Be. They are…unhappy that Baphomet seeks it. They will be even more unhappy that he is on the same plane as the book now."

"Can't they do anything?"

He laughed unpleasantly. "They don't do anything they don't have to do. That's why they have minions. Like me."

"So now you have to clean up the mess the Ordo made."

"Not just the Ordo. *Shabiri*." He said her name with the right amount of venom.

"Yeah. I'm gonna get her."

He must have detected the fire in my eyes because he sat up straighter with a cocked brow. "Oh?"

"She sent my grandfather away. Now we can't even talk to him."

"A shame. There was much we could have gleaned from him. Still, we have his notebook."

"But she got Doug that stupid spear. And she..." I shut my mouth. I wasn't going to mention how she looked at Erasmus. Because that was not part of the equation at all.

He seemed to read it on my face anyway and glowed with amusement. "Do you want my help?"

My synapses were screaming at me. I ignored them all. "Yes. I need your help. There's just no getting around it."

He smiled. "Good." Hopping off the table, he stood unsteadily for a moment. I couldn't help myself and reached out to support him. Abruptly, he grabbed me and pulled me against him. His eyes scoured my face, did a full inventory. "I *will* help you," he said, lips close to mine. "And when this is over, I will not take your soul. Do you understand me? I. Will. Not."

I couldn't speak. I could only nod.

He stared at my lips a moment longer before he released me and stepped back. "Then let's get to work."

When we walked back into the main room together, everyone stopped talking.

"Look who's the picture of health again." I said, thumbing toward Erasmus.

Seraphina looked ready to do battle, but Doc gently pushed her slightly behind him and approached. "Mr. Dark," he began.

"Warlock," said Erasmus. Funny, I didn't think he'd ever actually addressed any of the Wiccans to their faces before.

Doc controlled his expression nicely, though I could tell he was taken aback. "'Doctor Boone' will do."

Erasmus bowed. "Do I have you to thank for my current state of health?"

"Me and Seraphina."

He bowed to Seraphina, but she wasn't having any of it.

"You should go," she said sternly. "Thank you for saving Kylie, but you're not wanted here."

"Alas, dear lady, I am incapable of leaving the book. I *must* guard it."

"You don't have to do it where we can see you."

"Seraphina," I said kindly. "It's okay. I told him he could stay. We need him."

"But Kylie…" She was incredulous. "He…he…"

"He says he won't." His expression when he gazed at me was neutral, but I sensed something beneath it, something fiery that boiled under his skin.

"I make my oath to you all," he said, taking in Jolene and Jeff as well. "I will see that no harm comes to Miss Strange, from my own hand or from any other. I renounce her soul. And all of yours, just to be clear."

"Wait a minute," said Jeff.

"Later," I admonished.

"And what is your oath worth, Mr. Dark?" asked Doc.

Erasmus smiled. "Hmm. A good question. I…have never had to make an oath to a human before."

"There's another mark you could wear," Jolene piped up, her voice high and strained.

Erasmus swiveled toward her. "What mark?" he said slowly. I had a feeling he knew exactly what.

She turned her tablet to everyone. There was a picture of another strange sort of sigil, like the one he already had on his chest. "It would go on the inside of his wrist. It would mean you couldn't take souls."

"Would you have me starve for all eternity?"

"Yes."

He raised a brow. "What an unpleasant little girl," he muttered. "It is a proper solution, I'll grant you. But…I cannot agree to it."

I folded my arms over my chest. "Why not?"

"Because sometimes I am compelled to present myself before the Powers That Be and they will know instantly what I have done. Do you think for one moment I would survive that encounter?"

"Demons lie," said Seraphina. She was suddenly backed against the wall when Erasmus swooped in and cornered her, quicker than anyone could blink an eye.

"You have every reason not to trust me," he said in low tones, barely an inch from her face. She held her breath, trembling.

"Erasmus," I said.

He didn't back off. "You, who tries to recapture her youth with powders and blush but crawls ever closer to her grave, you dare tell me that *I* am lying, when you lie to yourself every day."

"Erasmus! Enough!"

He drew back slowly and looked at Doc. "Doctor Boone. I know you understand the onus under which I serve the book. I can swear upon it, if that will help. No? Then you have no choice but to believe me. You *need* my help. A god is loose amongst you. You need me."

"He's right," I said. "And not just Baphomet. But remember, the Booke will release something again too. We really do need him.

Whether...whether he's telling the truth or not. But just for the record...*I* believe him."

It was a litany in my head: *I have to believe him, I have to believe him*...Because I didn't know if I really did.

His eyes were shining when he looked at me. Pride, satisfaction? I didn't know.

"Then I will tell you all I know of Baphomet, and we must look at the weapons we have at hand."

I took up the spear, still black with Erasmus's blood. "All we have is this. The crossbow is broken."

"Broken? You *broke* the chthonic crossbow?"

"*I* didn't. Goat Guy did."

"Where is it now?"

"Back in Hansen Mills, I imagine."

"Wait here."

He was gone with just a bit of a breeze mussing my hair.

Jolene dropped her tablet to her side. "Be careful, Kylie."

"Everybody keeps saying that, but there doesn't seem to be any way to actually *be* careful."

"Well, I have an idea. If Mr. Dark won't put on the mark, maybe there's something else *we* can do."

"Yeah?"

"Yeah. Let me do more research. How do *you* all feel about tattoos?"

CHAPTER TWENTY-FOUR

It was barely a minute before Erasmus returned, the two pieces of the crossbow in his hands...and red blood spattered on his face.

"What happened?"

"One of the Ordo got in my way. I insisted on taking the crossbow. He discovered what it means to naysay a demon."

"You didn't—"

"Kill him? No. Perhaps I should have."

"Was it Doug?"

He studied the crossbow pieces "No. That other one with the pentagram on his head. Pity that was the only thing in it." He took hold of the pieces, fitted them together, and held it steady. I was about to ask, when the weapon began to glow. Smoke rose from the demon's shoulders and he gritted his teeth. Sparks flew from the place the halves were joined and then the glow died away. The crossbow was in one piece again. He examined it, then casually handed it to me.

I took it, felt its familiar heft. I hadn't realized how sad I was to see it broken until it was repaired. It had served me well. "I didn't know it could be fixed."

"Only I could. Shabiri may not know that. And speaking of which." He snatched one of the arrows from the crossbow's hilt, took it in his fist, and thrust the tip into his eye.

He yelled.

I screamed.

With a grunt of pain, he pulled it out. The arrow's tip smoldered, dripping something like acid, burning tiny holes in my wood floor.

"Erasmus! What did you…?"

But his eye was fine. With a leering smile he replaced the arrow into the hilt. "Specially treated. You can stop her with that now."

"From your *eye*?"

"Gross," said Jolene, though there was a light of curiosity in her own eye.

"What?" said Erasmus. "You can't poison *your* enemies with venom from your eye? What a waste."

Didn't even bother trying to wrap my head around that one.

"By the way," he added, "I returned your conveyance from the Ordo's property." I rushed to the window. There was my Jeep, parked in front. "And I took the liberty of removing the hexes and charm pouches they added to it." He took something out of his pocket, holding it with two fingers. "And this item. I thought you might want it back."

I took Ed's gun out of his hand. "Thanks, Erasmus."

He bowed. "My pleasure." Boy, he really had a charming way about him. If only he wasn't a demon bent on eating my soul…

An out-of-breath Nick burst through the door, slamming it closed and leaning against it. He jolted when he spotted Erasmus.

"It's okay, Nick. There's a truce going on."

"But what about…the soul-eating thing?"

"He says he won't do it." I shrugged. "I believe him."

His eyes darted from him to me. "Okay. If you say so, Kylie." He rubbed his arm and tried not to look at Erasmus. "Well, it's done. I sort of tapped the car into a tree to make it look more realistic. I didn't dent it or anything, and the car's still running. I'm sure he'll wake soon. He seemed like he was coming out of it when I moved him to the driver's side. But, uh…I couldn't clean out all the…the blood. Of course, it doesn't look like blood, so he might just think oil spilled back there."

"Thanks, Nick. I really appreciate it. But, uh…" I showed him the gun. "One item left. He's going to notice that bullets are missing."

Erasmus got that look whenever Ed was present. "I presume you're talking about your constable."

I ignored him. "You're going to have to return it as it is, I guess."

Nick took it and scratched his head, turning the heavy gun in his hands. "That might be a problem. I guess I've got to go back. Don't do anything interesting while I'm gone." He turned toward the door.

"Did you see Goat Guy out there anywhere?"

He paused, looking out the front window. "Not a sign of him. Mr. Dark, what do you think his next move will be? Will he try to attack us?"

"I haven't the foggiest. Perhaps your girl there should look in her portal to find a way to fight him."

Nick looked questioningly toward Jolene. "Her portal?"

"I'm not 'his girl,'" said Jolene. "And I'm already on it." She turned the tablet to show him and stuck her tongue out.

"Nick, you'd better go."

He nodded, tucking the gun into his pants and securing his shirt over it. "Okay. Be back as soon as I can." And he was out the door once more.

Jolene scanned her tablet. "Looking at the Hermetic Order of the Golden Dawn is only a start," she said without an upward glance. She probably hadn't even realized that Nick had left again. "But it led me to some of the secret writings of Aleister Crowley about the Law of Thelema."

"That's nonsense," said Erasmus.

"It's not," she countered. "Have you got anything better?"

"Baphomet feeds off of the energy of the earth—the creatures and plants. It is all food for him. He isn't a demon. He cannot be banished with pentagrams and spells. He is a *god*. I don't think your feeble books, or even that portal, can tell you how to banish a god."

She slammed it down into her lap. "Then, what? What do you suggest?"

"I…I will have to go for a time. To find out. Kylie." He turned to me. "Do you trust me?"

The word "no" was ready on my lips, but the truth of the matter was, in my heart of hearts, I *did* trust him. I wanted to, anyway. "If you have to go, you have to go."

"I have every intention of coming back."

"Wait, what does that mean? Is it…is it dangerous for you to go?"

"Yes. I must return to the Netherworld and…ask some uncomfortable questions, all without the Powers That Be discovering me. And that will not be easy."

"Maybe you shouldn't."

"It's the only solution. Baphomet must not be permitted on this plane. It is already ripping the fabric between the worlds."

"World*s*, plural? I was afraid that's what you said."

"Did you doubt that? You've seen the vortexes. The opening goes…somewhere. Where did you think that was?"

"I don't know. It's well beyond my pay grade."

"Wait, Mr. Dark," said Doc. "You said you needed a way to get to the Netherworld undetected. Maybe we can help with that."

He gave a full-throated laugh. My Wiccans exchanged glances with healthy doses of annoyance.

"You must be joking!" he guffawed. "Truly, I haven't laughed so hard in a long while."

I slapped him on the back of his head. His laughter stopped abruptly and he glared, affronted.

"Stop laughing, idiot. They want to help."

"That wasn't a joke?"

"No. Behave yourself."

He frowned and deferred to Doc. "Doctor Boone, I...appreciate the gesture, but what could you possibly do to help me?"

"Believe it or not, I have quite a few old books in my library at home. And between me and Jolene and her...portal...I think we might just be able to come up with something that'll work."

Erasmus stood in the middle of the shop while everyone followed Doc to his car. "He's serious?" he said to me when we were alone.

"Deadly."

"But he cannot possibly know..."

"What have you got to lose?"

"Time. Advantage over a god on the loose."

"I don't think an hour or two will make any difference."

He looked like he wanted to say more, but he had the grace to close his lips. Like a gentleman, he gestured for me to go ahead of him, and when I passed over the threshold, he closed the door. I heard the lock turn without him doing anything. Anything I could see, anyway.

We all piled into Doc's Rambler. Erasmus sat uncomfortably, crammed between me and Jeff. He could have magicked himself over there, but I sensed this was his way of trying to be part of the team. His hand lay in between our seats and I gave it a quick squeeze to reassure. He stiffened but didn't so much as look my way.

Jolene called Nick and told him to meet us at Doc's.

Doc Boone's place was less than a mile down the road. We walked into his darkened house. I didn't even want to know what time it was.

As soon as we settled in, Nick arrived, out of breath again, and peeled off his jacket. Erasmus stood as he usually did in the dark of my shop—stiff and uncomfortable. He surveyed the room with heavily hooded eyes.

Doc and Jolene scoured his library of old, leather-bound books. He'd take one down, thumb through it, and show Jolene, who was leafing through her own book from the shelf. They conferred quietly while Nick used Jolene's tablet for additional research. Seraphina sat with eyes closed, hands resting palm up. Feeling the vibration of the universe, no doubt. Jeff kept to himself. He had never been a research kind of guy.

I was about to say something to Erasmus when he moved toward Doc. "Wait, Doctor Boone! That book. I recognize it."

And speaking of Bookes, my own little shadow must've felt lonely, appearing beside me with a decided pop.

Everyone turned to look, then went back to what they were doing, as if disappearing and reappearing Bookes were an everyday occurrence. I guessed now they were.

Erasmus took the tome from Doc's hand and looked it over. Sigils were etched into the worn leather of what looked to be a very old, very well-traveled book. The pages were not parchment, but some kind of very thin paper.

"This is quite rare." He gave Doc a look of admiration.

"I did a lot of traveling when I was seeking the light," said Doc, "and I brought back a thing or two."

"From the Library of Alexandria?" Erasmus chuckled.

Doc looked decidedly dumbfounded. "You're not serious…are you?"

"Most assuredly."

Jolene peered over Erasmus's arms. I think he just made her millennium. I went over to look as well. Not paper, then. Papyrus. Maybe something that used to be scrolls now bound in a book.

"What *is* that?" I asked quietly.

"The Scroll of Banebdjedet," said Erasmus. "He was a god of Egypt. See here." He pointed out a painting among the hieroglyphs of a goat-headed Egyptian with a feather and cobra headdress on his horns like a pharaoh. "He was one of the first four gods to rule Egypt...before the others forced their way in. He is depicted with a ram's head. 'Ram' and 'soul' are very similar words in ancient Egyptian, making the ram sacred."

I couldn't help but touch the corner of the papyrus. "So... Baphomet is related to this god?"

"No. He *is* this god. This is his older self."

Doc's face lit up. "That's incredible."

"Indeed. He has used many guises over the centuries. When the Egyptians waned, he turned to the Greeks and became Pan. And when they, too, gave way to a newer religion, where there was no more room for a pantheon of gods, he faded. When they were no longer worshiped, the gods retreated to the Netherworld. And the Powers That Be entrapped them there. They would all be happy to escape and wreak havoc upon your world. If angered enough, the Powers might do it."

"So don't piss off the Powers," said an open-mouthed Jeff. "Good to know."

"Won't sneaking into the Netherworld incognito piss them off?" I pointed out.

"That's why I'd prefer they didn't know."

"Then we need a spectacular masking charm," said Doc. "Something that would work on all planes. That's why I was consulting this book. It talks about moving through to other worlds."

"Specifically, the Netherworld." Erasmus turned the pages and smiled at each scene, as if meeting an old friend. Maybe he had been there for the first signed edition.

"Then that's what we're looking for—Jolene, Nick."

"On it, Doc!" said Nick with a salute. His fingers worked furiously over the keyboard while Jolene flipped book pages double time.

Pacing, I watched them for a while, until I felt droopy and leaned back into one of Doc's comfy armchairs. Before I knew it, Doc was shaking me awake.

"Kylie, why don't you go home. We'll meet up at the shop early. I think we'll have a plan of attack by then."

I groaned as I rose. My bones were tired. I didn't think I'd enjoy that brisk walk home, but it had to be done.

Erasmus stood in my way. "I'll take you back."

"Oh. You don't…" but before I finished that sentence there was darkness, cold, and I was suddenly in my front room. "…have to do—Dammit, Erasmus! At least let me say yes or no."

"My apologies. You looked so weary…I thought I would help you."

I scrubbed at my hair and yawned. "Thank you."

As I stomped toward the stairs, I noticed Erasmus seemed to almost rock with nerves.

"Are you going to be all right?" I asked.

"Of course."

"G'night then." I could barely drag myself up the stairs. When I finally reached my bedroom, I did little more than shed my clothes, get into a long sleep shirt, and crawl under the covers.

~

I woke well before dawn. But there was the merest tinge of pink in the sky.

Erasmus stood over my bed looking down at me. I blinked sleepily. "You weren't there all night, were you?"

"Yes."

I pushed myself up to a sitting position and ran my hands over my face. "That's some of that creepy stuff I told you about." I was about to get up when he sat on the bed beside me, eyes intense.

"I don't wish to be melodramatic, but this might be the last time you see me."

I sighed. It felt as if I hadn't slept at all. "Well, it's a good thing you didn't want to be melodramatic. You're going to see me downstairs as soon as the Wiccans arrive, and then after you get back from the Netherworld."

"We must prepare for the possibility that I...may not return."

A sudden jolt gripped my heart like a stab of a knife. "But you will." I tried to slide off the bed, but he gripped my arm, stopping me.

"Kylie..."

"You have to come back, okay? Who will I harass if you don't?"

He said nothing. His eyes still held mine captive.

It was on my mind and I had to ask. "What happens, Erasmus, if you don't, um, eat?"

"I don't know. It's never happened."

"But...will you...die?"

"I don't know."

"What about other demons you've known?"

"We are all different. All created with a purpose."

"So demon taxonomy is a jumble?"

"We have some things in common. Other things...not." He drew closer. His hand came up and stroked my bed hair. He smoothed a strand from my cheek and tucked it behind my ear, as he had seen me do countless times before.

I licked my lips nervously. "Couldn't you try to eat something else? Like real food?"

"No." His fingers were still gently, barely stroking.

My hands moved toward him without thinking. I gripped the lapels of his jacket and soon I was running my hands up the hard muscle of his chest. "Have you tried?"

His breath hitched. I liked the sound of it. And so my hands traveled higher, touching the skin of his neck, knuckles scraping against beard stubble under his chin. "No. I was created as I am."

It was getting hard to concentrate. His gentle touches sent tingles over my skin. I really wanted to touch more of *him*. "But you, um, drink alcohol. And coffee. What about a...protein shake?"

He tilted his head. His finger traced down my cheek, under my chin, and down the smooth path to my neck. "And what, pray, is that?"

"It's…it's full of, uh, stuff that a body needs. Protein and vitamins and things."

"*You* don't even know what you're talking about, do you?"

I shook my head. His hand slid behind my neck and he cupped my head a moment before pulling it toward him. His mouth opened over mine and I was more than ready to receive it. We kissed like long-lost lovers. I clung to him, and his arms glided around my body, hugging me close. He angled his head to kiss me deeper, his tongue finding mine easily enough. The feel of his lips! It was a sensation I had never experienced with anyone else. Was it the demon or just his technique? I gripped him hard, tugging him against me, caressing him with my body.

He drew back enough to whip off his coat and pull open his shirt. I did him one better, shimmying out of my sleep shirt and underwear, and waiting for him on the edge of my bed with nothing on. I shivered at the chill in the room, but as he swooped in to embrace me again, all thoughts of the cold disappeared.

His mouth was at my ear, nibbling, breathing hard. My fingers were in his hair, tugging at him until he brought his face around and I could kiss him again.

His hands were everywhere now, callused fingertips gliding over me, causing me to shiver.

Driving forward, he pushed me back against the bed and quickly unbuttoned his trousers, shoving them down. His hands were hot on my backside as he lifted me up and thrust inside in one smooth motion.

He bent to kiss me and then dropped his face to my neck, teeth grazing my skin. I inhaled his scent, which wasn't quite like any man I had ever been with. There was sweat, but also something smoky—burnt logs in a campfire—and something earthy, like petrichor in a forest. I dug my nails into his shoulders and wrapped my legs around him, keeping him tight to me. He thrust harder, grunting with the effort. One hand was still beneath me, gripping a buttock cheek, while the other kept him balanced against the bed. Lost in sensation, I could escape the here and now. I could leave all of it—Baphomet, the Ordo…and even Ed—far behind a veil. There was only Erasmus. The hard feel of him. The hoarse murmuring in my ear as he repeated my name, as if trying to hold on to part of me before we separated again, maybe for all time.

His mouth traveled downward from my shoulder, nipping, licking as he went. His lips enclosed a peaked nipple and sucked as he grasped my hip and thrust harder.

His hot skin slid against mine, his hard muscles against the softness of my thighs. I pulled him in tighter, felt him deep within me. I angled my hips up, slamming against him.

I think I was already crying when release suddenly washed over me, his following soon after. Still he rocked into me, and I clung to him. He pulled his face from my chest and took my mouth with his again. We kissed until we both needed to breathe. He held my face with one hand and, with his forehead pressed to mine, we breathed each other in. "I thought it was the height of foolishness doing this once," he rasped, "but the most foolish thing of all was doing it twice."

"I don't regret a minute of it."

His breathing calmed as he gazed at my face. "Neither do I."

My heart flipped ridiculously but I tried to keep my expression neutral. "The Wiccans will be here any minute."

He drew back, taking his smoky warmth with him. He ran his hand through his long hair. "I know. I merely wanted to say… goodbye."

"This isn't goodbye. Stop saying that."

"It might be, Kylie. Be realistic. Whatever your witches come up with cannot possibly help. When I am unable to travel the Netherworld undetected, I will be forced to report to the Powers That Be and they will see into my mind. They will know everything and I will be instantly destroyed."

I clutched at his hand. "Then don't go."

"I must. I have to find a way to send Baphomet back."

I heard noises downstairs and Seraphina's voice yelling, "Kylie! We're here!"

We stared sorrowfully at each other for a long moment. The instant I let his hand go he vanished…along with his clothes.

It wasn't as easy for me. I had to drag myself from the bed into the shower.

I'd thrown on a cable knit sweater and jeans and was slipping my feet into running shoes when my phone rang.

"Kylie, thank God I got you."

I had to play the part. "What's going on, Ed? You sound terrible."

"I feel terrible. I blacked out yesterday. Behind the wheel."

"Oh my God! Are you okay?"

"Yeah, fine. Remarkably. As soon as I could drive, I got myself over to Doc. He was real nice about me coming over so early. He looked me over, told me it was from that fall a week ago."

"Really?"

"But it shouldn't happen again. He recommended I get a CT scan in Machias, just to be sure, so I'll be doing that today. I wondered…I know it's an imposition…but could you run me up there? If you can't, I'll understand. I'd have George do it, but I really need him here in case there's a break in the murder investigations. And then I thought…I mean, it's a helluva a date, but we could spend the rest of the day there. After you get done sitting around a doctor's office. Come to think of it...forget it. That's not the way I had this planned..."

Guilt swept over me, dark and heavy. "Maybe I can do that. I've got something going this morning but let me get back to you around ten to let you know. Is that too late?"

"No, that's fine. I stayed home from the station. But honestly, if you can't, Deputy George will help me out."

"Let me get back to you, okay. And Ed...I'm glad you're all right."

"I'll talk to you later, Kylie."

I closed my eyes and held the phone to my chest. I was the worst human being in the whole world. In *all* the worlds. What was I doing? Sleeping with a demon, making promises to Ed. Jeff was right. I needed to choose. But now was not the time. There were more important fish to fry.

I made my way downstairs. The coven was talking together in a circle. Erasmus, dressed again in clothes somehow cleaned of blood, hovered in the shadows as far away from them as the room allowed.

Jeff stood behind the counter, pulling out drawers and inspecting the glass canisters.

When she noticed me, Seraphina looked up and smiled. "I hope you don't mind I made coffee."

"You're a lifesaver." I retreated into the kitchen, Erasmus's eyes on me the whole time. "Subtle" did not seem to be in his vocabulary.

With a hot mug in my hand, I joined the others. They had a stone bowl on top of some kind of tripod set up in my fireplace, a fire going under it. There were roots, stems, and other bits of exotic herbs from my stores laid out on the hearth, and new sigils written in chalk there too. "So what's going on? What have you found?"

Doc was playing with something in his hand. "A way for your Mr. Dark to get around undetected. If you remember, we were trying to create an invisibility spell but we didn't have all the ingredients. This particular spell combines invisibility with memory. The person we cast it on will only be visible to those he speaks to, but anyone he stumbles across won't recall he was there. It's ingenious, really."

Erasmus drew closer. "It won't work on me. I'm not a human. I'm a demon."

Jolene squinted up at him from her seat by the fire. Her tablet lay on her lap. "That's why we had to find just the right one...*for* demons."

Doc threw the object in his hand up a little and caught it. "We've got this. It's an ancient Greek coin." He opened his hand. A misshapen thing struck with a lion's head. "It's made out of electrum."

"I see," said Erasmus. "You charm the coin and I carry it?"

"Not exactly. Here's the hard part. We have to melt the coin to embed our spell. And while it's still white-hot, we have to heat an iron poker and, well...thrust it into your chest."

Without thinking, I lunged in front of Erasmus. "*What?* Are you insane?"

"Now, Kylie, I know it doesn't sound very pleasant, but he isn't like a man. He can take a lot more punishment. And when dealing with demons and the denizens of the Netherworld, this is the safest method. Something in a pocket or sewn onto the clothes can be lost. This will be virtually undetectable."

Erasmus firmly pushed me aside. "I should like to point out that electrum is an alloy of gold and *silver*. And your poker is of iron... silver and iron can kill a demon."

"I realize that, Mr. Dark. Our spell will have protections to keep the silver and iron from killing you. As long as you return within the allotted time."

"And why should I trust you?"

"Well, that's not very neighborly. You entreated *us* to trust *you*. Can't you afford us the same courtesy?"

His gaze darted toward me before he squared with Doc again. "I see. If Kylie agrees, I will do it."

"Doc, I don't know."

"Look, the three of us stayed up very late to find just the right spell. You either trust us or you don't. And it's already been eight hours since Baphomet flew goddess knows where."

He was right. Who knew what the god would do next…or to whom? We were all in danger. Erasmus might end up being the safest out of all of us. "Okay. If Erasmus agrees."

He nodded slowly and faced Doc again. "Very well. What must I do?"

"Once the crucible is hot enough, I'll drop the coin in. The gold should serve as a shield to protect you, but I must also mention that while it is in your chest, it will be fairly painful."

He sighed. "Of course."

We all watched the crucible on its tripod. Doc held the coin tight in his left hand. Nick passed out printed pages to the coven. I glanced over Jolene's shoulder but couldn't make out what it said. Some sort of weird language. Jeff looked on casually, making sure he stayed clear of the silver.

When the crucible began to smoke, Doc dropped the coin in, where it sizzled and spit. He watched it carefully and began picking up the bits of herbs laid out on the hearth from left to right and popped them into the crucible. Smoke rose, and the room filled with a scent like a burnt car engine. I stepped back farther as the crucible's bowl began to glow with heat. Doc picked up one of my fireplace pokers and thrust it under the tripod into the radiant coals.

It was all a bit too medieval for my tastes. "Are we sure…"

"Shhh!" Nick shushed. He raised the paper to his face and the coven gathered around the reddening crucible. The fire threw them all into silhouette. They had never looked more like a coven than at that moment. It gave me a sick feeling. I reached behind me and grabbed Erasmus's hand. He squeezed, then quickly let go.

With papers in hand, the Wiccans chanted from the text while the fire flickered behind them. The crucible sputtered and steamed. They kept chanting as Doc bent over and grabbed a towel like an oven mitt to grasp the end of the poker. He whipped it out of the coals. It glowed red-hot.

As the chanting grew to a crescendo, he suddenly thrust it into the crucible. Something whined and the coven continued to chant.

Doc turned. "Mr. Dark, if you would open your shirt."

They faced each other boldly, as if challenging the other to flinch first. Was this really necessary?

The melted coin clung like a ball of fire to the glowing poker. Wispy smoke rose in a very strange pattern, almost like letters, elongating and shifting.

Erasmus held his shirt open.

"It would help if you knelt."

Stonily he got down on his knees, holding the shirt wide.

Doc nodded solemnly. "Now hold still. This is gonna hurt."

Before I could object, Doc jabbed the hot poker into Erasmus's chest. Erasmus threw back his head and howled. The windows shook. Books fell off of the shelves. Doc kept pushing the iron in, grimacing with the effort.

Erasmus's face was twisted in agony, teeth gritted. How long did this have to go on?

"Isn't that enough!" I screamed over the loud chanting, the fire that seemed to roar.

Doc held it there a moment longer before yanking it back. The ball of fire was gone. Erasmus's chest glowed where the iron had been, but there was no scar, no hole, and even now the glow was fading. He fell forward, head hanging between his heaving shoulders.

I tried to go to him, but Seraphina gripped my arm and held me back.

Doc breathed hard. "Mr. Dark, you have twelve hours. No more than that. Make good use of that time. If you don't return within the twelve hours, I won't be able to get that out and you'll die. Are we clear?"

It took a few more moments of deep breathing before Erasmus raised his head. His eyes glittered and he was plainly struggling with the pain.

"Crystal."

Slowly, he rose, closing his shirt. Without another glance toward us...toward *me*...he walked to the door. But before he left, he turned partway. "If I don't come back in time, look to that book from Alexandria. There might still be clues. I will send a message if I can. And Kylie, remember, the Booke of the Hidden is still your charge. There are more creatures to come. Beware. Good luck."

Instead of opening the door, he simply vanished.

CHAPTER TWENTY-FIVE

Twelve hours. That was all he had. Eight o'clock tonight. I almost called Ed and told him I couldn't make it, but Seraphina talked me out of it. It would help to keep me distracted, she said. And Ed needed me. Ed, the living, breathing human being. Like me. How could I argue with that?

I was reluctant to close the shop, and after wondering aloud, someone tapped my shoulder.

Jeff. His eyes and ears had morphed a little when Erasmus had been going through his ordeal, but they were slowly returning to normal. "Look, you should spend time with your…with the sheriff. I'll watch the shop."

"I can't ask you to do that."

"Look, I gotta do something. I can't wait around all day for Seraphina to finish that potion. And you should…you know. Decide. You should decide on…Ed." I lowered my eyes, unable to look him in the face. "And then later, I'll head over to your grandpa's place. Work on making it habitable. In the meantime, I can be useful here. I mean, I know how to run an herb and tea shop, right?" He sidled closer, wincing at the silver amulet, which I quickly tucked inside my shirt. "Doc doesn't have a TV. I can't read another book. Let me work here. You trust me, don't you? Hands off the till, I swear."

Should I? Jolene would come at three thirty and the shoe *was* on the other foot. I didn't need him—it was the other way around now. "Okay, Jeff. Thanks. Maybe I should make you a key. Since you'll be…staying."

He smiled that crooked smile that had gotten me in trouble all those years ago. "That would be sweet. But, uh, let's play it by ear for now. The wolf is napping, but sometimes it gets restless."

"The potion should help."

He swiped stray hair off his forehead. "Whenever it gets done."

When I arrived at Ed's, I told him the bad news, that I had to be back around six. He seemed disappointed but conceded it. "I realize it's a school night," he said good naturedly.

It was a good opportunity for me to see some other parts of Maine. I'd been so wrapped up in the shop—and then the Booke—that I hadn't had a chance to really leave Moody Bog. The only time I saw anything was driving straight through to my little village.

The day was pleasant enough, and Ed smiled a lot, which lightened my mood…until I thought about Erasmus's mission. He'd be fine, I kept telling myself. He knew what he was doing.

But he was also in pain and I hated that. *Have to stop thinking about it.*

As I glanced at Ed from time to time, I began to feel a little guilty. When I was with Ed, Erasmus fell to the background, but the same thing happened to Ed when I was with Erasmus.

Jeff was right. I was some piece of work.

Machias was only an hour away. Once there, I found it to be a quaint—there was no other way to say it—little town. Much bigger than Moody Bog, and with much more open sky than the claustrophobic forests of my village. Since it was along the coast, it had some charming wharves and waterfront shops. We wove around the roads till we got to the medical center. I felt bad for Ed. All this was so unnecessary. But I couldn't tell him it was a spell done by his brother…who had also walloped him in the first place.

I walked with him to reception and then the waiting room. "They said it will only take about half an hour," Ed said as we sat together in the pleasant waiting area. "Then we can walk around."

"If you're feeling up to it."

Doc had healed him of whatever bump Doug had given with magic, but no one knew if it would end up in the scan.

When Ed was called in, I stayed in the waiting room, nervously checking my phone every few minutes. Jolene said she'd text me if she got any word from Erasmus. It was nearly noon. Eight hours to go.

Ed came out of the exam all smiles. "Clean bill of health," he said and wrapped me in a hug. It was good to hug someone. It was even better to hug Ed. I pulled away, hiding my discomfort by fiddling with my purse and slinging the strap over my shoulder.

"Where to now?" I asked.

"Let's go downtown."

We bundled up in our coats. It was a cold, crisp day and the sky was clear. People milled along the streets, window-shopping.

Ed gestured toward the bay below us, surrounded by hills. "You might remember Machiasport from the second naval battle of the American Revolution, if you're up on your history."

"I was never one for history in school. More of a literature gal."

"Well, there are plenty of books on the subject."

"Where does the name Machias come from? Was it named after someone?"

"Nope, it's a term from the local tribe, the Passamaquoddy. It sort of means 'bad little falls.' The Machias River, in other words."

"Are the falls bad?"

"They're rapids, which probably made it tough to navigate by canoe."

"Is it an old town? I guess most are around here."

"From 1633."

"You guys don't mess around with your history. But what's with 'downeast.'" I'd seen that word on the sign coming into town.

"Most Mainers who live in this part of the state refer to it as downeast. Like you'd say 'socal.' I think it started as a nautical term."

"I see. So is Moody Bog downeast too?"

"Ay-yuh." He grinned.

Ed and I had an easy camaraderie. And he had made me laugh when everything had been so heavy. But I couldn't help but watch the skies for a large winged god or check my phone constantly for the time. It would have been a nice day if I hadn't been so worried.

When we got back to the car to see other sites, the Booke was there on the passenger seat.

"What in blazes is this?" said Ed, picking it up. An immediate uneasy feeling seized me. I wanted desperately to yank it out of his hands. My fingers griped the doorframe of the car so hard they whitened.

"Booke of the Hidden," he read. "Is this more of that Wiccan stuff? Oh, wait. This is that book you found bricked up in your wall, right? I remember you telling me about that when we first met."

"When you were accusing me of murder."

He blushed. It was charming. "Yeah. Forgot about that. Just doing my job."

"I know." I pulled it out of his hands. "It's old. I still need to get it appraised."

"You gonna sell it? Shoot, I thought it would be a great thing to keep around. A conversation piece, you know."

"I'm not as enamored with it as I was at first." *Now stay in the car!* I thought, placing it in the back seat.

"I don't know. Put it in a glass case in your shop. Another tourist attraction."

"I said no!"

He looked at me, questioning, and I blew out a breath. "I mean, I just think it would be a better investment if I sold it."

"Okay," he said, hands up in surrender. "It's your book."

And it was reminding me it still had creatures to release. Definitely not fun and games anymore.

My phone chimed. It was a text from Jeff.

Heading to your grandpa's. Jolene is here.

"Anything to worry about?" he asked after my long silence.

"No. Just Jeff letting me know Jolene arrived at the shop."

Ed seemed to puzzle at this. Obviously, something was missing. He wasn't remembering things…like how he was planning on going over to Doug's after learning his brother had beaten up Jeff. I watched pensively. Would Doug's spell hold?

Instead, he asked, "What's your ex-boyfriend doing working at your shop?"

Oh boy, hadn't thought that one through. *Think fast, Kylie.* "The thing of it is, Jeff got some bad health news. He's…he's going through some stuff and I agreed to let him stay at my grandfather's old place."

"What?"

"He'll be cleaning it out for me—doing me a huge favor really—and working at the shop a little. Like today so I can skive off."

"Your ex? That you ran away from?"

I postured with my hand on my hip. "I did *not* run away from him. I left to make a fresh start. And I'm giving him a chance to make good. Which he is."

"Sorry, sorry. It's just—this Jeff and that Erasmus guy. Seems a little crowded with your *male* friends always around."

Jealousy wasn't usually cute, but the crinkle of the bridge of his nose, the upraised brows—it was kind of a good look for him. I slipped my arm through his. "You don't have anything to worry about." Was that the truth? *You're still thinking about Erasmus.* But it was looking more and more as if I would be thinking further about Ed.

⁂

I drove us around the bay at Ed's instruction. He pointed out more sights, but when the time ticked toward five with still no texts from Jolene, I insisted we wrap it up.

Ed buckled his seat belt and settled in. "What's so important about getting back so early? We've been gone all day anyway, and the shop closes at six, doesn't it?"

"I have a lot of bookkeeping to do. Profit/loss and all that."

"It's just that…I thought that taking some time away…with your…ahem, new boyfriend…"

I bit my lip and stared straight ahead.

After a time of silence, he sighed. "I'm sorry. I didn't mean to be presumptuous. I was just hoping…"

"Don't be sorry. I…do think of you that way. It's all just new to me."

"You've seemed distracted today. I didn't want to mention it because I was enjoying your company. But it did seem that you weren't all there."

"It's Erasmus."

"Oh? What about…*him*?"

He had every right to use that tone. He didn't even know *how* much. "He had to travel today for a very important meeting and I haven't heard from him. It's…it's about his job. This could make or break him. I wanted to be there when he got back." I took the curve in the road a little too fast and winced when the tires squealed.

"Oh. You could have told me."

"I didn't want to bother you with it."

"Make or break him, huh? What kind of work does he do?"

"Corporate shark, that sort of thing. This could bankrupt him."

"Well, I hope it comes out okay. I know he's your friend and you worry about him."

"I do. And thanks."

"So I suppose that means the date is cut short."

"I'm sorry. And I'm sorry I've been a lump today."

"Don't worry about it. I'm grateful you could drive me to my boring appointment and that I got to spend at least a little time with you. And I've been a bit of a lump too, truth be told. Daniel Parker's murder has been weighing on my mind."

And on mine. "Any suspects?"

He shook his head. "A few vague suspicions. The lab in Bangor is taking a look at the DNA evidence, but that will take a while. Like I said before, George and I aren't exactly used to murders here and suddenly we've got four on our hands. It's likely the missing persons are homicides too. It really throws me. Are we looking at some sort of serial killer?"

I wondered if it would ease his mind to know that he didn't have to arrest anyone. Though the alternative was far more terrifying.

"Looks like it's probably a good idea for you to get back early too."

He nodded at the sunset. "It's just as well. I'll have to check in at the station."

"Let's come back here some other time and really make a day of it, okay Ed? Is it a date?"

"Yeah. I'll definitely take a raincheck."

We drove in silence. And it was comfortable silence. I didn't expect that. Even though I was worried about Erasmus, I still felt relaxed and safe in Ed's company.

You are one screwed up dude, Kylie.

We made it back to Moody Bog around six, just as the sky turned pink and gold and the trees on the ridge stood out like black cracks on the landscape. I drove to Ed's place, even walked him to his door.

"I know you won't come in so I won't bother to invite you. I can see that Erasmus is important to you."

"Yeah."

"So I'll wish him luck. Call me if you want to talk, okay? Anytime...Tonight, even."

"You're so good to me, Ed. I don't deserve you."

"Don't be so sure." He leaned in and kissed me on the cheek. Before he withdrew, he looked me in the eye and slowly pressed a kiss to my lips. He lingered there gently, not asking for more, but giving enough to let me know where he stood. He caressed my check with his knuckle and then disappeared inside his house.

I sat in my car, watching as the lights came on in his place. It looked so homey, so inviting and safe. Ed was sanctuary. What was Erasmus but chaos?

I scanned the sky again and saw nothing but birds heading home. I turned the car toward my shop too.

The gang was there, sans Jeff. I supposed he was making himself at home at Grandpa's place.

The Booke followed me in, which caused a few raised eyebrows.

"Any word?" I asked.

Doc shook his head and continued pacing in front of the fire. The crucible was long gone, but a fire was there and the poker was in the coals, waiting for Erasmus's return.

Nick went out for pizza and brought it back in about twenty minutes. I couldn't eat a single slice.

No one talked to me. Maybe they knew. It was probably telegraphed on my face. I wrung my hands, unable to sit still. I paced, too, but pacing in front of the fire was getting crowded so eventually I went out to the backyard.

My fingers traced the twisting, thorny vines of the dormant tea rose that twined around the leaning arbor. I looked up to the clapboard side of my house and couldn't help but find the scratches from the succubus. That was the first time Erasmus and I...

I sighed and sank into the rickety glider, pulling my jacket around me. Had he found the answer? Had they discovered him despite our best efforts? Was he in too much pain to make the trip back?

This wasn't like the last time he went missing. This was far worse. Because this time, I knew where he was and how much danger he was in. And time kept ticking.

⁂

Seven o'clock. I peered in through the window of my back door. The Wiccans were pretty much how I left them: Doc pacing; Jolene with her tablet in a wingback, though she was staring off into space instead of working; Nick munched absentmindedly on another pizza slice, cold by now; Seraphina's eyes were closed, palms turned upward on her lap.

I couldn't go in. The sunset had dispersed and it was cold, but I still couldn't go in. I couldn't be comfortable and warm while he was still out there, suffering God knows how much. I sat on the glider again, slowly rocking back and forth, watching night fall on the forest and hills above.

⁂

Seven thirty. "Erasmus!" I whispered into the darkness. "You're supposed to come when I call. Where are you? Are you okay? Come now!"

Silence. A lonely birdcall. A rustling in the underbrush—perhaps a mouse. But no demon.

⁂

Eight o'clock. I burst through the back door. "Where is he?"

Doc looked up forlornly and then down at his watch. Jolene bit her lip and lowered her face, pretending to read her tablet. Nick kept dog-earing an old book from Doc's library while he stared at me. Seraphina rose smoothly from her seat and laid her hands on my shoulders.

"Where is he, Seraphina?"

No one said anything. I wanted to scream at them. *You said this would work! You said he'd be all right! Where is he?*

A sudden noise outside startled us all. Snarling and howling.

Everyone rushed toward the window, but I got there first. The sheriff's Interceptor was parked skewed in the street. Ed stood in the headlight's beam, aiming his gun. He was shouting at something just out of the beam's reach, something making a horrific howling noise. No! Something else had come out of the Booke again. I wasn't ready. I needed Erasmus.

I cast open the door and ran out into the frigid night. The crossbow slammed into my grip and I felt a momentary sense of calm.

Ed flicked his gaze toward me. "Kylie! Get back inside."

"What is it?"

"Get back inside! It's a wolf."

The headlights flared over the blond fur. Jeff was a wolf again, snarling and snapping his jaws. I threw the crossbow behind me. It had armed itself with the silver-tipped bolt but there was no way I was going to kill Jeff.

"Ed, you have to believe me. It's okay. Just get back in your car."

"Kylie, goddammit! Get inside!"

"Ed, it's okay. He won't hurt me, but you have to get back in your car." I took a few tentative steps closer. Jeff turned his yellow eyes toward me.

Ed adjusted his grip on the gun, stance wide on the asphalt. "Kylie, please…"

My hands were reaching toward Jeff when suddenly I was on my back. I'd been slammed into the gravel, the wind knocked out of me. It made no sense. Stars winked and flew around my head. Something heavy sat on my chest.

The roaring snarl was closer now, and I looked up, expecting—hell, I had no idea what to expect.

An unfamiliar muscled man was pinning me down. Still dazed, I took in his appearance in flashes. High cheekbones and a square jaw. Large eyes set under curved brows. A sharp nose. Thin, tight clothing fit him like a seal's skin. Wings sprouting out from his shoulder blades. He almost reminded me of an owl.

A growl rumbled from his throat and vibrated his whole body.

"You are the human Kylie Strange," he said. He had a deep, rich voice to match his body…which was slowly crushing me into the ground.

"I…I…"

A swipe of a clawed hand threw his head to the side. Three stripes of black blood began to flow from his cheek. He slowly turned his head to the werewolf growling and barking beside him.

"He wants you to get off me," I said, trying to breathe.

"This is unusual," said the strange man. He rose, grabbing my neck and lifting me upright.

"Not helping the breathing," I choked, scratching at his immovable hands.

"Step away from her and put your hands up!" Ed ordered.

"Get away from here, Ed!"

"I'm going to fire if you don't let her go!"

Gunshot. The report echoed up and down the hills, dissipating beyond the forest.

The man released me and I fell. I hadn't realized how big he was, but I had been about a foot off the ground. I coughed and sputtered as I scooted back, feeling behind me for the crossbow. It slid into my hand.

The man…creature…whatever…turned. Though black blood was smeared on that tight shirt made of some kind of skin and across his pretty white wing feathers, it had apparently done no harm.

"Is that a weapon?" he asked.

"Officer requests assistance," said Ed breathlessly to his shoulder mic. His gun was still trained on the man. "Down on the ground. Now!"

"I do not understand."

Jeff rushed him. They tumbled on the asphalt, rolling, barking, snarling, blond fur and white feathers flying everywhere. The man just took it, not bothering to fight back.

What kind of creature was this? I looked at the crossbow bolt. It hadn't changed. I was afraid to shoot in case I hit Jeff.

He reared up suddenly and threw Jeff off. Jeff landed hard with a doggy whine and was still. I swung the crossbow at the creature's torso and didn't hesitate. I pulled the trigger and the bolt flew, hitting him square in the belly.

That got his attention. His eyes flew open and he cried out. He fell to one knee, yanking on the bolt and heaving it away from him. Black muck dribbled out of the wound, but there were no bursts of light and the Booke never appeared. He staggered back, glaring at me.

"They did not say you would resist."

"They? Who sent you? Who…*what* are you?"

"I am the Ancient One, the demon Andras, Killer of Men. You are to die."

"Yeah, well. I don't die easy."

"So I see." He swept us with his gaze: the Wiccans frozen in the doorway, Ed with his gun pointed, and Jeff still and silent on the ground.

He grinned, his mouth full of sharp teeth. "I have nothing but time," he said.

He leapt. I raised my arms for protection, but he wasn't aiming for me. Spreading his wings, he soared over my shop and into the gloom of night. The sound of his beating wings drifted into the mist.

So that was Assassin Owl Boy. Freaking great.

But then I saw Jeff. Scrambling toward him, I shook his shoulder. Maybe not the smartest thing to do with a werewolf, but…

"Jeff! Are you okay? Jeff!" He was breathing harshly, his dog tongue lolling out of his mouth. I hoped he was just knocked out cold. "Doc, can you help?"

He rushed over and knelt beside me.

The gravel crunched. Something cast a shadow over me. Shit. Ed. He lowered his gun to his side and stared past me at Jeff.

"Kylie," he said softly, uncertainly. "What the hell is going on? That's…that's not a wolf."

"I know, Ed. Help us get him inside and I'll try to explain."

My coven surrounded the blond werewolf and carefully lifted him, shuffling to get him inside. When I looked back, Ed was still standing on my gravel parking lot, gun hanging limply from his hand, his Smokey Bear hat askew, and a strange and faraway look on his slackened face.

To Be Continued in Booke Three

AUTHOR'S AFTERWORD

Thanks for reading! The story deepens. The characters are more involved than ever before. And there are even more surprises to come. Booke Three proves more horrendous for Kylie and her coven when mysterious trudging figures appear in a strange mist falling over Moody Bog. Doug and his gang are still up to no good, and a demon and a god wreak havoc.

If you liked the book, please review it! And don't forget to sign up for my quarterly newsletter and keep up with other news on my website, BOOKEoftheHIDDEN.com.

ACKNOWLEDGMENTS

Many thanks go to my publisher Keith Wallman and my editor Lydia Youngman at EverAfter/Diversion who scooped up the series and saved it from obscurity; to my agents Lisa Rogers and Joshua Bilmes for adding their own brand of magic; to the copy editors, cover designers, and publicist—I know you guys work hard with nary a glance, but *I* noticed and appreciated; to my husband who told me to write down this weird dream I had in the first place and who is the best support a wife and a writer ever had; and finally to my readers—long may you wave!—who are giving this strange supernatural world a chance.

CPSIA information can be obtained
at www.ICGtesting.com
Printed in the USA
BVHW08s1756011018
528943BV00001B/1/P